THE SECRET RESORT OF NOSTALGIA

Sahlan Diver

THE SECRET RESORT OF NOSTALGIA

ISBN: 978–17–87233–00–3

*Dedicated to my father, Edward Diver (1916–2002)
and my childhood memory of the spare bedroom
model train-set in our council house on the Kent coast.*

Preface

Unusual Mysteries

Unusual Mysteries, the series of three novels, and a book of stage plays, presents mystery stories like you have never encountered before. Unusual settings, unusual characters, unusual plotlines, with multiple misdirection and startling reveals.

(Mystery 1) The Secret Resort of Nostalgia
Shortlisted for The Yeovil Literary Prize 2017

A graduate is sent to document a remote Irish island community. What he discovers there may mean the difference between life and death.

" … unlike any other mystery novel I have ever read." *Sefina Hawke for Readers' Favourite*

(Mystery 2) For The Love of Alison
Finalist 2020 Indies Today Award

A journalist receives an invitation to visit a woman who was the object of his obsessive mental illness thirty years ago. That same evening, a murder occurs. Can the journalist prove his innocence, and his sanity?

"… very different from the countless other crime/thriller books that I have read…" *Reviewer at LoveReading.co.uk*

(Mystery 3) Sixty Positions with Pleasure

In the year 2050, a suspicious hit-and-run accident sets off a chain of deaths, each more puzzling than the last. A vision in a cave prompts a stampede of pilgrims. An Irish town declares its independence from Ireland and the EU. And twenty-something English engineer, Charlie Gibbs, is co-opted by fifty-year old Dutch company boss, Ilse Teuling, to assist in writing a sex manual.

"… a fun read … with an enormous cast of characters, most of whom are not what we think they are … Very enjoyable." *Lucinda E Clarke for Readers' Favorite*

**(Mystery 4) The Chapel in the Middle of Nowhere
(and three other stage plays)**

Members of a fading and obscure minor cult hold a party in an isolated location. None of them are prepared for the disruption that will be caused by three uninvited guests, one of whom may be hiding a dark secret.

All mysteries in the series available from leading online sellers. Further information and video reviews etc at:
https://www.businessassistant.biz/novelsandplays.htm

The Trickster God

In the summer of 1990, we didn't know it but we were at the end of an era, before the explosion of modern communications technology, before the omnipresent mobile phone, the Internet, universal email and social networking. Much easier back then to cut off people's access to information, if that's what you wanted to do.

TABLE OF CONTENTS

Prologue

The Trickster God returned last night and gave me the travelling dream. Always the same. I'll be walking the streets of a seaside town. There's never traffic, only people. Sometimes I'll be with the people, sometimes apart — observing from a distance. And *she* will be there: warm, friendly, sexy.

We take a boat trip together. I reach down into the water. That makes her angry. There's something concerning the sea I must not be allowed to find out. Back on the beach she slips away and I lose her in the crowds. My search ends at the wire fences. Through them I see the Dark Town, a grotesque reflection of my own. Where mine is day, the other is permanent night; where mine has people, the other has fleeting shadows; where I stand looking in, a Doppelganger of black stands staring out.

I have been to a place like that. I could return there now if not for the trick played upon me. In folk tales, the one who stumbles across a forbidden secret is visited by some terrible curse, transmogrified into a frog, imprisoned in a high tower, banished to the wilderness. My punishment was the place I knew and loved ceased to exist. But this is no fairy story. The place was real; the people were real; the conspiracy was real.

1

Chapter 1

The Dining Car

I saw everything. I saw nothing.

Right from the beginning, I got it the wrong way round. That, no doubt, was their plan. Did I know they had a plan for me, same as for everyone else on that journey? I must have sensed something wasn't right. Uncharacteristic of Mike Denning, twenty-two-year-old graduate from England, to be sitting in an empty dining car with the temptation of a lively Irish bar next door. Of course, there were the two women who'd squashed up against me in the crush of the one carriage devoted to serving alcohol. Their attentions had become embarrassing. I may be five foot eleven, athletic, reasonably good-looking, with a mass of black hair, but I wouldn't have marked myself down as a magnet for mature chicks. One of them, the one with the unfortunate laugh, like the noise of sheep being forced through a sheep-dip, she told me they were sharing a double bed, and winked as she added, "It's big enough for three."

Yes, I'd had to get away from the women. I made the excuse of wanting to listen to the pianist and pushed through the people to stand by the baby grand, where a man dressed in top hat and tails straight out of the nineteen-twenties furiously tinkled the keys in imitation of jazz-age music of the period. Stepping onto this train had been like stepping onto a film set; more than that, like stepping through a time warp and being sucked back into the past, the furniture and fittings of my compartment imported from a golden age of luxury, everything impeccably finished, bright and gleaming, like new. But at the same time, it felt old. It took me some time to figure out why: the total absence of plastic — anywhere. All you saw and touched: wood, metal, leather or glass. And the lighting — no fluorescents, the sleeping car corridors in particular strangely dim, evocative of those old thriller movies located on night trains, *Murder on The Orient Express*, and such like. Not that I expected a murder during the night but I *was* concerned about an accident. Apparently, we were to be confined to the tunnel for six hours. What would happen if the train derailed, or a fire broke out?

Maybe what bothered me also was the perfection of *the girl*: intelligent, sexy, gorgeous to look at. They'd promised she'd be with me in a couple of days. An offer they knew I wouldn't refuse.

Or maybe *the cloakies*. Four people arrived as a party, wearing a kind of uniform, imposing long dark cloaks with turned-up pointed collars having the look of the pantomime wizard. Could I be soon to enter the realm of some mysterious cult?

And the man in the customs hall who confiscated my camera. "I'm sorry, sir. You can't take the camera with you. We'll give you a receipt for it and put it in our strong room, for you to collect on your return." I informed him of my job with the estate, that they wanted me to take photographs as part of my assignment. He assured me a camera would be supplied. I couldn't figure out the problem. Why couldn't I take my own?

The crowding in the bar suggested the whole train must be there. I gave up hope of attracting the attention of the over-taxed barman and came in here, the curtained diner, empty at the moment, softly lit with pink-shaded table lamps, all gleaming silverware and crystal glass. At the far end, the galley car, clattering with preparations for the eight o'clock meal. As soon as a steward appeared, I'd order a drink.

An old lady entered from the bar. With her steel grey hair, tie-dyed skirt and beaded necklace, she looked every bit the aged artistic hippy. "Mind if I join you for dinner?" she said, as she sat down opposite me at the table for two. Her American accent had a tinge of Irish, suggesting a long-term residency. I knew her as Molly. She'd been standing behind me in the customs hall queue when an official asked obscurely: "Any rocks or pebbles?" Molly came to my rescue: "He's saying do you want to change your money. One Rock equals one hundred Pebbles. You can change money when you get there but the bank has its late night on Wednesdays. They won't be open till after lunch."

Something strange about Molly. That business when the man took her to the room for questioning. I met her on the platform afterwards. She rushed off to get on the train, though right now she seemed to have regained her composure. "I always go for first service," she said. "It doesn't worry you young people but at my age I get indigestion if I eat too late. So, what do you think ... about where you're going?"

"I feel I'm on information overload. So many facts to absorb at the interview this afternoon."

"You're happy with it all? There's nothing worrying you? "

"Only the long journey underground."

"Oh. That!" She laughed. "That's nothing! Here's the waiter. Let's order. We should get served first."

The restaurant car was filling up fast. Four guys dressed in blue security guard uniform took their place a few tables away from ours. A poker-faced waiter arrived with the menu. Surprisingly, it listed no meat, only vegetarian and fish dishes, though all flamboyantly described. "Men tend to favour the potato and lentil pie," said Molly. "It's cleverly done with herbs and spices, so it tastes more like cottage pie. It's the nearest thing they have to a meat dish."

I said, "I'll order it. The waiter doesn't look like he'd appreciate me asking for a cheeseburger."

Molly apparently thought my remark hilariously funny and laughed out loud, such that the couple on the adjacent table turned to see what was amusing her. Embarrassed, I looked around apologetically. I caught one of the blue guards eyeing me with an icy stare. He averted his gaze but not before I'd registered being under scrutiny. I mentioned it to Molly. She turned to look. "I don't know him. The guards are told about new people. He was probably sizing you up."

"What do they do?"

"They keep the peace. Look! We're off!"

The train had started moving, so gently I hadn't noticed our leaving the station. Within a minute we passed into dense woodland, the gloom broken only once, by a wide beaten-earth path crossing the tracks and leading down between the trees to the garden of a large house. Five minutes later, we entered the tunnel. If the smile Molly gave was intended to reassure, what she said next did not: "The last daylight we'll see till tomorrow!"

The train slowed and came to a stop with a prolonged squeal of brakes, which gave way to an eerie silence. The engine had cut out. The chattering passengers lowered their voices, out of respect for the situation.

"Have we broken down?" I asked.

"You're nervous about this journey, aren't you?" replied Molly, "You needn't be. See what happens."

We'd stopped about a minute when I saw the driver coming along the outside, slamming down shutters over each window.

"The tunnel is lit every few yards," explained Molly. "The flash of light past the window might give people a headache or prevent them from sleeping."

"Also, they don't tell you this," she whispered, "but it's better if anyone suffers from claustrophobia not to be reminded they are in such a long tunnel. The train doors are shuttered and locked also, in case anybody goes screaming mad and tries to escape." Then, out loud, "Oh My! I hope *you* don't suffer from claustrophobia. I shouldn't have told you!"

The slamming faded as the driver progressed towards the rear, then increased in volume and faded again as he passed by the windows on the opposite side. After a long wait with everyone talking sotto-voce as if in the presence of the dead, the rumble of the restarted engine gave permission for resumption of normal conversation. With its passengers now snugly cocooned, the train moved off. Through gaps in the shutters came a rhythmic waxing and waning as we passed the tunnel lamps. The light had taken on a curious glow. I'd already been told the tunnel passed through a salt mine; I guessed the pinkness of the light due to our now being deep inside the seam. Frustrating not to be able to see out.

"You'd soon get fed up of the view," said Molly. "For safety, we can't go any faster than the speed of a bicycle. That's why they only run as a sleeper. A journey through a ninety-mile tunnel in waking hours would be intolerable."

The waiter came round, closing the curtains.

"What's that rumbling sound?" I asked.

"We've changed to the undersea track, sir. You'll get used to the noise. Most passengers find it hypnotic. At least they get a good night's sleep. No fun for those of us who have to work with it half the night."

Molly and I ordered dessert then chatted over coffee. For a talkative person, she showed a curious reluctance to discuss our destination. Several of my questions she deflected with an irrelevant answer, or by asking me a question in return. On the other hand, just like they'd done at my interview, she asked many questions about my upbringing, in particular the seaside resort that had been my childhood home.

We conducted our conversation against the peculiar low rumbling from the train wheels and the visual backdrop of the waiter bustling in and out with his tray of drinks. At one point the train braked hard and he came flying down the aisle, refreshment tray held aloft. But he recovered his balance magnificently. The gasps of the diners turned to cheers and applause, which he acknowledged with a smile and a mock bow. So, there was a human being under the poker face, though the mask had returned when he came round next, clearing the tables.

I asked him, "Why does the train need to brake? There's not another ahead of us, is there?"

"Curves, sir," he replied.

Molly said, "Don't imagine the tunnel is a convenient straight line all the way. They had to follow the natural geology."

The staff wanted to lay for second service, so Molly and I parted. Back in my compartment, someone had delivered a glossy brochure welcoming travelers to the "Island Express". The spiel went into great detail about the undersea tunnel, describing how the health-giving effects of the salt rock enhanced air drawn into the ventilation system. Passengers often remarked passing the night on the train in an unusually deep and refreshing sleep.

I was unable to sleep, my mind turning over the events of the day, in particular the incredible story I'd been told at my interview that afternoon.

Chapter 2

The Beginnings

A week ago, there arrived the letter which had been the beginnings of all this, the letter from Publishing John:

Nostalgia
April 23rd, 1990

Dear Mike,

I believe your contract is due to finish soon. I'm hoping it's good timing. I've broken my ankle, badly, and am laid up in hospital. I can still write but I need an assistant. I've already negotiated the hourly rate you've been getting in Dublin, though they won't pay travel expenses. You know how I've always admired your writing ability.

The letter went on to give details of the offices of a large estate, situated way down in the southwest corner of Ireland, in a remote coastal area of West Cork. I'd had my eye on a bigger opportunity, in Singapore, starting in the autumn, giving me time to fill in the summer with what I fantasised would be a laid-back, Irish style, country house appointment — a posh suite of private rooms; an easy workload, helping them update their database or accounts software; leisurely strolls down to the village pub for extended lunch hours; traditional music in the bar in the evenings. Great craic altogether. And the family might have a pretty daughter, an eligible heiress.

Directly after graduating, I'd travelled to Ireland for my first job, a temporary contract in Dublin, where I shared an office with three guys named John. The label on their door announced: "The Johns". Two of them had a technical training, like me. The odd one out I called "Publishing John", because of his former career in journalism and because he took charge of all product documentation, my role being to liaise between him and the technical guys. I'd be asked to write the first drafts, handing them on for editing and polishing — an education in itself, because he tore into my use of English, invariably rewriting what I had written. October 1989, seven months ago, he left the company abruptly, in mysterious circumstances. I arrived at work to hear raised voices coming from the boss's office. John was handing in his notice, unwilling to say who had made him the better offer. A rumour that he'd sold out to our chief competitor cast a shadow over his departure, not helped by his refusal to divulge even the tiniest clue as to his new job.

Even now, I felt a holding back. At the top of his letter, where you'd normally expect the address, the single word: "Nostalgia". That strange inscription wasn't the only puzzling thing. Why the effusive reference to my writing skills? Blatantly untrue. I could put it down to John's taking-the-mick sense of humour but the sentence jarred with the business-like tone of the rest. The thought crossed my mind he was trying to send a message, a plea for help, or a warning to be on my guard, by adding a phrase only I would know to be out of place. Did he think somebody would intercept the letter? Was he being watched while he wrote it? I discounted these ideas as the product of my over-active imagination. How many times subsequently did I wish I had not.

Chapter 3

Road Trip

The journey from Dublin down to Ireland's far south west coast had been a long one, its tedium exacerbated by the scenery, the flat rural landscape of central Ireland dull and oppressive under a heavy blanket of grey with a drizzling rain. We reached the coast at Bantry, where I had to change coaches. The sun came out, and with it a rainbow, the terrain of rocky hills and sea inlets transformed in an instant from gloomy to glorious, the changed mood reflected in the new coach, packed full of lively locals, with just one free seat, next to a tiny old man wearing a light grey suit that looked like it had been specially miniaturised to fit. His face seemed fixed in a permanent grin. I guessed rightly the grin would be a prelude to a lot of talking. He opened by asking my name. "Michael, is it? Sure, you're an Irishman already! Or do you prefer to be called *Mick*?"

I replied my friends called me "Mike".

My companion lived in my destination town. When I told him the purpose of my visit, he said, "So, you'll be working for The Earl?"

I asked, "He's one of the Anglo-Irish aristocracy, then?"

The old man laughed, "It's a joke, an honorary title, first given to his great-grandfather because of the way he lorded it over his lands. He made a fortune and bought up a vast area to create a country estate."

"How did he make his money?"

"He started off with a patch of hilly ground. He got it cheap. Nobody else wanted it." The old man pointed at a muddy, boulder-strewn field we were racing by in the coach. "Like that one. Useless for grazing. He found out why. A rock-salt seam hiding just below the surface."

"There's not much money to be made from salt, is there?"

"Right! With the narrowness of the seam, they had to drive their tunnels for miles, the main problem being how to prevent the miners from suffocating. The first Earl was your typical nineteenth-century inventor. He patented equipment for deep tunnel ventilation. Then he hit on the idea of exporting his ventilation systems for gold mines. That's what made him rich."

From my talkative friend I got the entire family history. An eccentric lot. The first Earl spent his money buying up land between town and coast, turning it into a game-bird reserve for the amusement of his shooting friends. He also built the family home, a mock castle, where he hosted extravagant social occasions. By contrast, his son, the second Earl, a recluse, shut up everything, living out a life of isolation and mental illness. The third Earl tried to develop the land near the coast with a grandiose scheme for a seaport but the notoriously treacherous currents and tides and the difficulty of cutting a safe passage through the rocky foreshore rendered the project impractical. It was abandoned.

The incumbent Earl, the fourth, sounded the most eccentric. In the sixties he'd hosted wild parties and rumoured sex orgies for his hippy friends. An enthusiast for motocross, he held a competition each year on a two-mile course across his land. In 1970 the races were cancelled and the course dismantled. No explanation given. In the same year, he cancelled a planned hot-air ballooning event. Again, no explanation. The locals worried the Earl might be showing signs of his reclusive grandfather's illness, then new activities started up. He amassed an impressive collection of vintage cars, open to the public every weekend. And he established an agricultural research institute. The latter caused disquiet in the neighbourhood, with the Earl's land now ringed by tall security fences, sightings of "scientists in white coats", and regular patrols by "green guards". They carried rifles fitted with night sights, supposedly for shooting vermin but, on more than one occasion, people who'd got too near the land had warning shots fired at them.

I asked, "If the family are so rich, why stay here? Why not sell up and move to Monte Carlo or those other playboy places?"

The old man made a wry face. "The estate is entailed. They can't sell it. They can't disinherit. Ownership must pass from father to son. Some families might see it as a curse, a millstone round their neck, preventing them enjoying their money. Still, we're not complaining. The Earl's goings-on keep us entertained. Without him there'd be no local economy. Organic vegetables are the latest thing. They grow a massive amount on the estate. They're even exporting tomatoes to Holland. We see the Dutch lorry twice a week in the summer."

Extensive tomato growing in Ireland was news to me. I remarked they'd need to have a lot of greenhouses.

The old man replied, "There's a puzzle there. Nobody knows where the stuff is grown. The estate employs townspeople in the packing sheds. None of them have seen the greenhouses. They must be somewhere, of course but the land stretches for miles, most of it is fenced off and the last known map was made fifty years ago. Wherever they are, I say they are being worked by the outsiders."

When I asked about the outsiders, my companion hesitated, as if he regretted mentioning them to a stranger.

"Every Tuesday, Thursday and Saturday mornings," he continued at last, "a coach leaves the estate. A fifty-seater, full of people. Every Sunday, Tuesday and Thursday evenings, it returns, again full of people. It passes by my house. My street is narrow, a bottleneck, so traffic usually crawls by. I've made a point of scrutinising this coach. I'm willing to swear the same people are never on it more than once, either outgoing or incoming. Where do they all come from? Where do they go? What happens to them on the estate?"

I said, "I'm beginning to have second thoughts about this job."

The old man chuckled. "Ah, no! The Earl's a great lad. He's often in the town bars of an evening. I've had a drink with him many a time. You'll like him. I've never heard complaint from the locals who work for him."

"So you've never asked him about the outsiders?"

The old man paused to consider his reply. "There are things you can ask and things you can't ask. You understand what I'm saying?"

At that moment there happened the defining event of the day. Our coach had arrived at the town centre. As I stood on the pavement, waiting to collect my luggage, a 1920's, Type 39 Bugatti roared up the street, paintwork and fittings gleaming in the bright afternoon sunshine, at the wheel an attractive young woman dressed to match the period of the car. The old man nudged me. "You can guess where she's going in a hurry. The Earl's personal assistant — some say the Earl's mistress."

Chapter 4

Fourth Earl

I'd been advised to take a taxi to the estate. I found out why after we passed the gates. The driveway down to the main house must have been at least a mile and a half long. On the right, it bordered dense deciduous woodland. On the left, a patchwork of stone walled grass fields ran up to hills a mile distant. Access in that direction was denied by the high wire fencing the old man on the coach had alluded to, lining the roadside as far as could be seen. At intervals were notices: "Keep Out. Agricultural Research. Risk Of Contamination." But I saw no "green guards", nor "scientists in white coats", nor did I see any crops or animals in the fields beyond the fencing.

At the end of the drive, the road curved away from the fence, passing through trees, emerging to give my first view of the Earl's mock-castle home, grand and impressive, with a turret at each corner and ivy covering the walls. Parked outside, the Bugatti.

The estate manager greeted me at the front door and took me to his office. He had prepared the contract of work to be signed by both sides. Regarding the special conditions of the job, he told me I would be having tea with the Earl, who would discuss those with me directly, then, if I was happy to sign, they'd give me a day or two to settle in before starting work. When I asked about accommodation, he replied brusquely, "That's already been organised." At that moment his office telephone rang and he showed me into the library to wait.

The library had everything you'd expect from a stately home: high-ceiling, enormous fireplace, plush sofas, and walls lined with tall stacks packed with old books. A few shelves contained modern books, probably the only ones ever read. Unsurprisingly there was a whole row dedicated to vintage cars and another to organic market gardening. Otherwise, the Earl appeared to be a man of eclectic interests. My eye passed over *Economics of the Small Town 1900 - 1960, Quadraphonic Sound, Miniature Model Making, Hot Air Ballooning, Helicopter Pilot Training, Seaside Entertainments of Bygone Days, The Theatre Backstage Handbook, Murder on The Orient Express.* I settled into a sofa with a book on Bugatti cars but voices outside the window and the crunch of footsteps on gravel distracted me. Two men, dressed in green uniform, were crossing the driveway. So, these were the "green guards". Something odd about their appearance, the cut of their uniform severely dated, reminiscent of nineteen–sixties London Carnaby Street. I couldn't decide whether this made them look on the verge of camp, or sinister, or, if possible, both at the same time.

"I'm ready for tea, if you are." My host had entered the room without my hearing him. "Chilly in here, isn't it?"

About fifty, tall, his thick black hair slightly greying, the Earl possessed the kind of good looks that are a distinct aid to authority rather than an encumbrance to it. He opened the door to the office and spoke to somebody inside. "Tell them we'll have tea now, and we need the fire lit."

Sitting down directly facing me, he said, "Mike, I've read your skill-set. I'm happy with that but I'd like to know about your background. Were you brought up in a town or in a city?"

"In a town"

"Good! Inland, or by the sea?"

"A seaside resort, on the south coast of England."

"And how would you describe your seaside resort?"

"Run down. The main street full of cheap shops, a few seedy amusement arcades by the beach. High unemployment. Not much going on."

The Earl stared at me, fathoming my innermost thoughts. "But it wasn't always that way? Do your grandparents come from the town?"

"On my mother's side, yes."

"Do they ever talk about the past?"

"My grandfather does, all the time. He talks about the factories now long gone. In his words 'Full employment and no excuse to be a layabout'. And he tries to persuade me what a great social life they had at the old dance halls and theatres. He has postcards showing the seafront crammed with day-trippers down from London. He has others showing the fishermen standing outside their cottages. The fishing industry went years ago. The cottages are holiday lets now."

Curious to know why the Earl was showing such an intense interest in my upbringing, I almost risked the impertinence of asking him outright. Luckily, a middle-aged woman, entering at that moment with a tea tray, interrupted the conversation. After pouring out the tea, she set about laying the fire. Hoping to get a clue as to a certain younger female, I changed the subject. "That's a great Bugatti you have outside."

"Our most recent restoration," said the Earl. "We're running her in. The policy of our museum is that a car should be treated like a living creature, allowed to roam wild and free, not kept in a cage."

"Do you have many in the collection?"

"They keep our hands full. We have them running at the weekends when we open to the public."

I thought it prudent interview strategy to empathise with my host's interests, so I said, "The car is a magnificent machine."

I couldn't have judged it more wrongly if I'd tried. With a look verging on anger, the Earl replied, "The car is a curse!" Then, smiling, "You can't imagine how I, a well-known vintage motor enthusiast, could say that. Consider this: Better to ban cars from the roads and confine them to museums. You may consider it impossible for modern society to function without the car..."

He paused briefly, waiting for the housekeeper to leave.

"...I can show you a place where not only is the car banned but society is all the better for it. What I am about to tell you is in the strictest confidence and will need a witness present."

He picked up the telephone. "Saoirse? Good! You're in the office. Would you come through to the library?"

The door from the office opened, and the most gorgeous girl I have ever seen entered the room.

Chapter 5

The Experiment

Seen close to, in her flapper dress, the Earl's assistant was even more attractive than I'd anticipated, age about twenty-five, of above average height, with nice legs and a slim but shapely figure, her expressive pretty face and large green eyes set off by long wavy natural red hair, striking and flamboyant in its colouration. She had a presence about her: quiet, calm and intelligent.

"Saoirse is here as a witness," said the Earl. "I am relying on your integrity that none of what I am about to tell you will you pass on, not even to the people closest to you. I should add there's nothing illegal or immoral involved."

I said, "In that case, I agree."

The Earl motioned for us to come close. "I ask that we form a circle and hold hands to set a seal on the agreement."

I decided to go along with the proposed extraordinary rigmarole, to see what would happen next. We stood in a circle of three. Saoirse gave my hand a reassuring squeeze.

The Earl said, "Repeat after me: I agree to keep secret everything I will come to know about Nostalgia."

I repeated the strange incantation, as instructed. Then we sat down.

"Imagine an isolated place. Free of the motor car," began the Earl. "Having no easy means of conveying goods or people over distance, the community must rely on itself for most of what it eats, most of what it needs, most of what it enjoys"

"You mean a back-to-nature, hippy commune?"

"No, I don't mean that. I mean a place that has fully embraced modern technology, modern work and the modern lifestyle, but instead of technology being in the possession of faceless corporations and rapacious multi-nationals, that same technology is in the possession of, and in the service of, the people. There are companies and factories but everything is done on a small scale, locally. As dependence on the outside world is restricted, the community has to provide for itself, resulting in full employment, managed harmony with the environment, respect for the local ecology, people's lives given meaning, crime and social problems eliminated."

I said, "It's difficult to imagine how a place like that could avoid the influence of the wider world"

The Earl paused and glanced at Saoirse. They both seemed impressed by my remark.

"Precisely the conclusion my friends and I came to in the late sixties. We were hippies but becoming disillusioned. Shall I tell you what was wrong with the sixties? It was all 'Me, Me, Me!' Have you ever heard of Dr Timothy O'Leary?"

"Turn on. Tune in. Drop out?"

"Yes. What a pile of dog shite! You know those movements where people try to build a better world through spirituality? It turns out, when you get down to fundamentals, all their focus is on their own precious spiritual state. It's not possible to build a better world when all you are thinking about is yourself. That's narcissism. The alternative is a life of dedication and self-denial — 'altruism'. People think narcissism and altruism are mutually exclusive. Narcissism appeals to the many and benefits only the few. Altruism appeals to the few and therefore cannot benefit the many. The intelligent way is to benefit yourself and humanity simultaneously. Then, you are doubly motivated — you benefit, and others benefit as a by-product of your motivation. Do you follow me?"

"Can you give an example?"

"An Indian guru in the sixties tried to get his followers in the West to become successful at business. Each follower would keep three quarters of his business profits for himself and donate the remaining twenty-five percent to charity. A brilliant concept, a win-win situation for everyone. Did his followers embrace the idea? No! They were too busy massaging their spiritual egos to want to dirty themselves with the ways of the world."

The Earl continued, "We found our own conclusions about reforming society increasingly at odds with the fashionable wisdom of the sixties. We wanted a place, remote and isolated, where we could develop alternative ideas. One of us suggested we start an underground community in the salt mine — a joke, but some thought the idea had possibilities, so we got out an old map of the mine seams. My friend, Dr Jim Braben, a geologist from San Francisco, took the map away to study. The next day he came back in a state of great excitement, carrying several more maps, including a nautical map of the west

coast of Ireland and a map of geological strata. He laid them out and pointed to a small island, about ninety miles from the coast. '*That's* where your salt seam comes to the surface', he said, 'All the geological evidence points to it.'
"

"The island in question — I'm not telling you the name — had never been inhabited, owing to its impenetrable and dangerous rocky coastline and tall cliffs. We had a mad, crazy idea. We would drive the longest tunnel in the world through the salt rock, take possession of the island as squatters, and build a secret isolated community. We had the technology; we had the money from my family's estate; all we needed were people who believed in the ideal and had the will to achieve it."

I asked, "Wouldn't they have needed to become expert tunnelers?"

The Earl smiled. "Clearly impossible. We openly declared a new mining company project. We put it about that my workers were driving a long test tunnel for a new generation of mine ventilation equipment. They laid the single-track railway as they cut the tunnel, along with power cables and the ducts for the ventilation system. Jim Braben took charge of the geological surveying, so no employee need be informed of our intended destination. Of course, we couldn't let any of them witness the tunnel surfacing the other side, so Jim excavated the last mile himself, with a small team of people drawn from our circle of close friends. A driven man. He and the others actually lived in the tunnel for weeks on end. Imagine their relief when they finally broke through to the island."

"What would have happened if they'd got their calculations wrong?"

"If they'd missed the island and come up through the sea bed, the pressure of the water would have collapsed the tunnel roof before they'd time to wake up to their mistake. Their tunnel would have become their grave."

"You're telling me you have a ninety-mile tunnel under the sea, by far the longest tunnel in the world, that nobody knows about!"

The Earl laughed. "I don't blame you for not believing it. If you take the job, you'll see for yourself. We've kept this secret since the early seventies. Over two decades we have bit by bit developed the land. Five thousand people live in the island's town now, though it's not entirely isolated — the inhabitants travel to and from the mainland by the tunnel railway."

I asked, "Are they the people on the coaches? An old man from the town told me about them passing by his house. He says there's never the same people on them from one day to the next."

The Earl and Saoirse exchanged glances.

"Saoirse has tried to persuade me the locals are not as innocent as I think they are," he said. "I see she's right. So! Our turnover of people has not gone unnoticed? Our train is an overnight sleeper. It runs alternate days, arriving in the morning, leaving in the evening. It has bed space for fifty, maximum. You do the math. It's solidly booked months in advance. Most of the island's inhabitants only get one return trip per year. I can see we must be more discreet. What else did this old man tell you?"

"I got the full story of your ancestors. He was positive about the effect of your estate on the town, though he complained about a cancelled hot air balloon festival."

"We had to call a stop to those at the end of the sixties. The thermals from the hills round here are treacherous, and, as is usual on ocean coasts, sudden mists and fogs get up. We had a weather-related helicopter crash on our land, the pilot and the passenger both killed. I won a subsequent legal action to prohibit over-flying of my estate. I wasn't prepared to risk adding a balloon tragedy."

The talk of a hidden place that only its inhabitants knew existed, I found hard to accept. I asked, "One thing I don't understand. Concealing a whole town. What's to stop anyone giving it away?"

"And throw away the ideal lifestyle we have provided?" said the Earl, "This is no random crowd. Each resident is carefully chosen on the basis of a whole raft of factors. Firstly, he or she must be an idealist; secondly, they must have a genuine aversion to the negative aspects of modern society; thirdly, they must bring a skill and be a good worker; fourthly, their parents must be dead. Shocking, I know, but what are they going to do when granny wants to visit the grandchildren? There are many other factors we have to weigh up. Selection is stringent and by personal invitation only. Naturally, we don't advertise."

"You haven't explained the name," said Saoirse. Not only was this girl a fantastic looker, she had an appealing voice to match.

"Ah yes, the name!" replied the Earl, "We decided to call our town, 'Nostalgia'. It symbolises our objective: to get back to a sense of community, a sense of purpose in society, without rejecting the positive aspects of the progress of modern technology. You'll find it a fun place — a lively seaside resort at work and at play. Any other questions?"

It occurred to me the primary reason for my being there had not been mentioned. I asked, "How did John get involved?"

The Earl glanced at Saoirse. "I'm sorry. We have tea. Impolite of me not to offer you some." Saoirse replied she didn't want any. I sensed an awkward moment.

"For when in the future we go public with our secret," continued the Earl, "we need every detail of our story documented. That's what we employed your colleague to do. He made a brilliant job of it, going everywhere, interviewing everyone. Unfortunately, he had an accident and now he can't move from his hospital bed. So we need you to do the spadework, collecting the data for John to write up."

I felt some qualms about the term "spadework". I asked, "Can you be more specific? My university subjects were electronic engineering and computer programming — very different from John's journalistic background."

"John thinks you can do it," replied the Earl, "and one thing we've learned about John is to respect his judgement. You'll be required to interview people, archive the material, take photographs, maintain a database, type up reports, you name it. John was keen we should get you.

He says you're a fast learner, which will be vital — the work has fallen greatly behind schedule since the accident."

"What *was* his accident?"

"Your John unintentionally strayed onto a restricted area. How it happened we're not sure, as it's all fenced off. One of our security guards was racing down a path on his pushbike, not expecting anyone to be there. Turning a corner, he collided with your friend. John broke his ankle falling. I understand you've been shown your contract of employment? I'll go and get it."

The Earl went through to the office. Saoirse and I smiled at each other. I felt compelled to say something but my mind went blank. I could think of nothing more original than to lamely ask, "The building on the hill opposite. Is it the railway station?"

"The station is a mile further down, in the valley. I'll be driving you there later if you agree to work for us. I hope you will agree. The hilltop building is the agricultural research institute"

"What research are they doing?"

"Top secret!" she replied. I thought she must be kidding me but the look on her face told me otherwise.

The Earl returned and brought over the contract to sign. "It's time for you to make a choice. Either forget everything we have told you, leave this room and never come back, or accept our offer, join us, and become an honoured contributor to our experiment for a better world. I've freed Saoirse from her mainland duties for a while, so, as from Friday, she will join you on the island and show you round."

This offer of Saoirse's company, whether innocent statement of standard procedure or calculated ploy to secure my agreement, was the deciding factor. Impulsively, I signed the contract, sealing my fate.

Chapter 6

Night Train

The train taking me to the island didn't leave till evening. The Earl invited me to wait at his home and provided an impressive first floor guest room, overlooking the driveway. The room had a TV but the comings and goings outside the window interested me more. First, Saoirse drove away in the Bugatti. During her absence, several business types arrived in expensive cars. Vans and lorries came and went intermittently, their drivers emerging with chits for signing at the office. Obviously, a busy and prosperous estate. At one point, the Earl came out and spoke with his green guards. He pointed up at my window, though I couldn't hear what he was saying.

It had been arranged I would go down at seven, when Saoirse would drive me to the station. On the dot, I heard the Bugatti coming up the drive. She shouted for me to jump in, and we sped off. My fear of seeming a fool again by asking inane questions was quickly dispelled. We chatted away like we'd known each other forever. I could have thought this a promising indication of chemistry between us, although I was more inclined to credit Saoirse's relaxed personality.

After passing through deciduous woodland, the road emerged onto open ground, where a security fence blocked the way ahead, forcing us to pull up at a barrier and guard hut. Saoirse took a document from her bag and rushed inside, emerging a few seconds later with a green guard, who promptly raised the barrier and saluted as we drove on.

"That's to stop locals getting through and discovering the railway," said Saoirse.

Half a mile further we arrived at the station, a picturesque redbrick building of curiously old appearance, like something out of an Edwardian photo album. It even had an adjacent station master's house, which seemed to me hardly justifiable for what, according to the Earl's story, could be no more than six trains per week.

As I got out of the car, Saoirse said, "Enjoy your trip. See you Friday!" She pressed the accelerator and the Bugatti shot away in a cloud of exhaust fumes.

I entered the building at the customs hall. That's where I met Molly and she explained the need to exchange my cash for Nostalgia's Rocks and Pebbles currency. I handed over a bigger amount of Irish money than I felt comfortable about and watched it passed to a spotty young assistant who duly vanished through a door.

Molly and I exchanged pleasantries. I asked if she did the journey often.

"At that price?" she exclaimed, "Though I'm not complaining. They give you your money's worth. Pure luxury."

"Four Hundred Rocks and Two Pebbles! Catch!" I braced to intercept a large canvas moneybag hurled in my direction. The featherweight object I caught felt at first empty but at the bottom of the bag I found an envelope containing a bundle of Fifty-Rock bank notes and two tiny,

One-Pebble, coins. With a suppressed smile, enjoying his little, "heavy rocks" joke at the expense of the newbie, the spotty assistant disappeared back though his door.

We joined the line for the luggage check, no modern affair of a conveyor belt taking your case through an X-ray scanner, more like an old movie, a row of uniformed guys standing behind trestle tables, rifling through your suitcase. I noticed two officials scrutinising us with more than casual interest, so much so that I began to feel uncomfortable. One approached and asked Molly to accompany him to his office. Through the window I saw them in intense conversation. Every now and then, Molly gave me a worried glance.

"Is everything OK?" I asked the other official.

"Routine customs check, sir."

Released from the formalities, outside on the platform, a flustered Molly hurried past me. "Muddle over my ticket. All sorted out now," she said, breathlessly. In contrast with her former friendliness, she seemed anxious to get away, I assumed embarrassed by the customs incident, so I left her to board, while I hung around, observing the scene.

The railcars, beautifully painted a deep maroon, certainly gave out the promise of being luxurious. This was no ordinary transport, more one for conveying millionaires or royals. The bodywork tapered off at the front to a bullet-shaped nose cone reminiscent of a streamlined rocket from an old sci-fi film. Behind the driver's cab a powerful throbbing emanated from the engine car. Connected to it, some goods vans, followed by the galley, the restaurant car, the piano bar, and a chain of six sleepers. I stood watching workmen load the goods vans with stacks of boxes and crates. The sleeping cars began to emit a gentle hiss of steam from their heating system valves into the cool May evening. Reassured by this comforting sound, I boarded the train.

#

My watch showed midnight. Admitting the victory of my sleepless state, I dragged myself out of bed, dressed, and left my compartment. Treading quietly along the dimly lit corridor, anxious not to wake anyone, I stumbled through the covered joins between the rocking carriages, eventually reaching the bar, where I found only one other customer, the blue guard who'd been scrutinising me in the dining car. His friendly greeting defused a potentially awkward situation: "At last! A fellow insomniac! Can I buy you a drink?" I suggested red wine might help me sleep. He returned from the bar armed with two glasses and a full bottle.

Early twenties, unusually short in stature at five feet, my new friend possessed that stockier build of the Irish set against the English. However, he failed to impress as carrying significant weight or muscle. A bald head might have lent him a certain "Don't dare mess with me" effect but he enjoyed almost as much black hair as myself. Whatever these blue guards did, unless the man possessed clandestine martial arts skills, I couldn't imagine the job involved confronting physical threat. He introduced himself as Tadhg, a guard returning to work after ten days holiday travelling round the steam railways of Wales. An obvious buff, he talked enthusiastically about our tunnel train, explaining in laborious detail the locomotion achieved through special pods extended below the engine to pull us along an electro-magnetised track. Clearly, he wasn't technical, the physics of his muddled explanation pure nonsense, but the potent combination of his verbal ramblings and two large glasses of full-bodied Merlot had the desired effect of making me drowsy. I left him to finish the bottle, while I staggered back down the swaying carriages to my compartment.

I woke next morning to absolute quiet. For a brief moment I imagined the walls of my Dublin flat to be closing in on me — then I remembered. Drawing back the curtains, I saw the window shutters had been taken down and that the train was standing at a platform. The station clock showed eight minutes past seven.

A knock on my compartment door: "Six-Thirty call, sir."

I opened the door to the steward. I said, "The clock outside says eight minutes past seven."

"That's 'Island Time', sir. Thirty-eight minutes ahead of us. We keep mainland time here on the train. Don't forget to put your watch forward when you leave."

"Why is the island thirty-eight minutes ahead of the mainland?"

"I don't know *why*, sir. It just *is*."

Chapter 7

Island

I saw neither Tadhg nor Molly at breakfast. Most of the passengers had left early. Of course, as permanent residents, they all had homes to go to. By the time I quit the train, the dining car had emptied. The Earl's estate manager had given me the vaguest of instructions for getting to my hotel: "Take a canal boat to the town centre, then walk to the seafront," adding obscurely that I could either walk or take the ferry across the water. Not a man with any patience for elaboration, so I left it at that — how difficult could it be to find the only hotel in town?

The warmth of the railway cars hadn't prepared me for the damp chill island mist that clung to my face as I stepped off the train. The platform was deserted, the waiting rooms locked up, the customs hall in darkness. At the side of the building, I found an exit gate, which gave onto a broad cobbled square surrounded by woodland. A fingerpost, labelled "Water Taxi", pointed to a footpath leading down to a canal, where I could see a horse-drawn barge slowly drawing off. I shouted for them to wait, and made a run for it, culminating in a flying leap, which landed me squarely on deck before they had moved too far out. The bargeman's face registered his disapproval of the recklessness of my boarding. I joined a dozen people standing squashed together between the tiller and the cargo, I assumed passengers from the train because of their long dark cloaks with the turned-up pointed collars.

35

Had I truly arrived in the domain of an unknown cult? Too late now to reconsider.

The barge glided along, my fellow passengers standing cloaked, silent and inscrutable. An impenetrable mist enveloped our serene passage, deadening all sound, so you could hear only the gentle lapping of water against the barge sides, the regular heavy thud of the horse's hooves on the towpath, and early morning birdsong from the fields beyond. Then, like an image from a surrealist painting, there appeared, through the gloom, rows of luminous eyes, each row stacked on top of the other.

"The windows of the hill dweller houses," confided the bargeman. "That's the desirable part of the island. Everyone wants to live there because of the special amenities."

Who or what were these "hill dwellers"? A kind of displaced tribe? And what were these "special amenities" the other islanders so desired? An image of "pygmies with patios" came into my head.

I asked whether we would be negotiating any locks. "You need a river to feed locks," said the bargeman. "Hungry for water they are. We have to preserve our limited resources here. The canal follows level ground." He pointed ahead. "There's the town wall!"

Looming up in front, the fortifications of a bygone era, an ancient battlemented wall, the canal passing through an archway flanked by tall stone towers — except of course all fake — according to the Earl's story no construction on the island could be more than twenty years old. As our boat passed under the arch, two men in blue scrutinised us from above. Strange that on this isolated island it had been thought necessary to enclose the town in a guarded wall.

Inside, the scene could not have been more different, a densely built-up area, long terraces of houses lining the canal. With most of my fellow passengers I disembarked at the first stop. Passing down the town's main street, full of quaint shops, none open yet, I caught glimpses in the fog of cloaked figures unlocking their doors and stepping inside. The end of the street gave out onto a quayside, where I searched for the boat to the hotel but none of the several fishing vessels roped to bollards remotely resembled my expectation of a ferry. I peered out to sea, straining to hear the sound of an engine from within the vast misty expanse, the only vessel on the dead-calm water a rowing boat being slowly manoeuvred in my direction by an old man. Reaching the quay wall, he shouted up "You want the hotel?"

Bemused and horrified at the thought of him taking me onto the open ocean, I reluctantly handed down my luggage. The ferryman assured me the hotel was no distance and we set off. The mist soon swallowed up the receding quayside and I could see nothing but vaporous white. I marvelled at the old man's sense of direction as he rowed on, never once showing concern he might be off course. He had little conversation, apart from alluding at intervals as to how "fierce hot" it was, so much so that I felt obliged to offer to share the rowing. He brushed off the suggestion. "Not at all! You're grand! Fierce hot, though, isn't it?"

The hotel now coming into view presented an extraordinary sight. An impressive rectangular three-storey stone building, it appeared to be floating on the water. In front and to the right of it, a wide paved area; on the other side a garden set out with tables and sunshades. The surrounding water ran right up to the pavement and right up level with the lawn of the garden. No wall or drop separated water from land; the one joined seamlessly to the other. The ferryman noticed my amazement. "Clever, isn't it? It'll stay that way for another hour."

"Is the hotel on a raft? Does it float up and down with the tide?"

"With that weight of stonework! "

"Does it move up and down on jacks?"

"Impossible!"

I could see the ferryman enjoyed baffling newcomers with the mystery of the floating stone hotel.

"You're won't get it. I'll tell you. This isn't open sea. It's a bay. At the back of the bay is a wall. There's pipes through the wall at the height of the lowest high tide of the year. Any tide higher and the surplus drains through to a salt marsh the other side. So, high-water mark is at the same level all year round. The hotel and gardens are built on concrete foundations at the exact high-water level."

"Surely the ocean tide is too powerful to be defeated by a few drainpipes?"

"I can see you're a bright lad. The opening at the sea end of the bay is narrow. It's blocked by another wall, with sluice gates. They close those gates as soon as the tide has flowed in."

With a sudden jolt, the boat came to rest against the hotel pavement. Stepping out onto land precisely level with the water, I fully expected it to sink as I put my weight on it. Retrieving my luggage, I asked, "What happens at low tide?"

The old man rowed off, shouting back at me between strokes, "There's a sandy beach... But it's not natural... The sand's imported... A by-product of the salt mine... Nothing's real here."

The mist reclaimed his boat, and he was gone.

Hotel check-in was straightforward. They took me past the ground-floor dining room, full of blue-uniformed breakfasting guards, upstairs to a second-floor front-facing room, bright, clean and simply furnished. No swish modern decor here: a bed, chest of drawers, a clothes cupboard, some bookshelves and a writing desk. I stood for some time at the windows, looking out at the fog, and at the silvery sea, which enveloped and clung to the land as though threatening at any moment to spill over, engulfing all. Then, still groggy from my interrupted night on the train, I took off my jacket and lay down on the bed.

From somewhere down the corridor, I heard voices. A man: "Has he arrived yet? Who's been assigned?"

Answered by a woman: "Quiet! He's there!"

Chapter 8

Nostalgia Hotel

Midday I woke to the distant sound of excited children. Sunlight streamed in through my bedroom windows. The morning mist had lifted. The tide had receded a great distance, exposing a wide area of sandy beach. Mothers and fathers took advantage of the fine weather to sunbathe, while their children built sandcastles or splashed about in the shallow water's edge. I planned for the next two days to get to know the place. From hotel reception I purchased a map, which cost me three Rocks and fifty Pebbles of their island currency. Sitting outside in the hotel garden, in the warm sunshine, with a pint of the local brew for company, I congratulated myself on landing such a plush and unusual assignment — luxury hotel, food and accommodation all paid for, drink also paid for ("within reason" the Earl had said), generous wages, fascinating location, fine seaside summer weather, possibility of a girlfriend ...

The map showed the hotel to be at the edge of a small rocky hillock, unimaginatively entitled "Little Island". Behind the hotel, a network of a few short streets. An S-shaped curve, marked out on the map with parallel dotted lines, ran from the back of Little Island across the stretch of water to Nostalgia Town. I took it to be a tunnel but later discovered it to be a causeway that could be crossed at low tide. Further inland was marked the straight harbour wall, with an area behind labelled "Salt Marsh", the very same wall and salt marsh the ferryman told me precisely regulated the high-water mark. The wall cut right across the back of a horseshoe-shaped bay, two miles from end to end, a mile across at its widest point, tapering down to a gap of less than a hundred yards at its outlet through tall cliffs to the open sea. The legend "Sluice gates. Hydro Power Station" marked an embankment which closed off this outlet.

Across the water from the hotel was marked "Nostalgia Town". A magnified inset showed the streets in detail. I could easily appreciate five thousand people lived there. The wall, with its succession of twelve towers, or "gates", enclosed the built-up area. It formed a semicircle, terminating at each end at the long quayside. From the quays, a promenade and road ran along the side of the bay as far as the coastal cliffs, curving uphill through woodland and running back downhill to the railway station. Starting at the railway, the canal passed a steep hill built up with houses, which I judged must be the houses of the hill dwellers. The canal flowed into town under the wall, out again at the southern side, across the salt marsh, to an extensive area marked "Industrial". Various map symbols were obscure to me, but one I knew well from maps I'd used on cycle rides as a teenager in southern England: the symbol for a glasshouse. A vast area was marked off with glass, presumably the site of Earl's organic vegetable growing business.

On the far side of the water, a steep wooded escarpment ran the entire length of the bay. Another promenade was marked, stopping just short of the sea cliffs, with a building labelled "Lighthouse". Looking from the hotel garden towards the coast, I could just make out in the morning heat-haze the round glass lantern of a tower sticking out from the wooded cliff top.

At the back of town, the contours indicated hills. An unlabelled feature, marked with a dotted line, stretched across this part of the map from one side to the other, with a single building the only other feature in this area of open countryside. Some tracks were marked also, but no roads. I turned over the map to study the plan of the rest of the island. There was no such plan, only an index of the grid markings for the town streets. I asked at reception if they had a map of the whole island. They told me the far side was used exclusively by the agricultural research institute — nobody ever went there, except the Blue Guards, who had the job of patrolling the security fence marked on my map with the dotted line.

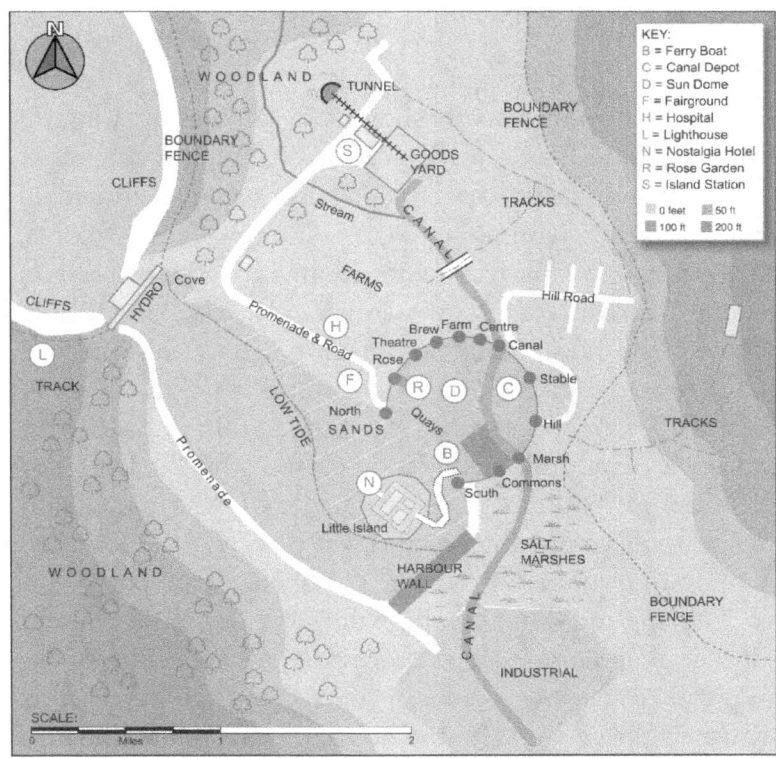

A Map of Nostalgia Town and Surrounding Area

I decided to spend the afternoon on a reconnaissance of the town. I now understood the estate manager's cryptic instruction when he'd said, "either walk or take the ferry". With the tide out, I could cross over by foot. The road behind the hotel rose steeply, winding its way between a jumble of quaint fishermen's cottages before descending from the brow of the hill down a long straight street of ordered Georgian-style terraced houses to a quay at the back of Little Island. Two shops faced the quay: one an aquarium, "Admission: 1 Rock", the other a typical seaside bucket-and-spade shop, with families queuing up for ice creams. Inside, an emporium of anything you might need for the seaside: beach balls, beach games, inflatable rubber rafts, swimming aids, swimming suits, bikinis, towels, bags, sun hats, sun creams, sun glasses, sun shades, canvas tents and windshields, food and drink, chairs, hammocks, loungers, fishing rods, fishing tackle, bait, beach carts, with stock spilling onto the already cramped floor space. As on the train, I noticed the distinct absence of anything made of plastic, the buckets and spades, for example, being made of tin and wood respectively. Was this an enforced policy of the town, to live up to its name by creating a pastiche of the past?

Leaving the shop, I walked the roadway to the far end of the quay. Here it sloped down to join the white stone-flagged causeway snaking across the golden sands towards the town. With the holiday atmosphere, the lure of the beach, the hot sun and the cloudless blue sky, I felt my enthusiasm for work rapidly diminishing. I decided my tour would go no further than the bay. Accordingly, I abandoned the causeway and made a half circuit of Little Island's rocky circumference. As I came back round to the hotel terrace on the far side, a pleasant light sea breeze tempted me to cross the sands and seek out the low tide mark. Close by the water's edge, knots of infants dug furiously with toy spades, flinging sand in all directions, creating little moated islands with towers and walls in imitation of their town. I took off my sandals and strode the shallows towards the coast for about a mile, then turned back, striking off in the direction of the quays. From out here I had a panoramic view of Nostalgia, with the two round towers marking the quayside termination points of the surrounding wall. The town buildings were mainly two-storey, the exception dominating the view an enormous round glasshouse protruding above the line of all the others and containing many trees growing up to the apex of its domed roof. I speculated it might have a religious function. It might even be the temple of the wizard-like *cloakies*. The hippy origins of Nostalgia and the verdant greenery inside the dome suggested to me some sort of nature-worship cult. I imagined naked women joining hands inside, ululating, dancing round in a giant circle.

Near the quays, the sand underfoot became dry and powdery, obliging me to thread my way between more and more, mainly female, sunbathers. One woman, a brunette, aged around forty, wearing a bikini, and with fantastic legs, smiled at me invitingly.

A concrete ramp led from the sands to the tower known as "North Gate". On the far side of the road, a building labelled "Telegraph Office" had a sign up saying "Telephone Anywhere! Free!" This gave me the idea to ring John at the hospital. Inside, I expected the office to be a hive of activity but the door opened onto an empty wood-panelled chamber, high ceilinged, lit by a skylight, and having a partition and counter across the back. Telephone booths lined the walls, each containing a shelf with an old-fashioned brass telephone and a leather-bound directory. No telephone possessed a dial. The woman behind the counter told me to lift up a receiver and listen. I did so and a well-spoken female voice answered, "What number do you want, caller?"

While I stood waiting to be connected, the woman from the beach stepped in from the quays. She had covered her bikini with a light blue summer dress. With the place empty, she could have chosen any booth but she took the one directly opposite mine. She stared at me as she lifted the receiver, her pixie hairstyle emphasising arresting blue eyes. Absently, she rubbed her right leg up and down her left calf, as if to relieve an itch, though I guessed a deliberate display, for my entertainment. She asked the operator for a number then abruptly turned her back to engage in conversation on the phone.

A crackly voice in my earpiece announced, "Hospital". When I asked to speak with John, they gave no response. I waited a few seconds, thinking I must have been cut off, then the crackly voice came back: Who was I and what was the purpose of my call? Another silence, then a different voice: "We're sorry. There are no telephones in the ward. You need to make an appointment." And the line went dead.

It shouldn't be this difficult to get in touch with John. The Earl's office might help. I asked the woman behind the counter for the estate number. She replied the network had no connection to the mainland. When I pointed out her sign, saying "Telephone Anywhere", she explained that meant anywhere on the *island*. She said I could send a telegram, and gave me a form to fill in. Not wishing to over-dramatise the situation of the aborted phone call, I wrote the estate office a courtesy note thanking them for the hotel accommodation and dropping a hint about meeting John. I handed the form to a man wearing a green eyeshade, who proceeded to tap out my message in Morse code on a hinged contraption made of brass, like stepping back into the American Wild West. Curiously ancient technology for a town I found out later to be advanced in so many ways.

Leaving the office, I stole a quick glance at the lady of the legs. Halfway back down the road, a woman's voice behind me said, "You're new here, aren't you?" The lady herself.

She invited me to go with her to watch the incoming tide-race, apparently a sight not to be missed. I stood surveying the scene while she sat on the edge of the quay, those legs dangling over the side. I noticed she wore a wedding ring, as well as fetching, light-blue strappy sandals, matching her dress. The tide was still out, families dotted all over the extensive sands, children playing, enjoying the summer sunshine, a tranquil scene soon to be disturbed. Several guards went down onto the beach, anxiously consulting their watches. Others sprinted across the sands from the hotel while some with pushbikes took off at speed in the direction of the coast. All along, from nearby to the far distance, the sound of guard whistles. "That's to warn families to take care of their young children," said my companion.

The water was coming in fast now, covering the sand at such a rate it was like watching a speeded-up film. Clouds of swooping gulls marked the advancing tidal edge, eager for food churned up by the rapid flow, the cacophony of their squawking making redundant any further use of warning whistles. The families had picked up their towels and things and hurried towards us ahead of the chasing wave. The children obviously thought it great fun, this daily race to beat the tide, their screams of delight mixing with the exultant bird cries.

Ten minutes later, with calm restored, where there had been a wide expanse of sand, now all was seawater. Fierce Hot came along, untied his boat and rowed two guards back to the hotel. I said goodbye to my companion and awaited the return of the ferry. Sitting in the boat, watching the receding quayside, I regretted I had not asked her where in Nostalgia she lived. She had told me only her Christian name: "Sally", the last thing she said to me, "We must meet again."

At seven, I went downstairs to get something to eat. The busy hotel dining room and lounge bar fronted the whole ground floor, taking maximum advantage of the view, the wide sweep of the bay out to the coastal cliffs. The muted decor of wood-panelled walls, plush sofas and country pub furnishings avoided the insolence of attempting to upstage the magnificence of the panorama framed by the windows. Just like on the train, the menu offered vegetarian dishes and fish, but no meat. Did they have a moral objection to meat, or did its absence from menus provide an indication of the size of the island, that it lacked the land area needed to support effective meat production?

Late evening, from the window of my hotel room, I watched the rise and fall of the glow from the distant cliff-top lighthouse. The lighthouse — now there was a funny thing! Who built it, and for what purpose? Wouldn't the lighthouse in fact draw attention to the habitation of the island they were so anxious to keep secret? With hindsight, I understand I was too absorbed at the time with my impending rendezvous with Saoirse to appreciate this question of the lighthouse was the first doubt in my mind about Nostalgia Island and the trust I should place in the people who controlled it.

Chapter 9

The Follower

Thursday began on a cloudless sky, with none of the mist of the morning of my arrival. I looked out from the breakfast room at the sunlight glistening on the clear blue sea. Uncanny how the high-water lapping against the edges of the courtyard gave you the impression of floating on a raft. I watched as the ferry from the mainland arrived, picked up a guard, and departed. By the time I got outdoors it had returned, Fierce Hot in charge, somewhat bad-tempered from his exertions under the morning sun. Sitting in the boat I have to admit my admiration for his navigational skills had evaporated along with yesterday's mist. The ferry merely travelled in a dead straight line between one quay and the other.

At the town, I took out my map and made my way down a random side street. I had devised no exploration plan.

How to describe my first experiences of Nostalgia? The traditional architecture I had seen so far, along the canal and quayside and in the back streets of Little Island, recreated the look of an old seaport but, away from those areas, modern experimental architecture predominated, though never on the scale of the office block. Nostalgia possessed no skyscrapers, no blocks of flats, nothing greater than three stories. The roofs, in particular, stood out, subject to a strict building code: business premises must have roofs sloping; residential premises must have flat roofs. Wherever a roof sloped, you saw no tiles, only a solid expanse of solar panelling, the type that collects heat from water flowing in glass channels. The flow of water shimmered in the sunlight like a myriad of waterfalls. By contrast, the flat roofs of the residential properties were reinforced to carry the weight of earth troughs, and planted as gardens, the combined effect, a city-in-the-sky. Along the street you'd see familiar shops, offices, homes; above, you'd see an alien nether world of foliage and light.

One feature of Nostalgia, different from the town of my upbringing, and foreign to me, was that most streets possessed a factory or workshop of some kind, normally at the street corner. They made no distinct separation between residential and industrial. Walking around, I encountered many such street corner buildings, including a glassworks, a boat builders, a mechanical engineering company, metalworkers and carpenters, two potteries, clothing manufacturers, bakeries, three microbreweries and a distillery. Most Nostalgia residents lived minutes from their workplace. Even those working in the industrial estate lived half an hour away at most. In the outside world, it's common for people to spend a quarter of their working day commuting. Over a forty-year working life span, that's ten years of their life wasted. And they call it progress.

Nostalgia had no supermarkets, no department stores, and of course no out-of-town shopping complexes, as no inhabitant possessed a car. To provide for the many needs of modern life, a great variety of small shops took their place. My exploration of the town took me past one such, an outfitters, with a window display of cloaks identical to

51

those worn by the passengers from the train. I went inside and asked the shopkeeper, "Do you need special permission to wear one of those?"

He looked at me for a moment, then burst out laughing. "Very funny, sir! You're new here, aren't you? I suppose they do look pretentious if you're not used to our island fashions. They're morning cloaks. Turn up the collar and they're brilliant for keeping out the damp. Being in the middle of the ocean, we get a lot of fog, even in summer."

My assumption about the "cloakies" had been without foundation. Their silence on the barge held no more mystery than an understandable reaction to the early morning chill. Next, I queried the man on the dome in the middle of town. He told me they called it the "Sun Dome", an all-weather recreational facility. He chuckled when I told him I'd thought it functioned as a temple. "There's no religion on Nostalgia Island," he said.

The man gave me an enthusiastic tour of his shop. I remarked on the unusual design of the clothes, whereupon he explained the situation to me. The train arriving at the island only three mornings per week limited the amount of goods that could be imported. The clothes retailers could never bring in sufficient stock. Instead, the train brought in the raw materials, from which they made up the clothes locally. The industrial area even provided a natural dye manufacturers and fabric print works. The shopkeeper told me that once the women of the town got hold of the idea they could influence the local makers, a mini fashion industry had sprung up, the designers giving free rein to their imagination, without the constraint of needing to fit in with mainland fashion. "It's high summer now," he said. "People are dressed for the beach, so island style isn't so noticeable but go to a formal occasion or to an entertainment and you'll see a difference all right. Come back anytime and we'll get you fitted out."

After leaving the shop, I turned my attention to the roof gardens. Steps led to these from street level. Until now I had not gone up — I'd assumed them to be private. A local put me right by pointing out the signage on the steps. The gardens inter-connected, forming an alternative and elevated right of way around town. Each garden occupied the space of the house below, informally demarcated with small trees, shrubs and flower borders. The public footpath threaded its way along the edge. Where roads needed to be crossed, bridges carried the path over. Even these were created for visual effect, not the ugly graffiti-strewn concrete flyovers suffered everywhere in modern urban development, but delicate traceries of cast iron, the design of each bridge highly individual, both a functional item and a work of art. Walking from roof to roof I felt like a character in a children's story entering a place of enchantment, everything strange and wonderful, with that slightly disconcerting feeling it's not real, it's all a set-up to lure you in, that round the next corner might lurk a trap.

I came across Tadhg, sitting at a table with two guards, playing cards. "We're on our break," he said. "We organise our round to bring us back near the house at lunchtime".

"I wondered why I hadn't seen you at the hotel," I said. "Some guards live outside, do they?"

"A lot of us do. Who gets the housing is decided by lottery whenever a place becomes free."

Their garden possessed a feature I'd seen in others, a tapered, obelisk-like, four-sided trellis structure, about eight feet tall, covered with a climbing rose. On closer examination, I noticed it disguised a tubular grey metal chimney at its centre.

"It's for ventilation," said Tadhg. "Come down and we'll show you the system. Time up, lads!"

The guards flung down their cards and put on their uniform jackets. I followed them down a staircase and along the street to their house. The interior exhibited impressive decor, obviously professionally done by the Earl's designer. The rooms were scrupulously tidy. "It's not normally like this," said Tadhg. "We've got three girls coming for a meal tonight."

Tadhg pointed to a metal grille high up on a wall, and another at floor level. "The one there is connected to the chimney on the roof," he said. "You saw it planted with climbing flowers. They act like an air freshener. The air's drawn in the low grill and goes out the high grill. Both pipes pass through a heat-exchanger."

"So it ventilates without wasting heat?"

"Yes. All the rooms have them."

I observed with interest as they collected up what appeared to be standard issue guard equipment — tide whistle, waterproof notebook and pen, miniature binoculars, a walkie-talkie handset each.

"Don't you guys sometimes carry rifles?" I asked.

"The green guards do," said Tadhg. "The island doesn't have the vermin problems of the mainland. We'd only need rifles for unusual situations."

I wanted to ask him what classified as an "unusual situation", but thought better of it.

The three of them paused to synchronise wristwatches, impressive chronometer jobs. It was evident they took their duties seriously. Tadhg fetched a camera from on top of a bookcase. Catching me watching him, he hesitated for a split-second before picking it up. "I've forgotten to put film in," he said, forcing a laugh. "I'll have to go and get some. Have you got your new camera yet?"

"How did you know they'd confiscated my old one?"

"I didn't. Standard procedure, though. I assume you'll be taking photos for your work."

"That's what they told me. I've no idea of what. I might start with the roof gardens. They're very unusual."

"Energy-saving is the main reason for having them," said Tadhg. "The earth covering keeps the houses warm in winter. Cuts down the amount of electricity the island needs to generate. Have you been to the Sun Dome?"

He showed me on the map the best route to get there, though I hardly needed his help, as you couldn't walk across Nostalgia's roofs without seeing the Sun Dome dominating the skyline. Following his directions, I arrived at a footbridge leading to a doorway at the dome's upper level. Sally came out, wearing the becoming light blue colour of the previous day, and accompanied by a man of similar age. I said hello but all her friendliness had vanished. She stared right through me without acknowledging my greeting. A jealous husband, I thought.

I entered the dome at the level of the first-floor balcony, to be immediately enveloped in tropical heat and humidity. Leaning against the balcony rail, I surveyed the ground floor, below. A tangle of hothouse trees and shrubs bordered onto ponds stocked with brightly coloured fish. To one side, a waterfall crashed spectacularly down a wall of rock, filling the place with the sound of its cascade amplified by the echo from the domed roof. The intense heat made airborne the scents from the exotic foliage and flowers. I imagined it would be a great place to go in the gloom of winter.

A young guy leaned against the balcony opposite. About my age, dark hair, average height, ordinary appearance. I'd seen him before: in the bar on the train, perusing the outfitters' window display, talking to somebody outside Tadhg's house, and now here. One coincidence too many.

I took the stairs down to ground level and left the building by its main entrance. In the forecourt, I encountered Sally, who had somehow made a quick change into a cream-coloured dress. This time she greeted me with a big smile. To her man she said, "This is Mike. He's the stand-in for the one who had the accident. You know — it was in the local paper."

I said, "You didn't recognise me a few minutes ago. We passed at the top entrance."

Sally laughed. "My twin sister! She married my husband's twin brother. We're Sally and Tom Macnamara and they're Jenny and Patrick Macnamara. We've been here six months and people still can't tell us apart."

We discussed Nostalgia town and the island. Their one complaint intrigued me — the lack of access to the ocean. When I suggested the mouth of the bay, beyond the tidal barrier, they told me the intervening power station was out of bounds. As to the cliffs, fencing blocked them off completely. In fact, the fences had been erected so far back from the cliff edge, nowhere could you get even a *view* of the sea, let alone access to it. Only from the top of Little Island could you see the ocean. "There's a telescope up there," said Sally's husband.

I suggested to be so completely ringed in on such a small island must take its toll psychologically.

"Once you acclimatise, you'll never want to go back," said Sally. "The fences are nothing compared to the problems of the outside world. Here, we can go anywhere, in the middle of the night if we want, and not have to worry about safety. There are no rough areas, no places to be avoided. No vandalism. No yobs. No menace of graffiti. Parents can let their children play in the streets. And we have the most precious freedom of all — time. No wasting our lives on the stress of daily commuting."

At that moment, we were joined by the twins, the men remarkably similar, the women also, though in personality quite unlike each other: Jenny, serious to the point of being prim; Sally, relaxed and familiar, one would even say permanently flirtatious.

While we talked, the guy from the Sun Dome came out and approached, but he passed on. I told Sally I suspected him of following me. She gave me a look questioning my sanity but I determined not to miss the chance of discovering the man's identity. I kept behind him in the main shopping area, then through side streets in the direction of the canal. At a house close to Canal Gate, he let himself in with a key. I took note of the number on the door, for future reference.

Chapter 10

Chess

After lunch at the hotel, I crossed the sands via the causeway and followed the quayside to South Gate. Here, the road comes to an end, blocked by the imposing bulk of the wall. Only twenty years since they constructed it of rough stone and flint, winter storms and ocean breezes had already weathered the masonry, furnishing an antique staining of yellow and grey lichen, making it indistinguishable from a genuine relic. Inside the gate tower, I ascended a spiral staircase. A walkway branched off from an opening halfway up but I wanted first to go up to the top, where a door let out onto a flat roof with battlements. I unfolded my map with the intention of identifying the island's agricultural institute. A mile distant, not quite at the top of a ridge, stood an isolated building, identical to the institute building I had seen facing the Earl's stately home. Running downhill, a network of stone-walled grass fields met at the bottom a long security fence. On the mainland I hadn't given a lot of thought to the fences. Having been told about them by the old man on the coach, I suppose I'd accepted their presence as a necessary part of the security arrangements. Here on the island, from my aerial vantage point, they made a quite different impression. The single unbroken span, fifteen foot or more high, topped with razor wire and flowing over hill and dale, spoilt the view the way a thick scar might mar a pretty face. There was something brutal about it. Surely, many townspeople must at times have wanted to know, as I did at that moment, what was on the other side of the island, beyond the hill with the institute, beyond the other hills that could be seen in the distance on the prohibited land.

"Can I help you?" Turning round, I saw a blue guard.

"Am I out-of-bounds?" I asked.

"Not at all. The tower roofs are open to the public between dawn and dusk."

He came right up to me, his face too close for comfort. "You were studying your map hard." It was spoken as an observation, but I detected accusation.

Being unsure of my ground, I judged it best to keep my temper. "I arrived yesterday. I'm getting my bearings."

"That way's no concern of yours. *That's* the limit of what you need to be think about." He swept his arm to cover the direction of the town and its immediate surroundings.

I said, "I thought it best to walk the wall, to get an aerial view"

Opening the door at the top of the steps and ushering me through, he said, "That's a good plan. You do that."

As I carried on round the wall, my mind kept coming back to the incident. It had rattled me. If I had a right to be on the tower roof, why should it matter what I chose to look at?

A short walk brought me to Commons Gate, where I considered going up on the roof again but at only two hundred yards from South Gate I would have been easily spotted. I waited till the next: Marsh Gate. This possessed two towers, between which the canal flowed out under an archway and on across half a mile of marshland to the industrial estate. Contrary to my bleak preconception of the salt marsh, the whole the area was carpeted in wild flowers, the predominant colour purple, resembling fields of lavender. A horse-drawn barge, laden with goods, was steadily pushing its way through reed beds in the direction of the industrial estate. I watched till it disappeared between the buildings. The estate showed evidence of sensitive planning. A frontage of attractive glasshouses obscured the more functional warehouse and factory units behind, with the tall grey chimneys of a chemical works being sited furthest from the town.

At Hill Gate, where the road leaves town for the hill dweller settlement, I saw something I hadn't seen till now, an opening in the security fence. From it, a rough cart-track wound uphill to the institute. Two blue guards manned an adjacent hut. I waited to see what might happen. Nothing happened. Traffic neither came nor went. The guards brought out deckchairs and lay back, jackets off, shirtsleeves rolled up, like a pair of sunbathing uncles on a beach. Clearly, they anticipated no drama this lazy hot summer afternoon.

Moving on past Stable Gate, where a complex of horse stables backed onto the town side of the wall, I came next to Canal Gate. In the street below I could see the residence of my follower of the morning.

At the wall's halfway-point, Centre Gate, I met Tadhg.

"I'm due at the beach for tide duty," he said. "I'll walk round with you."

We came to Farm Gate, the only gate with Hill Gate having a road leaving town — I assumed in the direction of farms, though I could see nothing but light woodland stretching to the far distance.

"You can't see them because they're all permaculture, said Tadhg.

I said I'd heard of permaculture. "Isn't it some kind of layered system where large trees shelter smaller fruit trees, which are under-planted with crops?"

"Correct," said Tadhg. "They scatter the crops, mixing them up. It's to fool pests. Pesticides are banned on Nostalgia Island. We don't agree with polluting the environment."

We came next to Brew Gate. I'd already found out, the first time I tried to order a drink in the hotel, that the island brewed and distilled its own alcohol, importation being prohibited, thus preventing the flow of money away from the economy, channelling it instead to local enterprise and employment. Tadhg gazed ruefully at the microbrewery that gave the gate its name. "Pity I'm in uniform," he said. "In this heat I'm dying for a beer."

After Brew Gate came Theatre Gate. Nostalgia had no television service, the island being too far from the mainland to pick up a signal. The absence of the means of entertainment we take for granted in the modern world had a galvanising effect on the town's cultural life. A constantly rotating program of plays, concerts and films kept the theatre permanently busy.

From Theatre Gate, we went on to Rose Gate, so named for the spectacular rose garden that thrived in the suntrap of the wall. When I'd started my elevated tour, the sun had been behind me. Now, having come round half circle, I faced directly into the sun's glare from across the bay.

At the wall's termination point, North Gate, we went down to the quays, from where Tadhg joined his colleagues on the beach. Shortly afterwards I heard their whistles announcing the tide. By the time I had walked to the ferry, the water had come in. The ferryman was Fierce Hot, as he reminded me several times during our passage across the water. Disembarking at the hotel, I offered him a tip, which he declined irritably. Then I had a brainwave. I asked if he'd like a cool beer from the bar. His delight at the suggestion showed me how slow I'd been in not taking the obvious hint. A quarter of an hour later, from my bedroom window, I saw Fierce Hot, still supping his pint, chatting away, oblivious to a queue of people impatient to get to the other side.

In the dining room in the evening, some blue guards sitting at a table kept staring at me. I felt under suspicion, an instinctive but irrational reaction to being stared at. One of them came over, the same who had challenged my presence on the tower but, just as with Tadhg on the train, he disarmed me with the charm of his off-duty self. He told me the guards held a knockout chess tournament in the hotel lounge on Thursdays and had been discussing whether to invite me to join them.

They set up chessboards on tables by the windows. While waiting for my opponent to make his move, I looked out at the water, first turning gold in the sunset, then as the night drew in, shimmering with the multicoloured reflection of the lights of a distant fairground. I thought heaven should be like this — good food, good beer, good company, great ambience, everything relaxed and at peace. Plus, of course, the availability of a good woman, which is what I hoped for the following day. Surely, if everybody in the world could have what I had at that moment, there would be no further motivation for political strife or religious nastiness, and people could learn to live alongside each other in harmony.

During the longest game, with my new guard acquaintance, Colm, an embarrassing incident occurred, embarrassing that is in view of our encounter earlier in the day. His new girlfriend, Orla, the evening barmaid at the hotel had never dated a guard before and, being a bit simple, didn't understand the strict protocol governing the guards' work. She came over in the middle of our game, pestering to be taken for a walk in the fields on the far side of the fence. He told her it was more than his job was worth but she kept nagging, asking what harm a walk along a few paths could possibly do. Eventually, he lost patience and dispatched her curtly, back to the bar.

One of the islanders told me the guards earned an enormous sum, considerably more than an average security guard could hope to earn. Danger money? Unlikely, in this safe, well-ordered place. Could it be an insurance policy, a tactic of the Earl to ensure absolute loyalty and commitment? "Mess up and you'll lose this exceptional salary you'll never equal elsewhere." If so, what was happening on the other side of the fences that the Earl was willing to pay way over the odds to protect it?

Chapter 11

Clocks

I had my shower running full blast the following morning when I heard three sharp knocks on my room door. Thinking Saoirse had arrived early, I leapt out, dislodging the curtain, bringing the rail down with a great crash. The knocks came again and a voice called out "Manager!"

Flinging on a bathrobe I opened the door. The manager smiled knowingly. "A young lady is waiting for you downstairs, sir. She asks would you join her for breakfast?"

The spectacle of me, dripping wet, trying to locate clean underpants, was not the suave image I'd imagined for this first meeting with Saoirse on the island. After furious dressing and grooming, I made it downstairs, mortally ashamed of my lateness. In the far corner of the dining room, I found her sitting at a table for two, wearing a thin cotton dress and being eyed appreciatively by a motley crew of guards.

"I'm disappointed with you. Your first morning on the job and you're still in bed! At the least I expected you to meet me at the station!" She laughed. "I'm only joking. It's not time for work yet. I forgo breakfast on the train to have breakfast with you here."

She had brought with her a suitcase full of bound documents, copies of everything John had managed to complete before his accident. "I'm sorry but you have to work your way through them," she said, "otherwise, the schedule I'm going to give you won't make any sense. It's doesn't have to be all pain, though. We can sit outside in the sunshine."

We took our coffees out to a table under the shade of a tree, the weather indeed fantastic, a hot morning sun, the air already warm, without even a hint of a breeze. True to form, John had been energetic with his output. While I leaned back in a lounger, wading through the mass of information, Saoirse went off to borrow the hotel's typewriter. She returned with it and sat at the far end of the table, working away at a variety of letters and reports.

Suddenly, she stopped typing. "Mike? Do you mind my asking how old you are?"

"I'm twenty-two."

Saoirse laughed. "I'm three years older than you."

I asked, "Why's that funny?"

Resuming her typing, smiling impishly, she said, "Never mind!"

By half past eleven I'd studied most of the documentation, my appetite for further reading flagging rapidly, increasingly distracted by the movement of the tide, which had relinquished its grip on the hotel terrace, and was slowly but surely drawing back, revealing ever more the firm wet sands underneath.

Saoirse had written out a detailed itinerary of locations. Pleased to hear of my efforts finding my way around, she accordingly crossed several items off her list. "The causeway should be passable by now," she said. "Let's walk across to town."

We climbed the streets at the back of the hotel, with Saoirse giving me a running commentary on the history the buildings, her encyclopaedic knowledge a testament to her dedication to the Nostalgia project. As we descended over the brow of the hill, we had a clear view across the bay to the town. The tops of the causeway stones could be seen showing clear of the tide. From this viewpoint, with its distinctive S-shape, it could have been some mystical white sea serpent threading its way across the emerald water. Down at the shore, it did not welcome our crossing. Here and there, the tide had lifted clumps of slippery black seaweed and deposited them on the stones. Saoirse grabbed hold of my arm with both hands, pressing close to me for support as we crossed.

In town, she gave me a guided tour of the locations important to my work: the town hall, newspaper offices, and so on. At one point, we turned off the main street into an alleyway and came out onto a broad square of houses. An attractive stone-faced building occupied the middle of the square, its slate roof crowned by a four-sided cupola with a clock face.

"Nostalgia's new museum," said Saoirse. "When your research is completed, we'll set up a permanent exhibition here."

For the afternoon, she gave me my first official task, interviewing the shop owners in Main Street, the road which ran from Centre Gate all the way down to the quays, the road I had walked down on the day of my arrival. Saoirse suggested the interviews as good practice; I'd get introduced to many people and it would help prepare for future, more substantial assignments. I started at the cheese shop, where they made all the cheeses they sold. Then the reconditioned pine furniture shop next door. Then a sign-writer, who also sold artists materials. Two hours later, I'd not progressed even a quarter of the street's length. Amazing, the number and variety of thriving businesses in this area, a stark contrast to the predictable boring aggressive chain stores and supermarkets that suck the lifeblood of the typical modern town. One has to credit the town's planners. They'd compensated for not having hypermarkets or indoor shopping malls by concentrating the town's shops into this one long street and the side roads radiating from it. The busy area, running all the way from the wall at one end to the quayside at the other, with the added focal point of the Sun Dome close by, gave the town centre life, bustle and sociability.

A young road sweeper, with a cart labelled *Liam Byrne Cleaning Services*, stopped me. "You're the new research lad! They told me about you. Come and interview me about my business some time." He pointed to his sign. "I do the lot: window cleaning; house cleaning; maintenance of drains; and I'm contracted to the council for road sweeping. Normally my employee does the sweeping. He's on holiday."

I asked him how he had come to be on the island.

"I used to clean the Earl's windows," said Liam. "He liked my speed and said he could give me the chance to expand my business into other types of cleaning."

"Does the town council provide many services?"

"A fair number," said Liam. "It all goes on the community tax."

"And how do the residents react to the money they have to pay?"

"Nobody likes taxes but they understand the necessity. Not like my home town in County Clare. Some fuckwit politician talking through his arse about socialism wanting to control us all and take away our freedom. Got the subsidised local refuse collections dropped. People had to pay private firms. The fixed charges got replaced with pay-by-weight. What happened next? The less well-off worked out they could reduce their bill by burning their rubbish or dumping it. Caused a hell of a pollution problem."

"Would you say the politics here are more left wing than right wing, then?"

"I'd say neither," replied Liam. "They don't do sides. They do intelligent politics. That's why the place is so successful. Take me as an example. When it comes to business, I'm right wing. I want to see enterprise given the maximum encouragement, because prosperity through personal initiative is good. When it comes to education or community services, I'm left wing. I don't see why people should be done down just because they're poor. They're entitled to the basics of existence same as anyone else. Don't forget that interview — my yard's on the industrial estate." He pointed across the street to a small shop with a window full of clocks. "The clock shop's worth a visit."

The signboard above said: *Cloghessy's Clock Shop*. A great noise assailed me as I entered. Shelves full of timepieces, all mechanical, all ticking. I thought a person could go mad working in a place like this. Mrs Cloghessy, the proprietor, a short fat woman, age mid-fifties, possessed a face so round she fitted in well with her stock. Already guessing what her answer would be, I asked the lady where she obtained her stock.

"Everything's locally made," she said. "There's a clock works on the industrial estate. We organise the export side of their business ..."

A great cacophony interrupted her. As one, a shop full of clocks whirred into action to strike the chimes of the hour. Seeing the clocks massed together, all showing precisely the same time, reminded me of the question I'd asked on the train. "Can you tell me why the clocks are thirty-eight minutes ahead of the mainland?"

"I've never thought about it," she replied. "I suppose it's because we're practically in a different time zone, out here in the ocean."

"But because you're further west, the clocks should be *behind* mainland time, not ahead of it"

"Then it must be like in Spain. Good for tourism with the evenings so much lighter."

"But you don't have any tourists."

"Then it must be for our agriculture."

"That can't be right either. Setting the clocks forward makes the morning darker. In the winter, I'm sure farmers prefer light mornings."

Mrs Cloghessy smiled. "You should have been here during the clock tower dispute," she said. "You'd have made a great advocate."

She described a scheme to build a clock tower on the opposite side of the bay, on the escarpment overlooking the industrial estate. The Earl had promised to donate the construction costs as a gift to the town. No sooner had everything been agreed than the town council dropped the idea. They replaced it with the building of the town museum and its four-sided cupola containing a chiming clock.

"Do you think Nostalgia's clocks are set forward to help our entertainment industry?" she asked. "We don't have television, so everyone goes out at nights. The lighter the evenings, the better."

"I can understand that," I replied, "but why not round up the time difference to forty minutes, or even forty-five? Or why not go the whole hog and make it an extra hour, as none of it bears any relation to what the time *should* be for your location. Why on earth thirty-eight minutes?"

Chapter 12

Saoirse

Saoirse called in at breakfast Saturday morning and gaily proposed a visit to the industrial estate. Then, in the afternoon, she'd take me to see the area of town known as "The Commons", and, for the evening, "I'll be your date," she said. "I'm sure you can afford to take me out to dinner on that fancy contract rate I know they're paying you."

Officially, I didn't have to work weekends but I had no cause to complain, having Saoirse to myself all day.

The ferry took us over to the quays, from where, joining a procession of shift workers, we walked the long salt marsh wall to the far side of the bay. The morning sunshine and fresh sea air were glorious and I wondered how the workers coped with the journey in the middle of winter. "Then they use the canal bus," said Saoirse.

At the industrial area we visited first the recycling plant. The manager took us to the factory floor, to watch cartloads of organic waste being loaded into giant heated drums for composting. I thought a bizarre first location to be building a relationship with a prospective girlfriend. I asked what they did with their plastic waste and was told that, with the exception of imported medical items, plastic was not permitted on the island. A revelation for me. From the time I'd got on the train, I had been aware of something different which made you feel well and truly back in the past. I'd assumed the insistence on traditional materials was merely to create atmosphere. Now I understood a more serious purpose. People constantly complain about how much politicians take from them in taxes, how much waste there is in government expenditure, while daily throwing away their own money on cheap shoddy plastic goods which sooner or later end up as landfill or polluting the world's oceans. The tour of the industrial area began my process of re-education. I came to understand the reason for what I would later observe to be the high standard of living on the island, even in the houses of ordinary working people. With the benefit of isolation, and protection it gave from the apathy, greed and stupidities of the modern world, the founders of this unique place had planned it down to minute detail. Maximum efficiency plus zero wastage had produced both an unspoilt environment and an affluent population.

Next, we visited the glasshouses. Whereas I'd expected to see row upon row of tomatoes, they'd mixed the crop with various flower species, to act as a deterrent for pests. The manager explained this made their operation more labour intensive but the money they spent on increased wage costs was counteracted, as he put it, by "not having to pay the chemical companies to destroy our environment with insecticides and not having to pay the government to keep people idle on welfare." Saoirse commented the mix of foliage, flowers and fruits was like the Garden of Eden. An unfortunate remark, as the hot, sweaty greenhouse humidity, plus the sight of Saoirse's firm body, enhanced by her clinging, flimsy summer dress, had been making me feel increasingly randy. I only needed to see an apple tree and a snake. Fortunately, there are no snakes in Ireland, nor were there any on Nostalgia Island.

The glasshouse tour finished, we traversed the extensive industrial estate, coming out at the wildflower meadows cultivated on the slopes running up to the wooded escarpment. "We try to maximise exports and restrict our dependence on imports to essentials," said Saoirse. "The island's never suffered the polluting effects of agricultural herbicides, so somebody suggested the bright idea we grow wild flowers to supply the town florists. Of course, in the winter they have to supply conventional blooms from the glasshouses but, in the summer, people prefer these, because they're so unusual."

Two women were loading up a cart with boxes of picked flowers. Mounted to the shafts, an extremely frisky snorting horse, kept under control by Tadhg. "I'll give you a lift back to town", he said.

We set off at a pace more suited to a Roman chariot race than a provincial horse and cart delivery service. Although clear from Tadhg's control of the animal that he was an expert, even so, our passage across the harbour wall sorely tested my confidence in his abilities.

"Aren't we too fast?" I shouted, above the noise of the cart wheels and the clatter of the horse's hooves.

"Trust the animal's instincts," shouted back Tadhg. "It's not about to commit suicide by plunging us off the wall."

After Tadhg had set us down at South Gate, not a moment too soon, Saoirse suggested we buy sandwiches on Little Island, and towels so we could lie on the beach and sunbathe. We walked back from the shop across the wide sands to the point where the low tide mark meets the harbour wall. Out here, we were alone.

After we had eaten and talked, and lain side by side, within touching distance, Saoirse asked, "Would you mind if I went for a swim?"

A strange question. Heat and sunshine, the sea at hand; why should I mind her swimming?

"That's OK, then," she said, and promptly pulled off her dress straight over her head. Bra and panties came off in quick succession, and Saoirse, all pert breasts, pointy nipples and luxuriant pubic hair, raced off, launching herself into the water. She called back at me "Come on down! The water's warm!"

I declined to undress, making a token effort by taking off my sandals and paddling about in the waters' edge while Saoirse swam back and forth in front of me. She had boundless energy for swimming, and I began to feel stupid, gawking at her naked buttocks rising and falling in the water. I went back to our towels and awaited the pleasure of her return. She came running back up the sands but, instead of covering herself, she stood looking down at me, drying her hair, her womanly assets proudly on display. "You should have come in," she said. "It's the warmest we've had since the summer started. Or don't you swim?"

I said that I didn't.

"I'll teach you. The beaches in the bay are all good. The water's shallow for yards wherever you go. I can hold you, to help you float."

Saoirse sat down, her body pressed up against mine. "Room for two? Move up!" She handed me her towel. "Here! You can help me dry my front."

As I took the towel from her, she grabbed it back, laughing. "Gotcha! I can do it myself, thank you!" Caressing her breasts with the towel, in a way nothing but provocative, she said, "So, now you know all about me. I've kept no secrets from you. Well, that is, *almost* no secrets."

She turned away, hiding some strong emotion.

I asked gently, "Are you OK?"

"Yes. Thank you," she said. "You're a very *kind* person, aren't you?" Recovering herself, she snatched up her bra. "Fasten me up! I know you'd prefer to unfasten it." Throwing on her dress and pulling up her panties, Saoirse hauled me off my towel. "Hurry up, Mister. The girlie show is over. You've got work to do."

In the afternoon, we visited "The Commons". In one corner of town, a wide-open space runs up to the wall between South Gate and Commons Gate. Tiny allotments divided up part of the land, with the remainder taken up by sports pitches and tennis courts. We met and spoke with many people out in the afternoon sunshine working their plots. Although in the middle of the ocean, the fertile ground benefited from the heat trap created by the shelter of the town and its high surrounding wall, as evidenced by the vigorous fecundity of their tended vegetables and flowers.

After touring the allotments, we moved on to the sports area. Each wall gate had given its name to a sports club, twelve clubs in all, with Hurling being the most popular of the sports played. Saturday afternoon wasn't like work. We spent our time watching the games.

At five o'clock, Saoirse returned home to change for our evening date. We agreed to meet back in town at *The Refectory* — a first-rate restaurant, though you needed to be sociable to enjoy it. The customers squashed up together on benches on both sides of an enormously long medieval banqueting table, cramped, noisy, and thereby extremely entertaining. Sally Macnamara entered with her husband. Seeing us, they came over. The husband sat down opposite me but Sally pushed him along the bench so she and I could sit facing each other.

When you'd finished eating, the restaurant didn't care how long you hung around. They had a selection of board games stacked up by the door. Saoirse asked the waitress to bring one over. "You'll like this," she said. "It's the Nostalgia game. Teaches you the street plan. You're given packages to deliver and you have to work out the fastest overall route. You can use any combination of Nostalgia transport. It's not easy, because there are random obstacles the throw of the dice puts in your way."

She set out the pieces on the board, an impressive representation of the town and its environs — with one noticeable omission: no security fences shown. About halfway into the game, Saoirse left the table to greet a friend. No sooner had she got up than I felt a woman's bare foot rubbing my trousers, working up towards my crotch. I looked across at Sally, talking animatedly to her husband as if unaware of my presence. Suddenly, she turned and fixed me with that same compelling stare she had given me in the telegraph office. "Are you enjoying the game, Mike?" Was she just having a laugh, teasing me, or was she taking advantage of Saoirse's absence to come on to me, with her husband by her side?

At one o'clock in the morning, the restaurant closed, shepherding a whole crowd of noisy, reluctant patrons out onto the street. I escorted Saoirse back to her lodgings at Canal Gate, where I discovered with alarm she lived at the very same house my Sun Dome follower had let himself in.

"Are you the only lodger?" I asked.

"Sean's here," she replied. "He told me he's seen you around town a few times. He said he saw you at the Sun Dome and intended to introduce himself but you were busy talking to some people, so he didn't."

"Who's Sean?" I asked with some trepidation.

"He works for the estate office. Technically he's my assistant, though recently the Earl has taken most of his time. I've hardly seen him."

I felt doubly relieved. Not a boyfriend. Not an enemy. Lucky I'd exercised caution and had avoided confrontation that day at the Sun Dome. What a berk I'd have looked, had the story got back to Saoirse!

Chapter 13

The Hospital

Monday. The start of my first full working week in Nostalgia. Saoirse and I spent the morning visiting factories. In her capacity as the Earl's personal assistant, she was well known to the businesses in town and they were more than pleased to give us a guided tour. The employees I spoke to expressed a high level of job satisfaction. In Nostalgia, one found no assembly lines with dull, repetitive, work. They had gone back to the apprentice system, with many young people under the instruction of older craftsmen. They trained their workers in all aspects of the production process, to give them variety and the satisfaction of being a maker of something, not merely a cog in a machine.

Most impressive of the lot, the engineering company, "Anything & Co", which had the motto above its factory gates: "If you can draw it, we can make it." They made all the mechanical and electrical goods of the island. In the drafting department they showed us how they could design any interconnecting and interacting set of parts by making a set of technical drawings on a computer screen. The same computers connected to robotically controlled machinery to automatically produce the drawn parts.

"Do you know nothing mechanical or electrical is imported to the island?" the manager said to me proudly, "Anything anyone wants we can design and make here, *and* it's not any more expensive."

I questioned how, even with their sophisticated technology, they could rival the economies of scale of mass production.

"Well of course, we can't," said the manager, "but we build things to last here, *and* we make repair parts on demand, so there's no wasteful obsolescence. Over the lifetime of the machine, the buyer will save money."

I asked, "Doesn't the high initial cost create a problem?"

The manager said, "Thanks to Nostalgia's banking system, no. The bank, which is underwritten by the Earl's millions, will make a long-term loan for the purchase of any goods manufactured on the island. The bank wins, the consumer wins, local employment and industry win."

Anything & Co had been the last stop on our morning tour. We had lunch at a pub in town before going on to the hospital for our first meeting with John. Being in Saoirse's company was a relaxing and pleasant experience, in no small part because of her natural openness, but I knew it would be premature to make romantic advances. Judged wrongly, it would not only spoil our relationship, it might even jeopardise my contract of employment. Also, I couldn't stop thinking about her sudden moment of sadness on the beach. Had she already developed feelings for me that could not be satisfied, due to some insurmountable personal obstacle of which I could not be told? Our visit to John might throw some light on the situation.

To get to the hospital, you followed the bay road out from North Gate. The Earl had promised me a town without the motorcar. Saoirse told me that wasn't strictly true — the ambulances and fire engine were motorised, and the doctors were permitted a car each. Subsequently I saw the doctors' cars around town often, quaint 1930's models, on loan from the Earl's collection. Outside of these few permitted vehicles, all travel was on foot, by pushbike, by horse-drawn cart, by canal boat, or, as we were now doing, by bicycle rickshaw taxi.

On our arrival, a surgeon took us to his office. "Your friend's accident has caused a number of fine bone fractures which, if not given complete rest and time to repair, could mean he will be stuck with a limp for the rest of his life. That's why we insist he must be kept here under observation, until we are confident of his full recovery. We can't risk him being loose with the rules and starting to walk about."

"You've moved him to a new room?" asked Saoirse.

"The office in the dispensary. Where the hospital records are kept. He can converse with you there without disturbing anyone. He complained the proximity of other patients made it difficult for him to concentrate on his work."

We found John sitting up in bed, left leg heavily encased in plaster held by a sling to the ceiling. Five years older than me, of similar build, with fair hair, though already balding, his alert face scrutinised us as we entered. I sensed an assessment of how Saoirse and I were getting along. Saoirse must have sensed it also, as her manner subtly shifted from casual to business-like. I stood on one side of the bed, while she chose the other.

"Welcome to your new office," said John.

We shook hands. Ever efficient, he'd made up a list summarising the work he'd done and itemising the tasks for which he needed help: interviewing people and taking photographs. We agreed Saoirse would meet me at the hotel each day, accompany me to the morning's venue, effect the introductions then leave me to get on with it. In the afternoon there'd be more interviews to carry out, or I'd go back to the hospital, to coordinate the results of my researches with John.

The conversation to plan my schedule proceeded smoothly but I couldn't help be conscious of an acutely strained atmosphere. Saoirse's natural manner became awkward when she spoke with John, and on his part I felt him to be somewhat offhand. Had there been a relationship that had come to grief? I'd have the opportunity to ask him later but I knew I wasn't going to — it would be hypocritical of me to offer sympathy whilst having designs of my own.

On leaving the hospital, Saoirse proposed giving me my first swimming lesson. "I know the ideal place. Not many people go there," she said.

We walked the beach in the direction of the coast, to where a rocky cliff brought it to an end, forcing us back onto the road just as it bent uphill away from the bay. Taking an overgrown path opposite a picturesque olden-style Irish cottage on the corner, we pushed our way through waist-high clumps of weeds until we came to a small wood leading to open meadow, with the cliff-top beyond blocked by a forbidding high wire fence.

Saoirse registered my undisguised distaste for this military-style eyesore. "They don't want anyone falling off the cliffs," she said. "Think about it. A tragic death on this island would cause us major problems. Come on! We're going this way."

A steep, rocky path led down to a sandy cove. In the distance, I could see the security fencing descending the cliff to join with the power station blocking the outlet to the sea. We were still within the confines of the bay.

"Get your clothes off, then," said Saoirse.

We sprinted out into the clear water like two fugitives from a nudist camp. Saoirse showed me first how to float. "The trick," she said, "is to arch your back and push your stomach up."

Standing by me, in the waist-high-water, organising the position of my arms, she leaned over my face. As she did so, her breasts brushed softly against me, one of her nipples coming to rest against my lips.

"Now, push up!" she commanded. Turning her head to look at my stomach, she suddenly broke off, rushed out of the water and lay down, huddled up on the sand.

I splashed out after her. "Are you all right? What's the matter?"

Her whole body shook with suppressed laughter. "When I said *push up,* I didn't mean *that.* Would you mind not getting an erection when I'm teaching you to swim?" She glanced at me and shrieked, "You've gone enormous!"

"It's only eight inches."

"Eight inches! You mean you've actually measured it with a ruler!" Saoirse lay back on the sand, convulsed, legs wide apart, not caring she might be turning me on even more with her wild, naked abandon. She'd stop laughing and ask, "Has it gone down yet?" look, and start laughing again. I felt a mixture of pride and dismay at her reaction. Eventually she calmed down but the swimming had ended. We dressed and started on our way back home. I offered my hand to help Saoirse up the steep path. She didn't let go until the end of our long walk back to town. I didn't know it then but there was to be only one more occasion we would walk that way together, holding hands.

Chapter 14

Interviews

My daily routine quickly established itself in the rhythm of my first week on the island, more a working holiday than work. After breakfast at the hotel, Saoirse and I would take the ferry, or walk across the causeway, depending on the morning tide. She'd introduce me to a factory or office where I would collect information and take photographs. Finally, I'd call in to John to report progress. Some afternoons I'd spend with John, typing up and indexing our material. In the evenings, Saoirse and I dined at the hotel or in town, before going on to the theatre or to one of Nostalgia's many cultural events. We'd finish the evening at the poetry pub or one of the music pubs, then I'd see her back to her lodgings at Canal Gate.

For my assignments I needed to buy a camera to take the place of my own, confiscated by customs back on the mainland. An intrinsically "Irish" arrangement: simultaneous sense and nonsense. "You're not allowed to take a camera but don't worry, we'll give you one when you get there." Like the time friends hired some wine glasses for an all-weekend Irish wedding celebration. They asked when they should return the glasses and were told, "Sure, wait till after the weekend. You'll be busy up till then." Or like the time a shopper in an Irish food market asked the price of fishcakes. "Two for six," replied the stallholder. "No! Wait! I mean six for two." Or like the Irish cattle rustler who invented a new method of stealing cattle: Don't load the animals into a truck; the engine noise will give the game away. Instead, quietly walk them down the lanes in the middle of the night. He was caught next morning by the trail of hoof prints leading directly to his farm.

It came as no surprise, after all I had seen so far, that the cameras sold by the photographic shop were made by "Anything & Co." Even the film was manufactured locally. "It has to be developed by a special process we do here," said the shop salesman. "Don't ever take it to a mainland film processor. They won't know what to do with it and you'll end up losing all your hard work."

The salesman talked about his cameras with great enthusiasm. He recommended a model with automatic exposure and automatic flash for low light conditions. "It's impossible to get the light wrong with this, night or day, outdoors or indoors," he said. "I'll leave it set on automatic, shall I? Don't forget to switch it off if you're ever in low-light and don't want flash, or you'll get a nasty shock *and* the embarrassment of a ruined picture!"

Another obligation for my work was to be interviewed on "Island Radio". Although the town council banned the use of portable radios, the island did have its own talk-radio, delivered to the houses by cable. A suspicious mind might have deduced a purpose behind their system — good phone and radio connectivity within the island but the only means for conveying messages to and from the outside world an antiquated Morse telegraph. Furthermore, importation of cameras banned, and film sold that could only be processed in-situ. In the summer of 1990, we didn't know it but we were at the end of an era, before the explosion of modern communications technology, before the omnipresent mobile phone, the Internet, universal email and social networking. Much easier back then to cut off people's access to information, if that's what you wanted to do. Having said that, I can categorically state in all my time in Nostalgia I encountered no evidence of censorship. The residents elected their town council democratically; the two island newspapers scrutinised the policies of their local politicians as closely as any newspaper on the mainland; even the policies of the Earl could be called into question. The townspeople were equally forthright in their spoken opinions. The only subject they wouldn't be drawn on was the security fences. The topic bored them. With a perfect working and living environment, they didn't care what went on beyond the fences. Why should they? The Earl's private business was none of their business.

The first Nostalgia businessperson I interviewed in depth was the owner of "The Bag Shop". The name might suggest they sold handbags, or travel bags. Yes, they did sell those, made to order in their own workshop, but they also did a strong trade in jute bags, imported from Bangladesh, which Nostalgia's inhabitants used for shopping and so on. Any time a mainlander might use a plastic bag, an islander would use one made of jute. The woman who owned the shop lectured me on the pollution problems caused by plastic bags in the wider world. I couldn't argue with her on that score; I did question the economics — on her own admission, her product was several times more expensive than the plastic version.

"Look what happens," she replied. "Because plastic bags are so cheap, the shops give them away for free. Because shoppers get them for free, they think of them as disposable, so next time they go to the shop they're given more for free. Which they dispose of again. And so it goes on. Better than the cost of giving away all those bags, sell a jute bag and encourage the customer to re-use it."

"You have a point there," I said. "Something for people to think about."

"People don't think!" said the woman, "That's the problem. They let others do their thinking for them, and the only thinking big business is interested in is 'Buy my product and damn the consequences'."

I found this same pattern of careful thought behind everything done in Nostalgia, not just in the many small businesses but also in the town administration. That afternoon, I interviewed the town's "Head Gardener". A tall spare man, you'd see him about, always dressed smartly in a tweed suit and flat cap which served to emphasise his authority over his employees. I asked was there ever a problem keeping his staff busy. He told me of a bylaw requiring all residents who owned a garden to keep it to a certain standard. If they had neither time nor inclination, they could request help from the council, who for a fee would send a team to do the work. This benefited the gardeners, by ensuring they'd never be unemployed, and it benefited the town, because everywhere you looked you saw abundant, beautifully kept gardens.

Later, I took my interview notes to the hospital to enter into John's computer. The absence of Saoirse created an opportunity to probe him for his impressions of Nostalgia in the nine months he had been living there. It turned out his experience had been identical to mine — the strange interview, the requirement for absolute secrecy, the unexpected train journey into the bowels of the salt mine, the fascination of arrival at the unique destination. Subsequently, just as for me, he had fully immersed himself in Nostalgia's special culture and ambience.

John urged me to walk the entire boundary fence. "It runs to many miles," he said. "You need to divide it up. You could start by walking the fence bordering the salt marsh."

Curiously, despite the importance he appeared to attach to the boundary, he evaded my questions regarding the circumstances of his accident which the Earl told me had happened when John violated the boundary line. I left on an agreement I would start by walking the fence bordering the salt marsh.

Returning to town, I called in to Tadhg's house. When I told him I intended to make a circuit of the salt marsh, he offered to show me round. "And I can do better," he said. "I can show you something spectacular but it can only be seen when it's dark. I'm on overtime tonight. Meet me at the guard post at eleven."

I informed Saoirse of the trip.

"I can guess where he's taking you," she said. "I want to come too. And Mary's sure to be there."

"Who's Mary?"

"Tadhg's new woman. Didn't you know? You men are so contained about these things. She's Dr Murphy's assistant."

"A nurse?"

"A biologist. Murphy's an ecologist, not a medic. He's in charge of all environmental matters in Nostalgia."

"No offence to Tadhg; wouldn't this girl be a bit bright for him?"

"They're both crazy about horse-riding. That's the connection."

In the evening, Saoirse and I enjoyed a Salsa class at the theatre, after which we spent time at the poetry pub's hilarious "spontaneous limerick" competition. At eleven we went down by Hill Gate, where we found Tadhg waiting with Mary, she even smaller than he, a sweet girl, pretty too.

Tadhg handed us a torch each.

"We'll follow the fence round the marsh," he said, "It will bring us uphill to the escarpment on the far side of the bay. We'll go towards the lighthouse then come back down to the promenade."

The cool night air put us in no mood for loitering. We started off at a brisk pace. With the two women deep in conversation, Tadhg and I walked ahead. I shone my torch all round, including through the fence to gauge Tadhg's reaction. He showed no concern for my curiosity.

Out on the marsh, away from the lights of the town, the slow-moving lighthouse beam swept the land beyond the fences with a surprising intensity.

"Why don't they mask the light?" I asked.

"You've not been outside the residential areas at night before?" asked Tadhg, "We don't have sufficient capacity to light the country roads. The lighthouse at least gives some background illumination. Without its beam, the island would feel a whole lot darker at nights."

We came to a cluster of low-fenced huts marking the dry land bordering the marsh. "Nostalgia's egg farm," said Tadhg. "Look, there's a fox!"

The fox, which had been trying to scratch a way under the chicken fence, froze in the glare of our torches, then raced off.

Leaving the salt marsh behind, we took a steep slope upwards through trees, coming out at the top onto open grassland, where we walked along with the brow of the wooded escarpment on our right and the lighthouse some two miles ahead.

"Are we going all the way to the end?" I asked.

"We're going back down again," Tadhg replied.

He led us between the trees to the edge of a clearing of scrubby undergrowth, telling us to turn off our torches and wait for our eyes to adjust to the dark. At first, I couldn't see anything, then I became aware of tiny yellow-green flashes of light all around.

"A glow-worm colony," said Mary. "The females emit the glow to attract the males. It's a first for Irish territory. We've no idea how they colonised this particular spot, nor why they're doing so well here. It's frustrating, being on Nostalgia Island, we can't publish a paper or invite experts to study them." She'd brought with her a magnifying glass and she and the others went down to the bushes to view the insects close up.

I waited before following them. A different kind of light had caught my attention — the research institute on the far hill, the windows brilliantly lit up. Nearly midnight. Strange they should all be working so late.

Chapter 15

The Mark

It had been organised for me to spend a day at the barge company, to learn how Nostalgia's distribution network functioned. Their offices and depot occupied the area fronting the canal between Canal Gate and Stable Gate. Saoirse came along to introduce me to the manager. She asked if we could visit the horses in their fields outside the town walls. With my limited knowledge I'd assumed these to be working horses. The manager put me right on that. "Only retired horses stay outdoors. Working horses get hot with their exertions — they have to be kept warm and dry in the stables."

I asked how they ensured the horses were never over-worked.

"That's the advantage of water-based transport," said the manager. "We can move a substantial weight and volume of goods with comparatively little effort, at least from the point of view of the capacity of a barge horse. Our running costs over the whole enterprise are cheaper per mile than a haulage company dependent on lorries."

"The lorry does have the advantage of speed."

"In Nostalgia, that would be a positive disadvantage. You'll have noted the high density of housing and industry in the town, and the remaining industry concentrated on the industrial estate. Without interminable ugly urban sprawl, who needs lorries?"

The horse tour done, Saoirse left us. I would be spending time with the bargemen, to see how they distributed the goods and raw materials that arrived by train. Pleasant, lying on top of the cargo in the morning sunshine, drifting lazily through the reeds and flowers of the salt marsh in the direction of the industrial estate. What I hadn't anticipated was they had no intention of allowing me to continue as idle observer. At each stop they co-opted me to lift boxes and crates onto the canal bank and drag trolley loads of goods to the factories and greenhouses. Midday, we lunched at a canal-side cafe but, within less than half an hour, we returned to the barges, loading them up with agricultural produce to be delivered to the station for the night train. The coordinated speed and efficiency of the workforce impressed me greatly, till I discovered they had an ulterior motive — as soon as they'd completed their work they could go home.

After we unloaded at the railway, we returned to the depot, where the men signed off. The manager called me into his office. "Did you have an interesting time?" he asked.

"Exhausting, but fascinating. I can appreciate why I needed to experience your distribution system first-hand."

"What do you think of this?" he asked, indicating a grey metallic box, about a foot square, on top of his desk. He sprung open the lid to reveal a revolving chamber fitted with glass test tubes.

"It's a laboratory centrifuge," I said.

"Correct. For the agricultural institute. Two came in this morning. They order them all the time. What are they for, do you know?"

95

"Could be anything," I replied. "The chamber spins round at high speed, creating a force on what you place inside it, separating solids from liquids. You could make skimmed milk, or get the cloudiness out of wine but that would be an industrial centrifuge. This size would be strictly research. They might put animal blood in the test tubes, or mashed up plant tissue. It depends on the research. Are you expecting me to tell you what they do?"

"No. Nobody knows what the feck they're up to and I don't suppose as a newcomer you'll be any wiser than the rest of us. But there's something about this gadget that bothers me. Turn it over. Be careful. It's heavy."

I lifted the centrifuge, which was deceptively heavy for its size, and stood it upside down.

"Notice anything?" asked the manager.

"Four feet and a label," I replied.

"Look to the right of the label."

Somebody had scratched a doodle into the metal, in the shape of a triangular shaped head having two eyes and a mouth. "Someone having a bored moment?" I suggested.

"That's what *I* thought," said the manager, "the *first* time it I saw it."

"You mean there's more?"

"Not in this delivery. The institute have ordered those centrifuges before. Each delivery has been a pair. We're conscientious with the goods passing through our hands. We inspect everything. One of my staff pointed out the mark right next to the label. I told him we'd go ahead and supply the centrifuge anyway. As it's so feckin heavy, nobody was likely to look under the base. When the next order came in, I inspected them before anyone else could get their hands on them. What do you think I found?"

"The centrifuges both had the mark on the base."

"Not quite. On every occasion, only one has had the mark. You know what I think? There's something inside. It's a smuggling operation. Drugs or something. The mark indicates which one has the goods. I'd like you to be a witness to my opening it."

I watched while the manager unscrewed a retaining ring and eased out the mechanism. Inside, the case was empty. "There goes that theory!" he said.

"The mark indicates which one *shouldn't* be opened," I suggested.

"Brilliant! I have a hunch you're going to be right." He pushed the dismembered centrifuge to one side and started to unscrew the other. Our expectation wasn't met. Neither had anything concealed within.

I said, "Maybe it *was* just a casual doodle."

"In the same place, next to the label, the same each time, and on those goods only? I don't think so!"

I asked, "Do you think it signifies something? Like a ritual symbol?"

"Wouldn't be the first odd thing I've known on this island," he replied. "You're at the hotel, aren't you? If anything comes up, I'll get in touch."

Chapter 16

The Rowing Boat

Saoirse and I always took a two-hour lunch break from work. The extended time allowed us to relax and amuse ourselves. Often, we'd wander around the rooftop gardens, walks that invariably ended up at Stable Gate, because Saoirse loved to pet the barge horses in their stables. On the hottest days, we'd lie the whole time under the shade of a tree in the rose garden. Or we'd go to the beach — in swimming gear to avoid another hiatus — for my swimming lesson.

One occasion, we visited the fairground, a determinedly old-fashioned affair situated beside the promenade between town and hospital, having quaint rides, a fortune-teller, coconut shies and the grating background music of a pipe organ. Usually there'd be a special event for young ones. We saw children queuing up for face painting, coming away in an assortment of disguises. A little boy, who'd just been given a white clown face, charged around boisterously, annoying the little girls. Watching him, Saoirse said, "I did that job once."

"Face-painting?"

"Supervising a children's activity. I enjoyed it. They were mostly no trouble, though there's always *one*, isn't there, who has to be taken in hand and told how to behave."

We came to the ghost train. Saoirse pressed me to take a ride, for a laugh. Our cart snaked round a creaky wooden tunnel, with an assortment of mechanical skeletons and ghouls leaping out making scare noises. As it rattled round one corner a giant black hairy spider dropped on a thread from the ceiling. Saoirse screamed, clinging to me tightly. Then we kissed. Inevitable it would happen sooner or later. Her kiss was pure Saoirse, warm and giving. But without passion. Something was being held back.

How can I describe the development of our relationship? We had become inseparable, outside of work obligations always together: at breakfast time, meeting again for the midday break, then spending the evenings in each other's company. That first kiss had crossed a line. Now we could relax over the matter of physical contact. Touching, holding hands, kissing; these came naturally, though with an unspoken agreement not to go too far. I knew Saoirse held a fear of something transcending our personal relationship, something she dare not talk about.

During one of our lunch breaks, an incident happened which greatly puzzled me. Saoirse suggested we hire a rowing boat. "You can row us out into the bay. It'll be fun eating our lunch, bobbing up and down on the water."

Some lightweight rowing boats, painted bright yellow, were moored near the fairground, their keeper none other than Fierce Hot, complaining, as usual, about the heat. I listened dutifully while he explained how to row. What I didn't let slip, in case Saoirse accused "Mister Eight Inches" of showing off again, was that, despite not being a swimmer, I had been a member of my university rowing team. Saoirse and I put on life jackets, got into the boat, and with my rowing skills we were soon making rapid progress in the direction of the coast.

"Rowing's not as difficult as it looks, is it?" said Saoirse, "I didn't think we'd be going anything like as fast and as far as this."

I said nothing, enjoying the familiar sensation of skimming across the water.

As we approached the sea wall, Saoirse said, "We shouldn't get too close. The outlet from the power station might upset the boat"

I said, "I'm aiming for the far side of the bay."

Saoirse replied, "I don't want to go over there. It's too far. How do we know the water's safe? I really must ask you to stop!"

She was shouting at me now. Saoirse, the friend, had disappeared. I found myself looking at Saoirse, protector of the island. I had no chance to challenge her on what she was protecting it from. A tremendous growl from the edge of the bay announced a speedboat, appearing from nowhere, racing towards us, driven by two guards, shouting and gesturing for us to go back. They circled at great velocity, creating a wash which rocked our boat alarmingly. I turned the boat, resolving not to be beaten. With my skill and speed in rowing I could return any time I wanted, under cover of darkness if necessary.

Saoirse said, "I'm sorry shouted at you."

I said, "It's my fault. Over-confidence. I acted stupidly."

And with that brief exchange we made up and put the disagreement behind us.

Chapter 17

Tracks

In the mood to get more outdoor photography done during the continued good weather, I obtained John's permission to bring forward the task of documenting the small-scale agriculture that provided the mainstay of the island's exports. I followed the road out of town from Farm Gate into the adjoining woodland. The air felt noticeably warm and humid here, compared to the open shore of the bay. Credit due to the clever tree planting, providing a windbreak but not so close as to block the sun. The sheltering plantations alternated with clearings covered by a great jumble of vegetables and herbs. The farm workers, predominantly middle-aged women, were out in number, busy weeding, their primary activity now the warm weather had started the growing season in earnest. These pioneer residents had planted the trees on formerly bare heath, nurturing them over twenty years, witnessing the land's transformation to the verdant, sylvan landscape it had become.

Impressive also, the simple wooden railway built to shunt handcarts full of produce as far as the canal. I walked the tracks to the terminus, at a wharf by a hump-backed bridge. I remembered passing under this bridge on the misty first day of my arrival, shortly before seeing the strange phenomenon of the hill dweller eyes. Now I could see the hill, with rows of porthole-like glass windows embedded in it, I understood the inhabitants to be "hill dwellers" in the literal sense — they lived underground.

I'd planned more farming photographs but this new discovery piqued my interest. Crossing the bridge, I followed a path going uphill through fields. The way forked, with a signpost pointing left to "Railway Station" and right to "Hill Dwellings". I took the right and came out at the top of the hill dwelling road, where it reached a dead-end blocked by a security fence. A group of little girls hopped around in a circle, singing, and playing a dancing game. A sudden whirlwind got up, blowing them in all directions, turning their singing to screams. One of them pointed me out to the others. They stopped, gathered together in a huddle with a lot of whispering and giggling going on, then, as one, stuck their tongues out at me and sped off, skipping down the hill. So light on their feet were they, you'd think they were on springs. That, and the whirling dust driven by a gusting wind, created a scene straight out of folk-lore, as if a white witch had magicked up a band of fairies to scatter to the four corners of the earth.

Retracing my steps, I took the path in the direction of the railway. It brought me down alongside the goods yards. An elderly black man sat on a tree stump, staring at the railway lines. I said "Good Morning" but he ignored me. He continued to stare straight ahead. I'd walked on another twenty yards when he called after me in an Afro-American accent, "Good Morning!"

I turned and went back.

The man continued to stare at the railway. He smiled as he spoke. "You know I've seen train yards all over the world but I ain't never seen a train shed like that one."

I asked, "Which one?"

He didn't reply. Out of politeness, I scanned the scene.

"My name's Ben", said the man.

"Pleased to meet you, Ben. I'm Mike."

"Hi, Mike." (Still staring ahead).

Another long silence.

"My daddy was a steward on the transcontinental railroad. He'd be gone from home seven days at a time. Three days to get to New York. A day off work, then three days back. He loved it. You know, he said to me once: It's funny. You're passing through all that territory, all those wide-open spaces, yet it's like you're not really there — your world for those days is the train, its corridors, the galley where you collect the food for your customers, your steward's bunk."

Another long silence.

I said. "I never thought of it like that. Quite a paradox isn't it?"

"Yep, I've taken a great interest in trains. Drafted into the U.S. navy. When my term of duty ended, I joined the merchant navy. Been all over the world. Whenever we got shore leave, other guys would waste time and money in bars. I'd seek out the rail lines. Sit on an embankment and watch the trains. Real mystical and spiritual experience. That's what I do here."

A long silence.

I was about to remark there weren't too many trains for him to watch on the island, with only three arrivals and three departures per week, when Ben started talking again. "Came to Ireland. Married an Irish girl from Cork.

Didn't work out. Drifted into working for the Earl. We got to talking about trains, and what my daddy done, and he said would I know how to do a steward's job and I said, yes sir, sure I would, so I got a job as steward on his train. Did it for fifteen years. Got promoted to head steward. Would have made my daddy proud. Retired now."

"Are you enjoying your retirement on the island. It's a great place to live, isn't it?"

Another long silence. This conversation was very hard going.

"The one on the right. See the long shed there, the one with the tin roof. That's where they park the train."

We were back to the subject of train sheds.

"What's wrong with it?" I asked.

"What's wrong with it! Nothin! It's the other shed that's wrong. The one after the parking shed. Ain't long enough to fit a carriage. And see the height. Two stories. Why would you need that? And it doesn't look right. Look how old it is."

"It's fake though, isn't it? There's a lot of buildings on the island they've made look older than they really are."

For the first time, the old man looked directly at me. He had a kindly face, but sad, I thought. "Why make that shed look old? The other doesn't look old. And see those doors it's got."

In the direction he pointed, the railway line ran from the parking shed to the second shed, terminating in roof-high double doors.

"I ain't never seen those doors opened," said Ben.

"Could it be from when they built the railway? They don't use it anymore?"

"It makes a noise. Kind'a whirring, grating noise. You know the noise you get in tall elevator shafts. Well maybe you don't, if you ain't never been to the States. You press the button. You get a noise down the shaft as the elevator starts and comes up to your floor."

His story aroused my interest. "When have you heard the noise, Ben?"

"Middle of the night. Couldn't sleep, so I came out here to watch the train come in. About fifteen minutes before train due, the noise started. And it kept going. Till the train came to the station. Then the noise stopped. Just like an elevator shaft. The elevator stops. The whirring stops."

I felt the old man needed reassurance. I said, "I expect what's inside the shed is a generating station. They need to boost the power when the train is at this end of the line. That would account for the noise you heard. It's the sound of a generator running."

"Is that so, mister?" said Ben, "Then tell me why I never hear no noise when the train's going out the other way, back to the mainland."

Up to this point I'd written him off as senile. Now I could see he was a lot more on the ball than I'd given credit for.

"Never? Are you sure?"

"I *have* heard it in the evenings."

"Well, there you are!"

"Only the evenings when the train isn't here."

"Are you sure?"

"First time I heard it. The train had gone back to the mainland the night before. I came down here with the doggy. He's dead now."

Silence again.

"You were saying you were walking your dog."

"He's dead now. Best dog I had."

"And you heard the noise?"

"Fifteen minutes, then it stops. No train in. Train's the other side of the ocean, on the mainland. Island station's all locked up."

"You're sure it's the noise you heard when the train arrived in the middle of the night?"

"I called him Benjamin."

"Who?"

"The doggy."

"That's *your* name."

"Dog's name as well." Ben laughed, then stared vacantly ahead at the railway.

I felt my cue to go. How much reliability could I put on this story? The man had come over as a combination of sharp-witted and muddled. The dog, for example. Residents weren't allowed to keep dogs. Was he coming out with a confused jumble of events from his past? I could think of no sensible explanation for a generator needing to be run at train arrival but not for departure. And why would the generator need to be run the evening after the train had left? Some kind of rehearsal? If so, for what?

Saoirse and I discussed Ben over dinner. I told her only the dog story; I didn't want to stir up trouble by passing on his train-shed comments.

"He's a nice old boy," she said. "You're probably right about his memory. We went to his house once, to present him with a medal for his services as chief steward. He'd got photographs of his dogs all over the walls. It's sad he can't have one as a companion here. I expect he misses the company. Misses them more than his wife, apparently. I didn't know he'd had a wife."

"Perhaps the Irish wife is a figment of his imagination."

"Do you think so? From what you say, it sounds like he was quite specific about how he met her. And that would explain how he ended up in Ireland. He doesn't strike me as someone who makes things up. He gets confused about time and date, that's all."

That same evening, Saoirse and I attended a reception for a new exhibition at the town art gallery. "I have to mingle and talk," she said. "Make sure you do likewise."

I got talking to a reporter from one of the two local papers. After enquiring about John and the progress of his recovery since the accident, he introduced me to a distinguished elderly gentleman, one of the artists being exhibited. In the course of conversation, it came out I had worked in Dublin, whereupon the man asked if I had ever come across a sculptress named Mary Cahill.

I explained sculpture wasn't my scene.

"We have some major pieces of hers here," he said.

"She lives in Nostalgia?"

"*Used* to live in Nostalgia. Come with me. I'll show you."

A few streets away we came to Nostalgia's outdoor art gallery, a walled garden filled with modern sculpture made of sheet metal, cut and welded into various forms.

"It's a pity you never met her," said the old man. "You might have set my mind at rest. You see, she loved this place, but then she went away. On my last trip to Dublin, I visited her. She refused to talk about why she'd left Nostalgia. In fact, she didn't want to talk about Nostalgia at all. It was clear my visit wasn't welcome."

"Do you think she had a falling out with the town council?"

"I don't know," said the man, "but what's unsavoury is the money."

"She lost money?"

"On the contrary, she'd come in to money. When I knew her, she never had money. She enjoyed a good lifestyle here but she didn't own property or anything like that. In Dublin she'd got herself set up in a cottage with a fantastic studio and gallery overlooking the sea in Dalkey. You know the area — millionaire pop-star land close by. I think she'd been paid to keep her mouth shut."

"About what?"

"Well, *that's* the question! If we could answer *that*! I come to this garden often to sit amongst her work. I feel she's left a message in her sculptures. *She's* been silenced but they can't silence her art."

Later, I returned to the garden. A giant guard whistle sculpture, about three-feet long, constructed of folded sheet metal, had been formed into a seat. I sat on it, alone in the moonlight, trying to decipher what coded information might be contained in the silhouettes of the strange forms before me. Several life-size human outlines, painted white on one side, black on the other, stood at the entrance to the garden. A weather vane sculpture, mounted above the gatepost displayed a large metal question mark, in place of the traditional cockerel. If the disappearing sculptress had intended to leave behind a message, it was difficult to figure out what.

Chapter 18

Ghosts

During my time in Nostalgia, I conducted more than one hundred interviews, with shop owners, factory owners, apprentices, bankers, bakers, railway staff, seaside entertainers, musicians, industrial workers, fishermen, restaurateurs, medical staff, people from all aspects of island life. However, the most important aspect eluded me.

Saoirse and I had been to the theatre to see a late-night set of one-act ghost plays. As we walked back in the darkness along the town wall, the brightly lit windows of the agricultural institute came into view.

"Does work go on there every night?" I asked.

"Yes," said Saoirse, "same as on the mainland. They work eight-hour shifts in rotation. Three shifts, for round-the-clock coverage."

"I've never met any of the research staff. Will I get to conduct interviews?"

"Unlikely. They have their own dormitories. They make it a rule not to mix with the town."

After I'd seen Saoirse to her lodgings, I went back up onto the wall. I wanted to think. I had been told by many townspeople that much work went on at the institute (though nobody could volunteer any knowledge of the nature of the work) but I'd not previously known they worked round-the-clock. To my mind, continuous shifts do not equate with research; shifts are what you need when you are making something, when it's unsafe to leave a manufacturing process unattended, when there is some urgency to complete, or when you are producing a bigger quantity of something than is normally required. I hoped for a clue, but I could not at that distance make out any detail in the glare of the fluorescent light emanating from the windows. Whatever they were doing there, I had an uncomfortable feeling about it.

Also, what Saoirse said about the workers wasn't credible. She could not possibly have seen it for herself. Monkish scientists, so dedicated to their work they never emerge from their dormitories to enjoy the delights of Nostalgia: the sandy beaches, the warm shallow water for swimming, the promenades, the fairground, the hotel chess tournaments, the restaurants and pubs, the music, the dancing, the theatre, the roof-gardens, the Commons sports clubs. If Nostalgia could not tempt these people, there must be some other, greater source of temptation keeping them away, something that could only be on the other side of the island. This idea didn't satisfy me either. Even should the other side of the island be more compelling, that the research workers should *never* wish to visit Nostalgia was inexplicable.

The nearest I could get to a plausible explanation was there had been a disagreement between the institute and the town such that staff had started a boycott of the town in protest. Even intelligent people can get involved in long-running, childish disputes, which do no good to either side.

A boycott would surely hurt the research workers more than the town. Each morning the horse-drawn cart would be parked outside one shop or other, loading up with provisions to be taken through the security gate and trundled up the rough path to the top of the hill. Many shopkeepers I'd interviewed derived substantial income from the patronage. Of course, the institute had no choice. Where else could it get its supplies from in this isolated place?

Something else puzzled me greatly. How did the institute workers travel between the island and the mainland? Presumably on the train, though no islander I'd spoken to ever claimed to have met an institute employee.

A blue guard, one of my chess playing acquaintances, came along the wall towards me from the direction of South Gate.

"Everything OK?" he asked.

"Fine. I'm on my way back to the hotel."

He glanced at his watch. "You need to be quick if you want to miss the tide."

The incoming surge envelops the beach at a frightening rate. When I got down to the causeway, the flow had begun to fold itself around the paving stones. By the time I had sprinted across to Little Island, my legs were already splashing through seawater to the height of my knees.

Chapter 19

A View of the Ocean

I'd expected Tuesday would be a good day, marked in my diary as "Theatre Day", my official visit to the town theatre, though it became eventful in ways I could not have anticipated.

An extremely busy venue, the theatre started work each morning at eight. I'd been warned to arrive on time, or they might not be able to fit me in. First, they took me round the backstage technical facilities; then I had the pleasure of interviewing the exceptional actors and actresses whose performances Saoirse and I had attended together. At the end of the morning, they took me to the manager's office. "I'm due for a meeting at the bank," he said. "Why don't you come with me? We'll go along the wall. It'll be easier to talk up there."

Aged early sixties, the manager possessed the finely sculptured face of the theatrically inclined. One wonders if facial type and acting ability are genetically connected, or they just go that way through years of moulding their visage to suit the variety of characters they're required to take on.

We went up the steps at Theatre Gate and along the wall towards the town centre. "You should understand Nostalgia is like heaven for actors," he said. "We have a full company who are never out of work. Sometimes we're running several shows a day. That's the staggering difference the lack of television makes."

I suggested their program, although mixed and varied, was a little more hi-brow than the average television fare.

"The funny thing is people get to like it," he replied. "I've had so many say to me, in retrospect they've been appalled by the time they've wasted watching rubbish on TV. People can develop an appreciation of quality, given the opportunity."

"And is their enthusiasm reflected in the economics?"

"Of course! Like this visit to the bank. We're requesting a loan for an ambitious equipment update. I don't anticipate any problem getting approval. I should imagine our account is as healthy as any of the town's larger businesses."

At the bank, the manger greeted us warmly. "Come into my office, gentlemen! Mike, we've got ready the document John requested on the bank's history. My secretary is out on an errand. She'll give it to you when she gets back."

I'd met the manager before, when I'd opened an account. Quite unlike the cliché idea of a bank manager, even more theatrical in manner than my present companion. In fact, he'd been a performer in an amateur production at the theatre. Predictably, they got their loan.

He picked up his office phone. "Sally? You're back? Mike's here to collect the document for John."

He sent me through to the outer office. Sally the secretary turned out to be Sally Macnamara.

"You work here full-time?" I asked.

"The regular is on holidays. I'm only a temporary. Where's your friend?"

"She's attending a working lunch at the town council."

"That's lucky," said Sally. "It's one o'clock. Time for my lunch and I have no-one to go with. If you were a gentleman, you'd ask me out."

"Where would you like to go?"

"The hotel. Then you can show me your room afterwards."

She pulled open a filing cabinet drawer and handed me the document for John. "What are you waiting for?" she asked.

"I thought you might be bringing a handbag."

"No. Only my body. That's all you need."

She grabbed my arm and wheeled me out into the street.

"What's the hurry?" I asked.

"Don't you read the tide tables? The water comes in at quarter past. It'll be a waste of precious time having to wait for the ferry. And I have to buy something first. Wait here!"

She disappeared inside the bag shop, returning within moments, holding a small cardboard jewellery box. We ran down the road to the quays and across the causeway, laughing together.

"Let's watch the tide race," said Sally. "We can go up The Knoll."

The Knoll is the high point of Little Island, a grassy mound set apart from the old cottages and having a viewing platform with a telescope. There's always a sea breeze up there, even in warm sunshine. We made it to the top just in time to see the advancing tidal wave speeding across the bay.

Sally asked if I'd tried the telescope. "You can spy on people walking about town."

I dropped a Pebble coin in the slot. The fairground appeared in the viewfinder magnified as if right close by. I swung the telescope round, tracing the line of the wall from North Gate, through Rose Gate, then Theatre Gate, Brew Gate, Farm Gate, Centre Gate and Canal Gate, as far as Stable Gate. Significantly, the Knoll's information board, mounted on tall metal posts, blocked the view of Hill Gate and the institute beyond. It occurred to me the placement of the board was no accident.

Swinging the telescope further round gave impressive close-ups of the salt marsh, the industrial estate, and the wooded escarpment on the far side of the bay. Scanning along the line of the trees to their end, I focussed on the far harbour wall and the power station. Directly behind, a tall rocky stack out at sea blocked any chance of a wider view. However, just to one side, a gap in the rocks offered a narrow window onto the ocean. A container ship slowly traversed the distant horizon. A small fishing boat briefly crossed the field of view. Then the shutter blacked out. It wouldn't be till later in the afternoon it would dawn on me — the incongruity of what I had just seen.

Sally reminded me of the time. "I don't want to miss seeing your room before going back," she said.

In the hotel dining room, she placed her little cardboard jewellery box to one side of the table.

"Do you mind my asking what's inside?" I asked.

She smiled. "Patience! After we've eaten."

I enjoyed being in Sally's company, her light, flirty conversation, with the constant sub-text of that inviting stare of her eyes, one of those women whom a friend had described as having a permanent "Come hither" look, simultaneously compelling and disturbing, like a mermaid luring sailors to their doom.

Upstairs, she sat on my window seat, admiring the view across the bay. "Now you can open the box, Mike."

It contained a gold ankle-chain.

"Put it on me, please."

Sliding her dress up well above her knees, she said, "Did you know some married women wear an ankle chain to signal they're available to other men?"

I said, "Sally, I think you're making that up!"

"No. It's true. But you have to know which leg. One side is completely innocent; the other isn't."

She kicked off her high heels. "Which leg will *you* choose?"

I said, "I'm choosing the left. Does that make you innocent or guilty?"

"I don't know," she replied. "And I don't know how to find out. It's not the sort of information you can ask for at a public library, is it?"

I knelt down before her, fixing the chain, enjoying the smell of her perfume mingled with the warm close-up odour of her body.

Turning her back on me, she said, "And please fix my dress. A button's come undone."

I told her the buttons were fine.

"Are they? Just a moment!" She reached behind with both hands, her long, delicate fingers and brightly varnished red nails flicking the buttons open one by one. Easing apart the folds of her dress, exposing her bare back and the clasp of her brassiere, she said, "We've still time."

I knew to go any further with this charade would be to slip rapidly beyond the point of no return. I said, "We should go down to the ferry now, or you'll be late for work and I'll be late for meeting Saoirse. Allow me to do up your buttons for you."

Later that afternoon, my thoughts went back to what I'd seen through the telescope on the knoll. A fishing boat— outside the boundary of the bay — so it could not be a boat belonging to the town, with all fishing being done within the bay and no inhabitant having access to the coast. However, I had sufficient knowledge of boats from my seaside upbringing to know what I saw could only be a local vessel, far too small for anyone to have risked taking across ninety miles of open Atlantic. Therefore, it must have come from somewhere else on the island. Who controlled this boat and what was its purpose in being there?

Chapter 20

Hotel Cat

I never knew whether I'd get downstairs in the morning before or after Saoirse's arrival at the hotel. A model of efficiency in everything she did, the vagaries of the tides and the clunky ferryboat service severely tested her punctuality. On this particular Saturday morning, she arrived much later than usual. "We've got a problem," she said, smiling, evidently amused by something.

"What's so funny?" I asked.

"Did we tell you at your interview you needed to be flexible to work for us?"

"I don't remember that being said."

"Well, you do. How would you like to manage a hotel for a week?"

"You mean *this* hotel?"

"The manager and his wife go away on holiday today. The husband in our replacement couple became unwell yesterday. Suspected appendicitis They're keeping him under observation at the hospital. In the circumstances we can't expect the wife to cope alone. All our reserve people are unavailable for one reason or another."

Saoirse reached into her bag and slapped a pile of telegrams on the table. "Total chaos this morning, with this lot going back and forwards between here and the mainland. It's not the easiest way to carry on a discussion. Then I thought of you — and me. We could manage it together."

"I don't know anything about hotels. Do you?"

119

"Nothing at all, but it's not like it's a tourist hotel with unpredictable guests arriving daily. It's a home for the Blue Guards, and the occasional new resident. The staff know everything they have to do. Management is administration, keeping records, doing the accounts, that sort of thing, keeping an eye on the bar, making sure of employee timekeeping, locking up at night. We only have to keep it ticking over. Of course, there's the regatta reception, but I've been going to those for years, so I know what's expected."

Sensing an opportunity, I asked, "Where will you stay? Will you take a room here?"

Saoirse smiled at me indulgently. "I don't think that's a good idea yet, do you? We both know what will happen if we sleep under the same roof."

I said, "John won't like it!"

"I've already told him you're doing it. He grumbled loudly about his schedule."

"How did you know I would say yes?"

"I couldn't imagine you saying no."

Saoirse had described the running of the hotel in routine terms. In truth, any number of incidents might occur which would test our joint lack of experience. We took on the responsibility with a shared trepidation. In fact, it turned out to be an idyllic time, with only one incident out of the ordinary. The tide had gone out, with many families already arrived at the beach. Through the windows we saw a cluster of small children in the distance, running excitedly around something, shrieking with delight.

"What do you think's going on?" asked Saoirse.

"They've found a crab," I suggested.

"I think I'd better check," she said. "We don't want any kid getting an injury."

I watched her walk across the sands. She stood talking with the children, then picked up a small grey bundle and came back, the children running along beside her.

"Let's give pussy a saucer of milk, shall we?"

I went to the kitchens to fetch the milk while Saoirse took the tiny tabby cat round to the hotel gardens.

"The chef says he's employed to feed humans, not cats," I said, as I placed the saucer down in front of it. "Should I buy a tin of cat food?"

"Here?" exclaimed Saoirse, "On the island!"

A stupid remark on my part. I'd forgotten the island authorities banned cats and dogs, out of concern for them contaminating the research institute land. Hence the children's excitement on seeing the animal, and why the adults who'd been sitting in the hotel garden also crowded round the novelty.

"We can at least get the chef to boil up some fish," said Saoirse. "You know we'll have to keep it locked up indoors until the tide has come in, to stop it escaping to town. Thank God, cats hate water. It's the only way you can keep them under control."

The cat leapt about under the tables, chasing pieces of string being pulled along by the children.

I asked, "Are you suggesting the hotel keep it?"

"We can't be seen to break island rules," Saoirse replied, picking up the cat and stroking it under the chin.

"This has happened before. You know how they get here, don't you — the only way anything *can* get here — on the train. They sneak inside when the passengers are embarking. We think the steam heating attracts them. They hide somewhere near the pipes, curl up, go to sleep, then slip off on arrival."

The cat purred loudly, in sync with Saoirse's stroking. I joined in, stroking the top of its head in unison. "Will we send it back on the next train?"

Gently placing the cat on the ground, Saoirse said, "You're clueless about animals, aren't you? How do you think we'll get it on the train when it's not going of its own free will? It'll be terrified, break free and run off. We'll need a cat box. I'll ask Anything & Co to make one. The only cat in the world with a custom-engineered cat box."

I said, "I'll take a photo for the archives. Knowing them, they'll want to do something fancy. A voice-operated cat flap — sorry, I mean a meow-operated cat flap"

Saoirse laughed. "Now you're being silly. We're trying to keep the cat confined, not help it escape. Anyway, it would be cruel on the children to take it away now. We'll send it back on the Monday night train."

The cat finished its saucer of milk and gave a pitiful mew, as though saying, "Is that all there is?" Saoirse dispatched me to the kitchens to tell the chef his terms and conditions of employment had been revised.

I found hotel managing to be an enjoyable occupation. In the future, I might abandon my career and become a hotelier but, right now, the position offered a special advantage. Six weeks into my time on the island, I had seen and heard enough to know something must be going on underneath Nostalgia's facade of the ideal town. I assumed something undesirable, otherwise why would the Earl and his collaborators be at such pains to conceal it? I had no confirmation of the situation with John but I suspected, like me, he had wanted to find out the truth. He had been caught in the act and incapacitated. To avoid a similar fate, my own strategy would need to be patiently and cunningly laid. Its success depended on a number of prerequisites. The first of these, I would obtain by means of the hotel.

Chapter 21

Eddie The Dalek

"Will you take me to a dance?" Saoirse had asked during my first week on the island, "I should warn you, there's a catch."

"Sounds ominous."

"You may be good at it already. It's a Salsa evening"

"I don't know Salsa"

"That's the catch. We have to go as a couple to classes."

Salsa was the favoured dance of the town, danced by young and old. For good reason. All music, by decree of the town council, had to be live, but un-amplified. Rock music, starved of its dependence on high volume, had become extinct. People still need to dance, and you can't dance to quiet music. Enter the Salsa band with its brass section, baritone sax, piano, and array of percussion. Latin had become the town's popular music.

The demise of packaged music enabled a number of talented musicians to get a full time living. It amused me to find that Alice, the violinist leader of the string quartet, who played for afternoon tea in the hotel, a lady of about fifty with her hair tied into a bun, let her hair down, literally, on Monday nights, transforming herself into the raunchy, blowsy, shouting lead singer of a wild blues trio that played in the hotel bar. Those same musicians also played in the salsa band.

The salsa classes mixed pleasure with ordeal, the pleasure of dancing with Saoirse being offset by the ordeal of coping with the teacher, Eddie, a small angular fellow with a curious high voice, like a Dalek crossed with an old-fashioned school gym mistress. You'd come out of Eddie's sessions feeling somebody had hit you with a sledgehammer, so critical was he of the slightest mistake. However, despite the pain, I do give him credit for forging me into a reasonably competent dancer.

Tonight, our class had been booked for the hotel dining room. We cleared the chairs and tables to the side to create a wide space, which was immediately packed solid with vigorous dancing couples. Eddie wheeled between us, yelling instructions. At the final chord from the band, a shout of appreciation went up from the bar. The customers had crowded unseen into the doorway to watch. Asked to date the high point of my life on the island, I would place it at that moment. From then on, everything began to unravel and it all started with the business of the keys.

The hotel managers take charge of the keys. The midnight routine, after the departure of the staff, involved checking the kitchens, locking the back door from kitchen to the outside, then locking the door separating dining area from kitchen. The keys went in the hotel safe overnight. Normally, only the manager and manageress had access. This week I had access and I wanted a copy of those keys. I planned a clandestine trip over to the town hardware shop. On the Wednesday afternoon, Saoirse attended a meeting in town, the ideal opportunity, were it not for my having to remain in charge. Tadhg unwittingly came to my rescue. He called in to see if I needed help. I asked if he'd mind manning the desk for an hour. Tadhg obliged, and I got my keys.

While in town, I called in to the bookshop to purchase a hardback volume on the most obscure subject I could think of. I found one entitled *Applied Mathematics*. Perfect for the job; nobody's going to look inside it, I thought. Later that evening, I used a Stanley knife to carefully hollow out the pages. I put inside the copied keys and pushed the book between the others on my bedroom shelf.

Chapter 22

Regatta

On the Saturday morning at the end of our week managing the hotel, Saoirse and I sat together on the window seat of my bedroom, watching the impressive rush of the tide race that twice daily cuts off the hotel from the mainland. Unlike at the town quays or at the more sheltered back of Little Island, out here in the exposed bay we faced full frontal onto the force of the incoming water. The gurgling tsunami slammed against the hotel's concrete foundations, sending up a towering plume of spray, which soaked the forecourt and rattled the windows.

"We won't see each other tomorrow," said Saoirse. "John's attending the regatta, so I'll be busy taking him round in his wheelchair. And there's another thing: I hope you don't mind but I've co-opted you onto one of the rowing teams. Don't worry if you can't keep up with their pace. It's just for laughs. Nobody takes it seriously."

Only half listening to the bit about the rowing race, I didn't at the time anticipate how near it would come to compromising my future plans. I was puzzling over Saoirse's willingness to spend time with John. Whenever I'd been on the way to the hospital, she'd find a reason not to join me. As our official supervisor on the island, she showed remarkably little interest in the three of us meeting together, being content to get all progress reports second-hand from me. Now, despite her clear aversion, here she was, cheerfully volunteering to spend the whole day with John.

Saturday evening: our big hotel event, the reception for the regatta organisers, the thank-you celebration for all their hard work. Saoirse and I waited by the hotel entrance, greeting the arrivals being brought across the sands in a procession of bicycle rickshaws and horse drawn carts, the men in black tie, the ladies extremely glamorous in the unique island fashions. Saoirse had chosen to wear a long midnight blue dress, the colour complementing her vivid red hair.

We had welcomed all the guests, when a curious incident occurred. While awaiting the arrival of the mayor, we saw a tall man walking alone across the sands. As he came up the steps to the forecourt, we could see he was young, mid-twenties at most, blond-haired, six foot four inches in height and powerfully built. As I stepped forward to greet him, he whisked a camera out of his pocket, announced "Say Cheese!" clicked off a snapshot and walked past us into the hotel without saying a further word.

"Who was that?" I exclaimed.

"Nobody *I* know," replied Saoirse. "Did you notice he had his camera pointed straight at you?"

It might seem a little thing, a triviality hardly worth worrying about, somebody taking your photograph without permission, springing it on you as some kind of trick for private amusement. I felt furious, as if someone intended to gain an ascendancy or control over me through possession of my image. I said, "I'm going inside to find him."

Saoirse gave me a worried look. "Please don't do it by yourself. Get Tadhg to help you."

The idea of enlisting Tadhg to tackle a ruffian struck me as highly comical, with him being only a little fellow, unlikely to scare anyone, let alone a giant almost a foot and a half taller than himself. To oblige Saoirse, we went in search of snapshot man together, hoping the authority of Tadgh's blue guard uniform might add some weight. We found the man in the garden. To my astonishment, his face showed genuine alarm when he saw us coming. He sprinted for the brick wall separating the garden from the street, made an impressive flying vault over and disappeared on the other side. Tadhg showed his courage by a leap of his own but with the disadvantage of height he failed miserably. Saoirse, who had come through to the garden to see Tadhg launch himself impotently at the wall, was trying very hard to stop herself from dissolving into laughter. In a last-ditch attempt to salvage his injured dignity, Tadhg ran off in pursuit via the hotel back door. Half an hour later he returned to report failure. Snapshot man had vanished. Whether still on Little Island or departed by beach or causeway was unknown.

Our plan had been to hold the proceedings in the bar but the calm evening air decided us to move the event outside. We instructed the staff to set up refreshments in the garden, while the hotel handyman strung coloured lights back and forth over a makeshift bandstand. The amazingly versatile town musicians started with Vivaldi,

129

to lend a touch of class, later morphing with ease to a blues band, then playing Cuban salsa. The infectious music got everybody up dancing. The perfect end to a perfect week — or so, in our over-confidence, we thought. The regular hotel managers would not have forgotten, as we did, to allow for the tide. The music at maximum volume, the dancing and conversation in full flow, nobody noticed the incoming water. Just as it had done twelve hours earlier, it slammed against the edge of the courtyard, the spray soaking everything and everyone in sight. The ladies ran shrieking for the cover of indoors, followed by the men, who crowded into the bar like a waddle of bedraggled penguins back from a fishing dive. Saoirse raided the laundry for a supply of towels, while I handed out free whiskies all round in embarrassed apology for our error.

Next morning, I got out early to scout my photographic assignment. Notwithstanding the town's nautical location, Nostalgia held its regatta inland, on the reservoir, the source of the island's water supply. I took the canal bus to the railway, where on the far side of the station square, I found the signpost for the reservoir. The uphill path ran alongside a steep-sided concrete drainage channel, dammed at regular intervals to drive generators, the water flowing out through metal grilles. By such means, the islanders took maximum advantage of the terrain to generate their precious electricity, extracting current at each step of the drop to sea level. The stream cascaded down noisily, though the width and depth of the channel indicated capacity to contain a larger flow, one of flood-like proportions.

A ten-minute walk brought me to my destination. This part of the island I'd heard talked about many times, the recreational facilities, rowing, fishing, swimming, and so on but I hadn't anticipated it would be such a sizeable body of open water — I estimated at least half a mile across and three quarters of a mile in length. Sailing boats criss-crossed, moving at some speed, driven by a strong wind. Dense forest lined one side of the reservoir, while on the other side a bare grassy hill ran up to a ridge.

I considered the ridge worth a climb, to get an overview of the area. At the top, beyond a plateau of open grassland, I saw a distant security fence enclosing woodland, the fence following round in a curve to join its twin on the cliffs. So now I knew the reservoir marked the limit of the permitted area on this side of town. Pushing across the plateau against a brisk cross wind and reaching the fence, I looked through to the woodland beyond. I caught, between swaying branches, glimpses of a white building in the shape of a classical temple. The momentary parting of foliage tantalised me with all too brief views of the structure. I felt the building must have some significance. Strange that it should be so near, yet fenced off.

Back downhill, crowds had gathered. So many people! On a general holiday like today you could appreciate just how populous was Nostalgia's community. I joined many others making a gentle perambulation around the reservoir's circumference. Ahead of us a footbridge, which took the shoreline path across an inlet to a large square pond. A wooden pier at the back of the pond connected to a hut positioned on stilts above the water. A crowd of people peered at it with interest. Suddenly, a body dropped from underneath with a shout and a capacious splash. The spectators let out a cheer. This performance was repeated several times. The swimmers floundered around in the water while the crowd waited in further anticipation. Walking on, it was only after hearing the laughter and wolf-whistles of the crowd and seeing the swimmers rapidly climbing naked up a ladder into the hut, that I understood it to be a sauna.

The rowing race started at twelve, with teams made up of young guys from the businesses on the industrial estate. I'd been co-opted onto a team of glasshouse workers. The townspeople considered it the most exciting event of the morning. It ran the full length of the reservoir, starting at the far end. However, the pace of the rowing disappointed my expectation, painfully slow compared to the near Olympic standard of my university team. I could certainly have propelled us out in front of the others. But, recalling the incident in the bay with the speedboat, I thought better of showing off. I preferred nobody to be aware of my ability, including any watching guards. Nevertheless, I took a risk by playing a game. As we neared the finishing line, my team gained second position. Without me they would have had no chance of coming first. I supplied pressure to the oars, bringing us tantalisingly close to overtaking the leaders, the crowd yelling its appreciation. The mayor commended us in his prize-giving speech for our courage in defiance of obvious exhaustion.

As we came down off the back of the podium with our second-place rosettes, a strong hand grabbed my arm and pulled me to one side. My blond snap-shooter of the previous evening. "I rowed for my college," he said, in an English accent. "Balliol. Who did *you* row for?"

I hesitated. He shook my arm. "Come on. Your secret's safe with me. I'm on your side."

"Birmingham," I answered. "How did you know I rowed?"

"That super-smooth action of yours. Beautiful. Stands out a mile, *if* you know what to look for. Though I bet you weren't also in the university drama society. You forgot to pant for breath like the others. Look, I know you're hiding your skill. I'm not going to give you away. What I'm interested to know is *why* you're hiding it?"

I said, "First, I want to know who you are and why you took my photograph last night."

He laughed. "Melodramatic, wasn't it? Escape by leaping over the garden wall!"

Someone called out my name. John, parked in his wheel chair at the refreshment tent, with Saoirse at his side.

"We'll speak later," said my acquaintance, and he vanished into the crowd.

Seeing John and Saoirse together, I pondered whether her volunteering to be his carer for the day was in fact a ruse to keep us from conversing alone outside of the supervised scenario of the hospital, and whether this action was out of obedience to the island authorities or motivated by some private fear of her own.

At two o'clock, I returned to the railway to take photographs. Row after row of watercraft of all shapes and sizes packed the square in front of the station. Following tradition, each Nostalgia business entered a float. I got offered a ride on one with an ingenious display demonstrating the re-processing of waste vegetable oil to create diesel for the few motor vehicles on the island. I declined their offer, because I aimed to take photographs of all the participants, hitching a lift to town with the last ones to leave.

A team of volunteers started to wheel the floats by trolley to the dockside, where I took photos of a crane lifting them into the canal. The reservoir sluice gates would be raised on the hour to create a surge of floodwater. Down at the harbour, the gates had been opened already, to begin the process of draining water into the bay. The combined flow created at each end would propel the lightweight regatta craft the entire length of the canal.

The chimes of the station clock announced three. A hush descended on the waiting crowd. At first you could hear nothing, then from the direction of the reservoir came an ominous murmuring, increasing in volume until it had become a roar. The crowd cheered as a wall of water slammed into the canal. The floats tossed about wildly, their occupants clinging tightly to the fragile superstructures to prevent themselves being thrown off. Then, as each craft settled into its journey downstream, furious activity struck up on the quayside, with a group of volunteers queuing up floats for the crane, while others raced back to the railway to wheel in yet more.

I joined the final float to leave, which belonged to the natural dye works. Who should be in charge but none other than snapshot-man. He introduced himself as Dave Wilson, assistant chemist at the works, an immigrant to Ireland from England. He told me how he'd been working for a pharmaceutical company near Cork city when the Earl poached him away to work in Nostalgia. This year was his third on the island.

If you've never seen natural dyed cloth, you won't appreciate the subtlety of the colouring that can be achieved in comparison to modern aniline dyes. It's like comparing natural light to glaring neon. Onboard, a bunch of extremely pretty women modelled island fashions made up from the dyed fabrics. They included the leggy Macnamara twins, both dressed beautifully in a patterned beach wrap. As we drifted downstream, I first took pictures of the models, then pointed my camera at the spectators. The most boisterous crowds clustered around the canal-side pubs inside Nostalgia's walls but, when we left the town behind, at Marsh Gate, all was still and silent. With the balmy air, the warm late afternoon sunshine, the purples and yellows of the salt marsh flowers, the pretty women and the gentle motion of the boat, I was suffering from sensory overload. If that wasn't already enough, Sally Macnamara flirted unashamedly by sitting on top of me, putting her arm round my shoulders for support. She did that thing again of drawing attention to her legs, this time slowly rubbing her hand up and down her calf muscles, staring wide-eyed at me as she did so.

We docked at the industrial estate, where a crane raised our craft from the water. I helped them with dismantling, loading the contents onto a cart. Dave told the women he and I would push the cart back to the works. They went off up the road, leaving Sally, who stood conversing with us. As soon as the others had gone out of view, she said, "Well, goodbye then", put her arm around me and engaged me in an extended kiss. To say it would have been unkind to resist would be to wholly misrepresent the situation. Directly tasting the desire of this older married woman was for me an unfamiliar but intensely erotic and compelling experience.

"Obviously your lucky day!" commented Dave.

The town planners had situated the dye works, like all the other chemical businesses, far from the residential areas, half a mile on the other side of the estate. Dave and I trundled our cart down roads a hive of activity, with businesses packing away their floats.

"Did you ever see a town like this?" he said, "A proper town. One that doesn't depend on the car. Most towns would die without the car. Either they're dormitories for city commuters or they're destinations for tourists. Nostalgia doesn't need the outside world to give it an excuse to exist."

"But you're hardly self-sufficient, are you?" I replied, "Look at the amount of goods and materials imported on the train."

"Self-sufficiency's a myth," replied Dave. "It's not even a good idea. Better to have networks of people and specialist communities, supporting each other through supply and demand."

We'd arrived at the dye works. Dave unlocked the gates and we pushed the cart inside a small warehouse for unloading. "Now we can talk in private," he said. "I heard about you coming to the island. If you're as bright as I hope you are, you'll already have suspicions something is going on."

"I'm not answering till I know more about you."

"You're right to be cautious. First, the photograph. I knew today we could talk without drawing suspicion. But, with all the crowds, I anticipated you might be difficult to locate. That's why I took the precaution of getting a snapshot, in case I needed to ask anyone whether they'd seen you." He reached into his pocket and took out my picture. "Here. Take it. I don't need it anymore."

A group of young guys walking past the gates came in to congratulate Dave on his idea for getting models on his float. One I recognised from the winning rowers. Unfortunately, he recognised me also. "Here's yer man!" he said, "We want to talk to you about joining our team." I was beginning to regret my rashness in giving away my abilities.

When they'd gone, I asked Dave, "You have friends here. Why are you so anxious to talk to me, specifically?"

"Because you're an outsider," he replied. "I have to be careful. I expect you've noticed how nobody will talk about the other side of the fences. I can't even discuss the matter with my wife. She's worried we'll get thrown out. She'd be heartbroken to leave. But, I'm uneasy. Your colleague's injury was suspicious don't you think? How did he get onto the land? Not over the fence. No way! With that razor wire! In my opinion, there's only one way he could do it: concealing himself underneath the goods on the institute supply cart. His was no accidental straying. That's not possible. It must have been deliberate. I think he found out something and, what's more, I think you know what that something is."

"If I did, I might want to keep it confidential."

"It's the girl getting in the way, isn't it? You're protecting her. I only hope she's worth protecting. Have you ever noticed her doing anything unusual?"

"She always goes swimming naked."

Dave laughed. "Yes. I've seen her doing that. She's not the only one. This is Nostalgia-by-the-sea. Saucy seaside syndrome. People here don't have the inhibitions of mainlanders. The result of our cultured, egalitarian prosperity. You might say we're like an Irish Scandinavia. *Sally* swims nude — when her husband isn't there. She asked me to join her once. She was quite put out when I said my wife wouldn't like it. Last month, walking along the wall, I saw your Saoirse coming towards me. With one hand, she was swinging one of those jute bags. Very pleased with herself, I thought. In her other hand, she was twirling a bright metal object. You'll never guess what. A car key!"

"So? There are some motors on the island."

"There's nothing outside of emergency and medical vehicles. Why would she have a key for one of those?"

"The key for a car she drives on the mainland?"

In that case, why when she saw me did she drop it into her bag?"

We dragged the big iron works' gates shut. They scraped and screeched on the concrete. While Dave secured them with a padlock, he turned to me and asked, "Does she drive a Land Rover?"

"Not that I know of."

"I drove one for a summer job once, identical maroon colour key tag to hers. I only got a quick look but I'm sure her tag had the logo as well."

I asked, "Where on the wall did all this happen?"

"At Hill Gate. She'd just come up steps from ground level."

"That's where you take the road to the hill dwellers, isn't it?"

Dave looked at me significantly. "And it's the nearest gate to where the supply cart goes, up the hill to the research institute."

Chapter 23

The Inventor

Next morning, Saoirse asked my plans. I told her I'd be picking up the regatta photographs to take to John for his approval. Afterwards, I planned to call on some previous interviewees.

"You haven't had a swimming lesson for ages," she said. "We can't let you get out of practise. Island Radio said this morning is expected to be the hottest of the year, too hot to do anything else at lunchtime."

The trip out to John and the visits to my interviewees were over by eleven, with an hour to kill before meeting Saoirse. The weather forecast had been accurate — a deep blue sky without a cloud to be seen. Too good to be indoors. I ascended the wall and walked round in the direction of South Gate, enjoying the panorama of the roof gardens in full bloom, positively Mediterranean in the sweltering sun. At Stable Gate, I spotted the canal depot manager down in his yard, ticking off newly arrived goods on a clipboard. I called to him, and he gestured for me to come down.

"You have something to tell me?" I asked.

"You remember the mark on the centrifuge?"

"The weird triangle shaped head? You've had another?"

"Yes, but something more puzzling has occurred. That one I showed you, I noticed later had a small chip knocked off the plug. We're conscientious with our quality control, as I've told you, but the chip was so tiny I decided the damage didn't warrant sourcing a replacement, so I sent it on and forgot all about it. That was, until this morning, with the arrival of more centrifuges. They're over here."

He led me across the cobbled yard to a box singled out from the rest and placed on its own in a corner. The open lid revealed two centrifuges inside, cushioned with paper straw. "Naturally, I looked for the triangular face mark scratched on the base. The one on the left has it. Would you like to take a look?"

Remembering their weight, I said, "I'll take your word for it."

"Now here's the curious thing. That one also has *this*." He yanked the gadget's mains cord from the box and showed me the plug, slightly chipped on one side.

I said, "Why would they need two identifying marks? Have you unscrewed the plug to see if there's anything inside it?"

The manager wound up the cord and replaced it in the box. "You're not getting it," he said. "Don't you see how we got it wrong? We assumed a succession of marked centrifuges. In fact, there's only one. *This* one, with the doodle drawn on its base and the chip knocked out of its plug. It's the same one, being endlessly recycled. It's coming into the island, going up to the institute and somehow finding its way back to the mainland, though not through us because we've never transported any centrifuges in the reverse direction; I checked our records to confirm."

I suggested the centrifuge was being used to smuggle out something valuable. "If we could have intercepted it and unscrewed it on its return journey, we might have found something incriminating inside."

"There are a lot of questions to be answered. How do they get it off the island? You know how diligent customs are. Concealing from them a feckin great heavy centrifuge would be nigh on impossible. And how come the institute people don't know this one keeps disappearing? Or is the institute in on the scam being perpetrated? If they *are* in on the scheme, why couldn't they send the item out officially, which would be unlikely to raise suspicion?"

I studied the plug, in futile expectation of a sudden light-bulb moment solving the conundrum. I asked, "Do you think it's being smuggled out by boat? We're told the coastline's too treacherous for access. There's no proof that's true, is there?"

The manager shook his head impatiently. "If they could get it out by sea, they'd bring it in by sea, wouldn't they? Why risk discovery by sending it through customs? In any case, the coast *must* be inaccessible or we would have had uninvited visitors to the island by now. That's never happened in the twenty years of Nostalgia' s existence."

I asked, "Then how do would you explain the fishing boat I saw off the coast through the telescope on the Knoll?"

He hadn't expected that piece of information! "Could have been from the mainland. Passing by."

"It was far too small to have been anything other than launched locally."

"That could prove my point," said the manager. "Why shouldn't the research institute have a boat? I'm not saying there isn't access somewhere on the coast for a local boat, just no safe route in and out for an ocean vessel."

"But an ocean-going vessel could rendezvous with a local boat or could launch their own small boat to land on the coast."

"A small boat can't be able to access the coast safely, or we would have had outside visitors."

"Now you're contradicting yourself," I said. "You agreed the small fishing boat I saw must have been local."

"We're going round in circles," said the manager.

I asked, "What do you plan to do next?"

"Some new residents told me things they'd seen which didn't add up," he replied. "I'll tell them about the centrifuge. See if they can suggest anything."

Leaving the depot manager to his puzzle I killed time walking round the colourful roof gardens, until the sound of Irish music caught my attention. Unlike the live music commonplace in Nostalgia from musicians and bands employed in the streets, cafes and pubs, unusually this music sounded like a recording. And I could hear laughter.

I descended a staircase to street level. On the opposite side of the road, a group of people stood around a large wooden box, colourfully decorated with red and white stripes, raised up at eye level on a plinth, like an old-fashioned Punch and Judy show. A banner across the top proclaimed "The Irish Dancers".

The music stopped. Someone said, "Let's run it again. Anybody got five Pebbles?" I called out, "I've got five," and went across to join them. They showed me the slot where I had to put in my money. As the fifth Pebble dropped, the box sprung to life. A panel at the base slid back to reveal an old 78 player with a record spinning round. An automated puppet hand picked up the stylus arm and lowered it onto the record. It played the Irish reel I'd heard earlier, the quaint scratchy soundtrack amplified by a giant horn protruding out of one side of the cabinet.

Next, the curtains at the top drew back to reveal a troupe of Irish dancers, arms linked, alternating man and woman, giving kicks into the air, the figures meticulously carved in wood, with jointed limbs worked by some invisible mechanism. This was no toy but a sophisticated piece of miniaturised engineering. As the music played on, the kicks of the dancers got steadily higher. The crowd started laughing at the joke I had not yet seen. The grossly exaggerated high kicks of the women lifted their skirts to expose knickers in a range of garish colours. And the man and woman at the end of the line actually blushed. How the maker had achieved that astonishing trick with faces carved from solid wood I couldn't imagine. The crowd were killing themselves laughing now. The end female figure wore no knickers, flashing her bits, which had been realistically carved with great attention to detail, while an exaggerated protrusion in the trousers of the blushing guy next to her slowly pushed forwards. Suddenly, the curtains swished closed, the music stopped and the panel at the bottom of the cabinet slid shut to hide the record player. The spectators dispersed, still laughing.

From the open windows of the premises behind the automaton I could hear the sound of machinery. A sign on the door said, "Bad Taste Toys". Too good an interview opportunity to be missed! Inside, a big, broad-shouldered man with a mass of wavy white hair, stripped to the waist and sweating profusely in the heat, was bent over a bandsaw cutting up blocks of hardwood. I waited till he switched off the machine, before knocking on the door to draw his attention.

He swung round, "Ah! Mike!" he said, "I hoped we'd get to meet. Don't look so surprised. I know *everything* going on in Nostalgia. Would you like a beer?"

He disappeared into a back room and came back with two chilled bottles of local brew. "I bought three crates yesterday," he said. "Amazing the bottles you get through working in this heat. Take a pew."

He kicked a footstool across the floor. "Have you come to interview me?"

I told him how I'd been attracted by his automaton in the street.

"I had a lot of fun building it but that's not my main business. You saw the sign on the door?"

"Bad Taste Toys?"

"It's my new enterprise. I worked for Anything & Co. Did some great things there, then got fed up of working for others. The Earl kindly set me up with the money for this business."

"You make toys?"

"Toys for executives, the kind of thing you might see sold in an upmarket catalogue at a price, limited edition, collectors' items, that sort of thing."

I asked, "Where does the 'Bad Taste' come in?"

He laughed. "Ah! Now there's a story!"

Clearing a space amongst the wood-shavings and tools on a workbench, he hitched himself up on top. "On holiday with the wife once. Some place with a tenuous connection to *Titanic*. Playing it up like mad: Titanic ashtrays, Titanic tea towels, Titanic pottery, cut glass engraved with the Titanic, themed fridge magnets, Titanic table-maps. Loads of stuff. All feckin Titanic. Tacky. Complete tat. Feckin Titanic feckin cat-dish, would you believe! And to add insult to injury: *Made in China*. Nothing that profited local industry — in a town with high unemployment, too! I knew I could poke fun at the faux sentimentality *and* make some money out of it. The Earl liked the idea. So *Bad Taste Toys* was born."

"Do you have any products I can look at?"

"We've just exported a crate to Holland. One of the Earl's veggie customers saw the toy and liked it. I can show you some bits. Come through!"

I followed him to a back room, where a variety of items had been laid out on tables, ready for assembly.

"See! No plastic. All quality materials. Hardwoods, stainless steel, etc. We have all the pieces here." He picked up a carved replica of the famous boat. "It's hollow. We've hidden some music electronics inside, with a weight at one end and a water-sensitive switch. Put it in water and it will slowly sink, prow first, playing *Nearer, My God, To Thee* as it goes down. Here, lift up the flap and you'll see the electronics."

He handed me the boat, a miniature work of art in itself — I could see why they'd need to sell these limited-edition at a price.

"Here you have the other pieces," he said. "Replica iceberg. Insufficient detachable lifeboats, and lead-weighted drowning passengers — not to scale of course. And here's the instruction leaflet.

I picked up a small slip of paper elaborately printed in an Edwardian font: "Place passengers at back of boat. Place boat in bath or fish tank and wait for results. Collision with iceberg, if required, must be carried out manually."

"Don't you worry people will say this is in bad taste?" I asked.

"Precisely. Load of feckin hypocrites. What do they care? Their only interest is the money they can make from their cheap tat. How many tears do you English shed over your losses at the Battle of Hastings? It's ancient history now."

I asked if he had any other toys. He told me he was working on *The Tay Bridge Disaster* but what he really wanted to simulate was the destruction of Pompeii by the eruption of Mount Vesuvius.

"Now, let's get down to more serious matters," he said. He left the room momentarily to close his front door. "I can see you're an intelligent man. What do you think's *really* going on in Nostalgia? No lies, now!"

Caught off guard, I hesitated.

"I knew it!" he exclaimed, "You have suspicions. Have you worked it out yet? What's going on here?"

I paused, not sure what to say. At length, I said "No."

"I started at four o'clock one afternoon, thinking it through, going over everything, fitting the pieces of the puzzle together so they made sense. Twelve hours it took me. Four in the morning I had it all worked out."

"Have you told anyone?"

"We're all having so much fun, I don't want to spoil it. It would spoil it for me, as well as for them."

"Don't you have a conscience?"

He laughed. "That's precisely why I'm not telling. I'll tell you something, though. There are others here who are in the know. I don't mean they worked it out like I did. There's not many bright enough for that. I mean people in Nostalgia who are in on the plan, who are actively working it."

"Won't you tell me what it is?"

"I'll do a deal with you. If you think you've seen the light, come back. If you're right, I'll confirm what you know. Otherwise, I'm giving nothing away."

I thanked the inventor for the entertaining tour of his premises and made my way to North Gate to meet Saoirse. A man with the brains to figure out a puzzle, for sure, but what put a doubt in my mind was why he would want to brag about it with the Earl being chief backer of his business?

That night, in my hotel room, I took stock with notepad and pen. Others shared my doubts about the island, Dave Wilson, for example, although he had no more clue than I. And that strange centrifuge business reported by the canal depot manager. Then the railway noises heard by Ben, depending on the reliance one could put on his muddled ramblings. Finally, the claims of the inventor at *Bad Taste Toys*? Yes, the inventor worried me. Too intelligent to be a gullible conspiracy theorist, no way would he risk ridicule by laying claim to wild conclusions without strong supporting evidence. You could read him two ways and both meant trouble. If he were indeed in cahoots with his backer, the Earl, then his suggestion of a conspiracy could only be to pump me for my opinion, i.e. there *was* a conspiracy and they wanted to find out how much I knew. On the other hand, if his conclusions were independent and he was genuinely seeking my opinion as an ally, it again suggested a conspiracy, one which he had uncovered.

I gave it up, tore the paper from my notepad, scrunched it up into a ball, and went outside in the black of night to the tidal edge. There, in the darkness, I set fire to the evidence, dropping it on the water to float away into the bay. But Nostalgia hadn't finished playing tricks with me yet. A freak gust of wind whisked the burning boat off the sea, sending it spinning into the air, where it hung for a moment like an orange Chinese lantern, before vanishing into the oblivion of the night.

Chapter 24

Salsa Night

Salsa Night — the big social event of the year, the opportunity for the fashion designers and clothing manufacturers of the town to gain publicity by outdoing each other with the glamour of their outfits. The women looked fantastic. You could be forgiven for thinking yourself at the Oscars, not at a provincial dance on a remote island ninety miles off the Irish coast.

Saoirse's costume had been specially designed for the occasion. Peach coloured, made up in layers and fringed, it rustled seductively as she danced, with a swirling motion that had a life of its own. Not all the costumes had been made professionally, however. A dark-haired girl who couldn't have been more than seventeen years of age came in the most amazing outfit. She'd wrapped and pinned a single length of white towelling round her body, only just hiding her bits. A big girl, she displayed sumptuous cleavage at the front, and at the back. Not the prettiest costume; unquestionably the sexiest. Even more incredible, it managed to stay on while she danced.

"Typical male!" said Saoirse, "You're waiting for it to fall off and reveal all, aren't you? You're going to be disappointed. You can bet she knows what she's doing."

Later on, while Saoirse and I took a break from dancing, I caught sight of the girl in white, dancing with an old man pulling off some flashy Salsa moves with great skill and gusto. At that moment, he spun round to face us.

"Look over there," I said to Saoirse. "Look at Fierce Hot. He's having the time of his life!"

"And *she* is, by the look of her," said Saoirse. "He's a great dancer. Did you know, two years running he won the 'All-Ireland' in his youth?"

"No. He never told me. Explains why he's so fit and capable with his ferry boat."

When the dance finished, I went over to the unlikely couple. "Great dancing!" I said. "Saoirse tells me you were once All-Ireland champion."

"Irish dancing. I only dance Salsa now," and he whispered to me, "I can tell *you*, because you're not Irish, I wish I'd done Salsa instead in my youth. You get to see a lot of bare flesh. Gets you fierce hot, though."

The band started up again, with a slow piece, a contrast to the energy of before. I noticed musician Alice coming off the bandstand, making straight for me, while Sally advanced from the other corner of the room.

Sally won the race. "Mind if I dance with your partner?" she said, sweeping Saoirse away in a close hold, leaving me to face Alice and her distinctly grinding dance moves. When the music had come to a stop, Saoirse came to my rescue.

"Does she always go for younger men?" I asked.

"Yes. She has a reputation for taking one home with her at the end of every dance night."

"I had a lucky escape, then?"

"Or not," said Saoirse. "From what I've heard, her bedroom repertoire is even more impressive than her musical versatility. Apparently, you can rely on her to deliver a virtuoso performance in the fast movements and her slow movement always builds to a well-orchestrated climax."

I asked, "How did you enjoy dancing with Sally?"

Saoirse laughed. "She's funny. Always flirting. Even with women. There's not something going on I should know about, is there? I noticed your disappointment when she didn't choose you."

I replied, untruthfully, "Only because you two left me stranded with Alice."

At the end of the evening, Saoirse and I walked along the wall to her lodgings. We met up with Colm, patrolling in his blue guard uniform.

"You couldn't get to the dance tonight?"

"No. A real bummer. Someone has to be on duty."

"This is Saoirse. I'm seeing her back home."

We left Colm on the wall, writing something by flashlight in his notebook.

"Do you know him?" I asked.

"I don't know every guard. I'm not that sort of girl."

"You know what I mean."

"I do know a lot of them. I haven't come across *him* before."

We'd arrived at the door of Saoirse's lodgings. "I've prepared a special event for you tomorrow evening," she said. "Dinner with Jim Braben and his family at their house."

I remembered the Earl talking about Jim Braben, his close friend the geologist who'd planned the tunnel and excavated the final secret mile. I asked, "Will you be there?"

"I can't go," said Saoirse. "Work to catch up on. I won't see you at breakfast or midday either. Meeting Jim is a great opportunity. Don't hold back from asking questions. He knows everything about the early days. You'll find he's the number one idealist, the king of the island. All major policy decisions emanate from him, despite the town councillors liking to pretend otherwise."

"Which gate does he live near?"

"He doesn't. He's one of the hill dwellers. You'll get to see inside their living space. It should be a fascinating evening."

"I'll let you know all about it."

Giving me a long kiss, and hugging me tightly, she said, "You do that some time."

Chapter 25

Shadows

 When I got back to the hotel, the manageress handed me an envelope. "This came for you earlier," she said. "We don't know who delivered it. We found it on the front desk."

A typed note inside said "Two A.M. TONIGHT. SUN DOME." No signature.

I tried to think who might have information they wanted to convey. The canal depot manager? The Tasteless Toys inventor? Then I thought of a more likely possibility — Dave Wilson. A clandestine, dead of night meeting would be just his style.

On occasions like Salsa Night, the guards ran an all-night ferry service. Shortly before two o'clock, the ferry pulled in from the other side of the water, Colm at the oars. "*You're* out late," he said.

"Getting some dead-of-night photographs of the town," I replied, relieved I had thought to take my camera with me as a convenient alibi.

I had never been to the dome after midnight. I considered it would be locked, though no reason why it should be, as modern curses: vandalism, graffiti and assault, were unknown in Nostalgia. I opened the main door, cautiously peering inside. The cascade of the great waterfall had been shut down for the night, the place deathly quiet and in darkness. The cloak and dagger situation warranted stealth. I entered the building as noiselessly as I could but made the mistake of letting the door go prematurely. It swung to with a crash, multiplied tenfold by the cavernous echo from the roof. I quickly attained the perimeter path, where under cover of foliage I could observe anyone coming in. I walked quietly and deliberately, keeping my eye on the doorway. Suddenly, some bushes ahead started to wave their branches alarmingly. A woman stepped out from amongst them — Alice, still dressed for the Salsa. "I hope you don't mind," she said. "I really needed to see you."

"Alice, you know I'm already accounted for."

She laughed. "Is my reputation really that bad! Let's go back to my place. I'll make you supper, then we can relax and talk together."

Linking her arm in mine and leading me out through a side door, she said, "I'm only two streets away."

I asked, "Why so late at night and why the mysterious typed note?"

"Why not? I was bored. I wanted fun. In any case, if I'd signed my name, you might not have come, or *she* would have wanted to come along, to keep you out of my clutches. You're never been a performer, have you? You can't appreciate what a let-down it is to have to go home alone after the high of a major session."

We arrived at a terraced house considerably wider than the average Nostalgia home. "I live here all on my own," said Alice.

She showed me into a large room, one half furnished with sofas and carpets like a typical living room, the other half having a raised wooden platform with a grand piano.

"This is where I work and play. It's a dual-purpose building. Private house and public rehearsal room."

I followed her through to the kitchen, where she set about preparing a multitude of small dishes: salads, cheeses, breads, dips and so on. The opportunity to look after a man seemed to be causing her a great deal of pleasure. Telling me to open a bottle of wine, she announced she'd get changed, and rushed upstairs, returning in a long, slinky black dress.

We took the food through to the living room, sat together on the sofa, and talked. During our conversation it transpired we had been students at the same university. After we had reminisced for well over an hour, Alice said, "Let me play for you. What would you like?"

I told her to choose and she sat at the piano, effortlessly reeling off a selection of Bach sonatas. I asked if I could take photographs. The rehearsal space had some freestanding spotlights, which I dragged into position, one to create a strong highlight on her profile, the other to backlight her hair. Alice launched into a wild, shouting blues, while I leaped about, like some pretentious David Bailey caricature, getting the best angle for my shots. I felt ashamed for my previous shallow opinion of this multi-talented, sensitive woman.

Later, as dawn began to break, I told Alice I would have to go, or I would be wrecked for work and for my dinner appointment with the Brabens in the evening.

"Don't leave yet," she pleaded. "The sofa pulls out to a double bed. I'll get you a duvet."

Arranging the bedding, she said, "I enjoy a fulfilling life here, excepting one thing. No eligible men. Most my age came here with partners, and the younger guys don't want you long term. This isn't like a normal town where you can take a city break in the hope of meeting somebody. You're stuck with what you can get. They promised us single ladies they'd improve the balance but of course our priorities aren't the island's priorities."

After the evening of non-stop dancing, then drinking wine and talking all night I felt totally zonked. I have a vague memory of Alice switching off the lights and her treading upstairs before I lost consciousness. In a vivid dream, she smothered my whole body with kisses.

I woke at eight with Alice next to me under the duvet, naked, her womanly body pressed against mine, her arm over my chest. Gently easing out of her embrace, I kissed her on the cheek. She smiled at me, murmured "Thank you" and went back to sleep again.

I spent the day at the hospital, indexing and sorting masses of notes and photographs. On hearing of my dinner invitation, John filled me in on the story behind the hill dwellers. The original founders of Nostalgia, being of a hippy bent, wanted to live literally in the bosom of Mother Earth, so they constructed houses buried in the hill. The surrounding soil insulation made the living space cool in summer, warm in winter, and a sophisticated ventilation system, as I had seen in Tadhg's house, pumped waste air out, exchanging heat with fresh air drawn in, thus keeping energy consumption to a minimum. John told me the houses had many other novel features, though he had not yet been inside one. Like me, he'd also been invited to dine with Jim Braben, several months ago, but his accident and hospitalisation had prevented it.

A bicycle rickshaw taxi took me to the hill dweller district. The windows of each house, let into the turf of the hillside along with a single door, provided the only evidence of habitation. They looked more suited to garden gnomes than homes for people. Each window was made of a special, bulging lens-shaped glass, not a window in the conventional sense, instead a prismatic light conduit that conducted daylight underground to an indoor garden at the centre of each dwelling. All the rooms faced inwards to this central garden. At night, with the house lit by electricity, the flow of light naturally reversed and the lensed windows glowed like so many eyes on the hillside, those same eyes I had observed from the canal boat on the misty first morning of my arrival.

Jim greeted me pleasantly, apologising for running a little late, that he and his wife were still getting ready. I glimpsed Mrs Braben, in her bedroom sitting at her dressing table, brushing her long hair. "In the meantime," Jim said, "the children can entertain you." He opened the door to a room in darkness, apart from a wide, bright opening to a lush sunny garden filled with an incongruous jungle of exotic plants. The door shut behind me and I fell to the floor in terror as a growling tiger came leaping in through the window.

Chapter 26

King of the Hill Dwellers

Mrs Braben opened the door of the room to find out the reason for her children's hilarious laughter. I'd recovered sufficiently to say "Just playing 'pouncing tigers'," and dived for cover again as another tiger leaped through the remarkable 3D television screen on the wall. The children screamed.

"I can see you'll make a great father someday," said Mrs Braben, "but we mustn't get them over-excited. They're going to eat soon."

The 3D "hole-in-the-wall" TV was the first topic of conversation at dinner.

"It's the invention of an islander who used to work for Anything & Co.," said Jim.

"I think I've met him. The Bad Taste Toys man?"

"The same. Their chief electrical specialist. Discovered an ingenious way to project light from conventional light sources to create a thoroughly realistic 3D image that doesn't require wearing special glasses."

I agreed. "It's certainly realistic! Will it be patented?"

"We hope so," replied Jim, "but there are technical obstacles to overcome. One is you need a big box fitted outside the wall of your house to contain the equipment. It's not practical, except here, where the houses are underground. The 3D TV is one of the reasons everyone wants to live on the hill."

"Island Radio interviewed me. I didn't know Nostalgia had a TV station also."

"The 3D process can't do live TV," replied Jim. "They have to buy in the programmes and convert them for their system. So, what we get are reprocessed outside shows — there's nothing specifically 'Island'. The emphasis of the program content is on keeping children entertained and educated, as most people on the hill have young kids."

Despite the relatively young age of his children, Jim was in his mid-fifties, the chief topic of town gossip the ease with which the men amongst the hippy founders had slept around. Their status gave them the sexual kudos of rock-stars. When they did settle down, they found partners many years' younger than themselves, hence the great number of young families living on the hill.

Jim's short stocky build and bald head confounded my expectation of the "King of The Hill Dwellers". The only feature true to type, his voluminous hippy beard. The contrast with his Irish wife could not have been greater, she taller than he, an attractive woman in her early forties, with a superbly endowed figure.

The conversation moved on to their house. I asked did they mind living buried in the earth. They replied the daylight channelled down to the indoor garden made you forget being underground. They loved the cosy environment. No drafts. Jim's only complaint, the single bathroom. "My wife's far too long in the bathroom in the mornings," he said.

"Whatever you do," said Jim, when the children had finished eating and Mrs Braben had taken them off to put them to bed, "don't mention Irish politics to my wife. You'll get an earful."

Jim's warning was to no effect. Mrs Braben raised the subject herself later in the evening. "Irish politicians! A load of useless feckin cronyistic wankers, the lot of them! Just looking after their own. I'm telling you, Jim, the sooner we can open up the island, the better it'll be for Ireland. Make them come here, so they can learn how the country *should* be run."

Mrs Braben asked my opinion of the state of politics in Ireland. It's always a problem for me when Irish people criticise their politicians, which they do all the time. As an Englishman, given the past history between Britain and Ireland, it doesn't seem "quite the done thing" to join in and agree. On the other hand, I don't want to disagree when some politician or other is being justifiably lambasted. I usually do the tactful thing, as I did on this occasion, by coming up with a parallel example of the state of politics in my own country.

The political conversation led to the related subject of unemployment, or it would be more correct to say *full employment*, experienced by the island's inhabitants. "The trouble is," said Mrs Braben, "Irish politicians only think in terms of the next big pharmaceutical company they can attract to Ireland, the next big computer company. If they can't induce a foreign company, usually American, to come here, they sit around helpless. They need to stop thinking big and start thinking small. Get the economy vibrant and bump up employment with Irish-owned small businesses that trade with each other, as we do here in Nostalgia."

161

"That's another way Nostalgia differs from the mainland," said Jim. "People can't rely on social welfare here, so island rules enforce a high minimum wage. The knock-on effect is positive of course, the money supply goes up, people have more to spend at the local businesses, shared prosperity for all."

"Like your wife was saying, Irish politicians could learn from you."

"Spineless bunch of turds," interjected Mrs Braben. "In hock to multinationals. Worried they'll threaten to pull out of Ireland and go elsewhere if the government stop licking their arses. The government's wonderful income support for the low-earner is nothing more than Irish money lost from the country, subsiding the profits of overseas feckin' fat cats. They should be made to pay better wages."

I steered the conversation away from politics as quickly as I could, because I didn't want to waste this chance of hearing the history of the island from its founder.

"My friend and ourselves had an agreement," said Jim. "Nostalgia would get the land most suited to building the town and setting up our industries and farming. The remaining land would be reserved for his agricultural research project."

"Which building went up first?"

"The hospital. The island is unapproachable by boat, and its terrain is unsuited to an aeroplane runway. With the mainland six hours away by tunnel railway, we needed the capability to treat people in case of emergency. You understand money's no obstacle to the Earl. He gave us a generous budget to equip the building. Finding the staff was more problematic. You know about the stringent islander selection process? Also, it was difficult to persuade people to make a new life here in the early days, with the primitive living conditions and the constant noise and disruption of construction work."

"What did you build next?"

"The hotel and those tiny cottages on Little Island. We needed somewhere for the pioneers to live until the houses in the town became available. Many of us lived on the beach in a tented village. Freezing in the winter! That's all gone now. Tough times, but it gradually came together. In the beginning, everyone helped with the construction, then as the town took shape, a whole service industry of small businesses sprang up."

I asked, "Do you think the community is practical in the modern world? Isn't it all a middle-class hippy dream?"

"How many people have you interviewed?" said Jim, "A lot by now, surely? Do you not see the real winners in Nostalgia are what you British refer to as 'the working class', those people who would have been forced into near permanent unemployment by modern technological advances, or, if lucky enough to get work, having to settle for being exploited in a routine job. We're not afraid of machines on the island. We have learnt how to use technology to *create* jobs, not replace jobs. We've proved it's possible to have a thriving economy *and* full, meaningful employment. You can see it reflected in the attitudes of our young people, in contrast with the average young person on the mainland."

"My worry," said Mrs Braben, "is how it will be for our young people in decades to come if we continue to prioritise rampant consumerism in preference to a decent living and working environment. If we continue to suck all hope and meaning out of our young people's lives, I worry there's a danger they'll embrace extremism to fill the gap."

Next the conversation turned to the subject of women working, on which Mrs Braben had her own take. "You know what the problem is with women working? A woman used to have a choice whether to work to help the family. Their total income went up, so they could afford a better house. But increased money supply forces house prices up. More women obliged to work. The money supply goes up again; house prices are driven even higher. It's a vicious circle. Prices go so high you arrive at a situation where a woman no longer has a choice between working or giving time to her family. She has to go to work, or they won't be able to afford a home. There's only one winner in that vicious circle — fucking estate agents!"

"In Nostalgia," said Jim, "we have a scheme to buck that trend. Have you interviewed any of our all-women companies yet?"

I said I hadn't.

"Then you need to correct that serious omission as soon as possible! These companies are run exclusively by women and staffed exclusively by women. They have two sets of managers and two sets of staff. One set go to the office in the mornings; the other go in the afternoons. And they mix which shift they do. So we don't give women an ultimatum — work full-time or don't work at all — they get a compromise where they can have a career, earn money *and* enjoy more time with their children, important in a child's formative years, don't you think?"

I spent several hours talking with this fascinating couple, taking down copious notes. At one point, Jim went off to read his children bedtime stories, leaving me alone with Mrs Braben. Being a woman, she had picked up what her husband had failed to notice — my feelings for Saoirse. Her inquisitive probing was beginning to get uncomfortable, when Jim returned and we resumed the conversation about the island. Several times I nearly came out with questions about the research institute. Why did we never meet the workers? What were they working on 24/7? However, I felt it would be rude for me to appear confrontational.

At the end of the evening, Jim took me to his office to show me a fascinating set of photograph albums, the pictures arranged in chronological order, so you could see how, bit by bit, the march of civilisation took over the wild and bare land. While I perused the albums, which Jim had piled up for me on his desk, his wife called him away. I pulled one out clumsily from the middle of the pile, causing the top album to fall off, disarranging a stack of papers. Saoirse looked out at me from a photograph that had been underneath, a zoom lens close-up of the two of us walking along the town wall, smiling and laughing together. I saw more photographs but heard Jim returning at that moment and had to hastily cover them over.

After such a pleasant evening, I did not want to think ill of my hosts despite this disconcerting discovery. What was the purpose of these pictures? Was Saoirse was being kept under observation by a jealous lover in the form of the Earl, and Jim had been tasked with sending back reports on our developing relationship? Could Mrs Braben's probings have been not just an innocent expression of female intuition but a calculated attempt to secure supplementary information? What concerned me was the furtiveness with which the pictures had been obtained. We could not have failed to see the photographer, unless he or she had taken the picture from with the concealment of a gate tower. We had been put under surveillance. I planned to raise the matter with Saoirse as soon as I met her the next day.

Chapter 27

Despair

Ancient peoples believed in omens. Had I been an ancient, I would have been forewarned as to what happened next. But I am not an ancient, I am a modern, so to me, sudden bad weather is merely sudden bad weather, nothing more.

A notable feature of a home buried deep in the bosom of the earth, which some might consider an advantage, others a considerable disadvantage, is that you don't notice the weather. When I stepped out of Jim Braben's house, it could not have been more contrasted to when I arrived, the sky black night, with a ferocious gale and a driving rain. Several times on the way back to town, the wind blew the rickshaw taxi sideways, on one occasion perilously close to the edge of the canal. I shouted to the driver above the noise of the rain covers flapping in the wind that he should take a safer route. To my relief, he agreed. We struggled for a while down a lane until the gale started to blow us backwards. We had to dismount and tow the vehicle on foot, me pulling on one handlebar, the driver on the other. Twenty minutes later, exhausted, cold, and drenched, we entered the town through Farm Gate.

Within the windbreak of the narrow streets, the rickshaw became usable again but, as we came out onto the quays, I doubted the hotel crossing would be safe. Even with high tide not due for three hours, already the water was at its highest, with a swell on it like an open sea.

167

I met some fishermen observing the storm. They told me the power station wall couldn't prevent the powerful head-on waves from spilling over into the bay. Flooding would be unavoidable unless the wind dropped. I gladly accepted their offer to take me across in their boat. Without the power of its diesel engine, no way could I have made it to the hotel that night.

On Little Island, the sea had submerged the hotel forecourt. I waded through water a foot deep to the heavily sandbagged front door. A notice said to use the kitchen entrance. The rocky slope on which the hotel had been built had forced construction of the kitchen and back door at a higher elevation, thankfully keeping the ground floor from inundation. Back in my room, I stood at my window, observing the worsening storm, certain damage would be done during the night.

I came down to breakfast on Saturday morning to find the place crowded with blue guards who had been active all night, securing property against the gale. Worse hit, the greenhouses, where flying debris had smashed many panes. The wind tunnel thereby created had flattened the crops inside. The town itself had escaped harm, with the exception of the more exposed roof gardens, where locals were already about, cleaning up. The guards had principally occupied themselves repairing damage outside the walls. Two island structures went unscathed: the hill dweller settlement, weatherproof under the earth, and the security fences, built never to fail.

I expected Saoirse to call in for breakfast to question me on my evening at Jim Braben's house but the seat opposite at our regular table for two remained empty. My mind explained it away as her being detained by urgent business in the aftermath of the storm. My heart already told me otherwise.

By low tide, at ten o'clock, the wind had blown itself out and the weather turned fine. Little Island remained cut off from the mainland, owing to the floodwater not yet drained back to sea. Making a circuit of the island's rocky shoreline, I spied one of the fairground's yellow boats beached on the rocks. The storm must have broken it from its mooring and swept it across the bay. I put it in an empty hut, which I assumed belonged to a cottage opposite. I thought of knocking on the door, to tell the owners I'd collect the boat later, but another idea occurred: speak of the boat to nobody; I could use it for a plan forming in my mind.

Returning to the hotel, I left a note for Saoirse, then took the ferry across for a meeting with John. When I returned in the afternoon, my note remained uncollected. Romantic longing eclipses all. I crossed back over and walked directly to Saoirse's lodgings. The lady of the house answered the door. "I'm sorry. Saoirse went back to the mainland on last night's train. Did you not know she was going back? She told us at the beginning of the week she wouldn't need the room after Friday."

I went up onto the town wall, my mind in turmoil. The problem was not Saoirse leaving — I had anticipated the Earl calling her back on business — but the fact she had said nothing. Now I understood why she held me so tightly when we kissed goodnight after the Salsa evening.

169

Was she not returning to Nostalgia? Had I been merely a temporary amusement? Was she the Earl's mistress? She always talked of him with the greatest of respect, though I'd never detected any infatuation. I felt cheated, convinced she had deliberately arranged my evening at the Brabens as cover so she could slip away.

With thoughts like these spinning round in my head, I came to the garden at Rose Gate, where I lay on the grass for hours, desolate, losing all track of time. When I went back up onto the wall, I heard the town clock striking eight.

I met Colm, wearing plain clothes, so I didn't recognise him; I'd only ever seen him in uniform. "How are things?" he asked.

"Not good. Woman trouble."

"That pretty girl? I've seen her on the estate. Isn't she the Earl's secretary?"

I couldn't tolerate company at that moment. I crossed the harbour wall to the opposite side of the bay. A walk along the far promenade helped clear my head. I listed all the positive reasons why I shouldn't give up hope: Saoirse was obviously upset on Thursday night about our parting; hard to believe she was currently having an affair with the Earl, nor that she might be reviving a past affair with John; she hadn't formally broken off our association; there might even now be a telegraphed apology waiting at the hotel; or there might be some other reason for her behaviour, something connected with the island.

Approaching the sea wall that closed off the bay, I saw the high fencing topped with razor wire, descending the slope of the cliff, crossing the road and running out as far as the power station control building. With the road ahead thus blocked, I took a track going up the side of the wooded escarpment. Halfway up, a tree trunk brought down by the storm had flattened one side of a wide enclosure fenced all round with wooden panels. I guessed the guards had been so overloaded repairing damage in the industrial area they'd no chance to check on these remoter structures. Notices said, "Pumping Station — Keep Out" but within I could see no machinery, only an enormous mound of brambles and creepers. At one point the vegetation had been torn through, revealing the fabric of a tarpaulin stretched over an object of substantial size. I pulled at the plant stems with the aim of accessing what lay underneath. How I wished for a machete or other implement to make quick work of the task. My hands were getting badly scratched by brambles and stung by the nettles that had grown up around the crash site. For crash site, it was. There had been not one, but two helicopter crashes, the one on the mainland estate, public knowledge, and this one on the island, hidden from view. Had the helicopter been brought down deliberately? Did the same thing happen on the mainland? The old man on the coach had told me of the cancelled ballooning festival. What thing on the mainland and on the island should not be seen from the air? Surely, it had to be connected with the institute, the one thing both locations had in common.

I applauded these wonderful conclusions but then my mind was thrown into doubt again. If they wanted to hide a crash, wouldn't they cut it up with an oxy-acetylene

171

torch, disposing of the evidence as scrap metal, like any self-respecting criminal? Why risk future discovery by leaving it in-situ, with an elaborate enclosure built round as a monument to your crime?

At the top of the hill, the trees gave onto open grassland leading to the cliff edge. Ominous clouds had gathered, threatening a repeat of the previous night's storm. They blocked the sun, turning the previously fine summer evening to dark grey. Fifty yards ahead, the chalk white lighthouse stood out in stark relief against the blackness of the sky. From my vantage point I could see right into the mechanism of the lantern — the usual array of Fresnel lenses and reflectors. Lighthouses had always impressed me, ever since my parents took me as a small child to visit one on the cliffs of southern England, though this was no regular lighthouse, interrupting as it did the line of the security fence. Perhaps I could get inside the building and cross to the other side. Definitely worth a try.

As I approached, the beam came on, an hour premature even allowing for the change in the weather. I hoped it signalled a test run and they would be too busy tending the mechanism to notice my intrusion. I tried the ground-floor entrance and found it to be unlocked. Inside, a storeroom. Tall cupboards stood against the circular wall; boxes of equipment and coils of rope littered the space. A spiral staircase ascended to the upper floors, from whence came the dull thud of footsteps on floorboards. I swiftly exited the back door onto forbidden land. Frustratingly, a second fence, thirty yards further on, thwarted my hope of getting a view out to sea. Not wishing to compound my failure with being spotted trespassing on their land, I turned, with the intention of getting out as quickly as possible. That's when I saw something astonishing. There was no light on the seaward side!

Whether done by electrical, optical or mechanical means I could only guess. As the beam swung round from the land, its intensity rapidly faded, reappearing only as it pointed back towards land again. With the angle of the sea cliff, the lighthouse effectively had its back to the town. From a distance you wouldn't see the cutting off of the light as the beam circled. Even close up you might mistake it for an optical illusion.

So, they had not built the lighthouse to shine out to sea. I had correctly surmised they would not want to draw attention to their island. Instead, it served to illuminate the land beyond the fences on the far side of town. Now, a new riddle took the place of the old, a riddle with no easy solution. High fencing, razor wire, powerful searchlight shining inwards, guards. Surely, a prison camp. What prison camp was this where the inmates were prosperous and happy, certainly happier than the average citizen in the outside world, free to do as they pleased, free to come and go by train, free to leave for ever if they wished, where the guards kept the peace rather than beat the prisoners?

Chapter 28

Carnival

Fearful of being detected, I hastened back through the ground floor of the lighthouse to gain the cover of the wooded escarpment. At the bottom of the hill, as I came out onto the promenade, the daylight was beginning to fade. Consequently, I didn't see, until about half a mile from the harbour wall, a solitary man sitting there, fishing with rod and line. I felt he was waiting for me, that we had an appointment. Worried my clothes might give me away, I made a futile effort to look clean, brushing off bits of vegetation and rubbing off mud stains.

Up on the harbour wall, Tadhg was the fisherman. "You look in a state," he said. "Colm told me about Saoirse. We're very sorry. Where have you been?"

"All the way to the end."

"Did you go up to the lighthouse?"

"I started, then tripped over a tree root. Went flying into a patch of nettles and mud. The weather looks bad for the carnival."

"It'll clear," said Tadhg. "The forecast is fine for tomorrow."

I thanked him for his sympathy over Saoirse. A thought occurred to me. Round his neck he wore binoculars. Had he been observing me, following my progress to the far end and puzzling over my belated return? What if he had? What interpretation could he possibly put on it? Anyway, I was sure Tadhg was OK, one of a small number of guards, principally the chess players, easy to get on with, the remainder a taciturn and aloof crowd, although they lightened up considerably in the evenings when the local girls came into the hotel bar.

Sunday morning, I lay on the beach in the hot sun. At every passing step, I looked up, expecting to see Saoirse. An impossibility, as the next train from the mainland would not arrive till Monday.

The afternoon carnival provided a welcome distraction. Like the regatta, the whole town took part, the primary event being a costumed procession along the promenade. I called in to John to receive instructions for taking pictures but he told me he'd already assembled an extensive collection of past photographs. He declined my invitation to wheel him to the event. Two nurses had insisted on taking him, John reckoned a good excuse for them to get a free afternoon in the sunshine, so it would be mean to refuse their offer. That suited my plans better anyway, because Sally had phoned me at the hotel, suggesting we meet up near the fairground.

I left the hospital and walked along the promenade. Joining the crowds of spectators. I heard Sally's voice calling out my name and turned to see her walking away from me, arm in arm with two young guys. Typical, I thought! But then she turned to me anxiously. One of the guys pushed her roughly into a rickshaw taxi, while the other took the front. Something wasn't right. I asked a cyclist waiting for the procession if I could borrow his bicycle. Following the rickshaw along the road, I kept my distance, careful not to make too obvious a pursuit. They travelled the full length of the promenade, turned to the right past the old-style Irish cottage on the corner, and continued in the direction of the railway. At one point the woodland road rises steeply, then dips before rising again. When I reached the top of the rise, I saw the rickshaw parked on the left, next to a path going off through the trees.

Leaving the bike by the roadside, I followed. I must have been walking the track for at least ten minutes with no sign of Sally or the men. If forcing her against her will, they could not have been walking at my swift pace. I had expected to overtake them. That I did not, suggested they had gone off in some completely other direction. Almost on the point of turning back, I came to the reservoir, at the point where the pier runs out across the square pool to the sauna. Through the open hut door, I heard a woman's voice crying out in distress. I rushed in, expecting the worse. I found Sally, wrapped in a bath towel, sitting on a bench, smiling. "Hello, Mike," she said. "I'm so pleased you came."

The hut door slammed shut behind me. A key turned in the lock from the outside.

"I think I should take up acting," said Sally, reaching down and stroking her legs. "I was sure you'd see through me. I must be better at it than I thought."

She stood and removed her towel. "You'll need all your clothes off as well," she said, as she started to unbutton my shirt. "It's going to get very hot and wet in here." Leaning forward, her breasts pressed against my torso, she whispered softly in my ear, "Stop being so British. You don't have to wait for permission to touch."

With a realisation as to why I had been brought here on the one afternoon we could guarantee not to be disturbed, I asked, "Sally, who were those guys?"

"Friends of mine. They played the part of 'suspicious character number one' and 'suspicious character number two' well, don't you think? I knew you had a taste for the melodramatic — that time you went off stalking some random guy from the Sun Dome. Turn round, so I can pull your shirt off."

I asked, "How did you get here so quick? I worried I'd lost you."

"We ran, of course. That's sweet of you. Now I can thank you for your concern." She tugged at my shorts. "There's something in the way." She reached inside my now distended underpants, her eyes even bigger than usual. "Wow! I knew you wouldn't disappoint."

Sally lay on her stomach on one of the benches. "Relax. Nobody will disturb us. The carnival goes on for hours."

Torn between the offer of immediate sex, my loyalty to Saoirse, and, dare I say it, a nagging conscience re Sally's poor husband, I decided to have some fun *and* put a stop to Sally's advances once and for all. I told her to close her eyes while I kissed every inch of her gorgeous body. The far wall of the hut had a wide bench, a suitable bed for lovemaking. I lifted Sally in my arms, carried her over, kicked up the nearby floor hatch and dropped her through to the water below.

"YOU FUCKING BASTARD!" she shouted back at me.

I jumped in after her.

"That was dangerous," she said. "You didn't know I could swim."

"Dave Wilson told me. He said he'd seen you and Saoirse swimming naked."

Sally swam around me like a shark circling its prey. "Not at the same time, though. Pity. She's hot. Did she tell you we enjoyed a long kiss at the dance?" Sally laughed. "The look on your face! My girlfriend's a secret lesbian! I bet there's something Dave Wilson *didn't* tell you about my swimming."

I asked, "What's that?"

Silence. She'd vanished behind me. Trying my best to stay afloat, treading water, I looked all round. Seconds passed. Still no Sally. Had she passed out under water?

Then a splash as she resurfaced, "I hold a record for underwater gymnastics. I'll show you what I can do."

She took a deep breath and went down again. I felt her wrap her arms round me and start doing something with her lips and her tongue. I didn't know a woman could use her mouth like that when fully submerged. Disengaging with difficulty from the suction of her octopus-like embrace, I swam away towards the edge of the pond.

She resurfaced and called after me, "Come back! Where are you going?"

"To unlock the hut and retrieve my clothes."

Monday morning, I regretted so much as having touched the woman. She arrived at the hotel at breakfast time, sitting opposite me in the place previously reserved for Saoirse. I noticed several guards watching, no doubt wondering what the hell was going on. Tuesday morning,

I found her waiting on the quays. We went to a cafe and talked. I tried to make her understand the risk to us both, the threat to her marriage, the threat to me of losing my job.

Matters came to a head on Wednesday when I returned to the hotel after work and found Sally taking her clothes off in my room. We agreed an arrangement. We'd meet for sex the following day. After that, we'd remain good friends with no more physical contact.

Thursday midday we kept our assignation, at the ridge above the reservoir, where nobody could see or disturb us. When it was over, we lay back, enjoying the afterglow, with the heat of the sun on our naked bodies. "Admit it!" said Sally. "You've wanted to give me that since the first time you saw me."

I said, "Sally, I want to ask..."

"No need, *uh-kush-le*. You can take me any way you want."

"Be serious for the moment."

Sally rolled over on top of me. "I'm *being* serious. What then?"

"Well. Don't you think everything's a bit too perfect in Nostalgia? In all the time I've been here, I've not met one unpleasant or annoying person. I wonder if it's real, that people aren't putting on an act."

"Definitely not an act!" said Sally, "I know what that's like from when a boyfriend took me along to his religious group. Everyone so feckin precious. Ugh! I couldn't wait to get out of there."

"What happened to the boyfriend?"

"I dumped him. Nostalgia's genuine. Why wouldn't the people be pleasant when they're all having such a great life? Even work is more fun here. You're forgetting the selection process. They filter out anyone who wouldn't fit in."

Sally lay on her stomach, peering over the top of the ridge. I lay back on the grass behind her.

"Are you enjoying the view?" she asked.

Later that afternoon we went swimming at the far end of the reservoir. Sally thought it best we not be seen returning to town together and told me to leave ahead of her. However, when I got down to the clubhouse end of the water, some rowing team guys accosted me and kept me talking. I saw Sally approaching. As she passed, she whispered in my ear, "A token of your conquest", and pressed something metallic into my hand. I did my best to look bemused, shrugging my shoulders, as if to say to the guys, "She's not with me." When I got back to the hotel, I took down *Applied Mathematics* from my bookshelf and placed inside it Sally's token — her golden ankle chain.

Friday, I headed for the station to take the evening train back to the mainland. When I'd signed the contract to work for the Earl, I'd asked for time off to return to Dublin, for a job interview for a bank in Singapore. I now hoped, naively, my absence would give the Sally situation a cooling-off period. And I had another purpose in mind — researching newspaper cuttings and library archives to try to find any indication of the real story of Nostalgia.

Chapter 29

Dublin

A steward greeted me on boarding the train. "A reminder, sir: we're on mainland time. Set your watch back thirty-eight minutes, so you don't turn up at the wrong time for dinner."

In the dining car, I sat opposite the manager of one of Nostalgia's clothing factories, a friendly and enthusiastic man from whom I had gleaned useful interview material. Maybe because of the effect of the wine before dinner, or maybe because he felt he now knew me better, he said he wanted to confide something he had not wanted to mention at his interview. It concerned his previous trip to the mainland. In a street market in Dublin city centre, he came across a stallholder selling a Nostalgia research institute white lab coat, as made by his own factory. He asked the trader where the coat had come from. Apparently, it had been purchased in a batch of a dozen from a dealer who often visited the stalls with a range of assorted second-hand goods. Three months after this incident, the manager received another order from the institute, the twelve sizes as before.

"So, those new lab coats replaced the old?" I asked.

"Yes, but what did the institute do in the three months between disposing of the old and buying the new."

"Well, presumably they didn't just have one set, they must have had at least two, so one could be washed while the other was used?"

"All the same, I could understand them disposing of coats *after* they'd received the new batch," replied the manager. "Why *before*?"

I suggested, considering the vast sums the institute must be spending on research, you'd hardly think they'd go to the trouble of selling a few tatty second-hand lab-coats.

"You're wrong about one thing," he said. "The coats were in perfect condition, neither soiled nor damaged in any way. But I agree with you. Even 'as-new' a market wholesaler could only be expected to pay pennies for them."

We had ordered dessert, being brought along by a waiter, when the train braked heavily, propelling him forward precipitously. It looked for a brief moment like he'd drop the lot. "Don't worry," he said. "We've not lost a plate yet. You need the balance of a tightrope walker to work on this train. Why do they always choose to brake hard when we're serving?"

Why indeed? And why did everything connected with the estate and the island come in pairs? I remembered on the outward journey the sudden braking of the train and the applause of the passengers for the skill of the waiter. Two braking incidents, two helicopter crashes, two hilltop agricultural institute buildings, two security fence installations, two types of guard, blue and green. Even the waxing and waning of the lighthouse beam had a twin in the waxing and waning of the tunnel lights as the train passed them by. Then a fantastical idea occurred to me: supposing there were two Nostalgias?

Leaving the train in the morning, I joined a waiting coach. Though certain Saoirse would not be there to greet me, I held out a faint hope, though no sign of her, nor of the Bugatti when we drove past the Earl's stately home. In town, the coach slowed to engage a narrow street. The old man who'd first told me about the Earl could at this moment be peering through his window, wondering where on earth all these new people had come from. Would he see my face, and recognise me?

The experience of being in heavy traffic was an unfamiliar one: the grinding of the engine, the constant braking and accelerating, the lurching at speed around corners. By the time we reached Cork city, I'd decided to opt for the railway to take me on to Dublin.

My interview with the Singapore bank went better than expected. They made an offer of a permanent job, with a generous relocation package, an offer they said they would leave open for a month. Luckily, they didn't require me to give them an answer on the spot. I was in no fit state for that; my thoughts lay entirely elsewhere.

Following the interview, I visited newspaper archives and libraries. Their records confirmed everything I had been told on the subject of the Earl, his family, the salt mine and the mine ventilation company. No anomalies, no hint of distorted or falsified information. I did, however, come across one interesting fact. Many newspapers had reported the tragic helicopter crash on the Earl's land but a search of the microfilm index revealed a second incident. A helicopter had vanished while flying off the Cork coast in fine weather, no wreckage found, presumed "lost at sea".

I hoped to find out also in the reference library the meaning of the strange symbol scratched on the research institute centrifuge. The librarian handed me an illustrated book of European symbols containing the full range from chivalric through to black magic. Given the resemblance to a mask, I asked if they kept books of tribal motifs. There I found it — a rounded triangular face, with two eyes and a mouth, the symbol of "Eleguá, The Trickster God" — *the god of opportunity, a benevolent god, but a god who can, if he's in the mood for it, deliberately create confusion by making something very simple into something complex.*

In a bar, I sat with a pint of "the black stuff", mulling over the helicopter mystery. Had the first crash been a rehearsal for the second? Realising a potential threat to their secret, the islanders had developed defensive technology? This they had tried out successfully on the Earl's estate and had called into action again when the unfortunate pilot of the second craft chose to fly over their island. Admittedly, all far-fetched and improbable but I could come up with no better explanation.

Sitting in that Dublin bar, I became aware of a growing irritation. At school, we once went on a biology field trip to a study centre in Suffolk, England. The centre had banned all music, which back then meant not being allowed to take transistor radios. We spent a week away from civilisation, netting invertebrates from fast flowing streams, collecting plant samples, digging muddy estuaries for buried worms. On the way home at the end of the trip we stopped at a motorway cafe for refreshments. A record playing on an old-fashioned jukebox felt like hearing music for the first time in our lives, an experience of heaven. This was the opposite. The maudlin throbbing of canned electric rock music ground into my consciousness like a track from *Hell's Greatest Hits*.

The city of Dublin too had lost its appeal. Where before I had seen charm, now I saw only litter-strewn dirty streets. A hundred and one other things I could list; unnecessary annoyances of modern life we could easily do without. I had to admit, Nostalgia Island had got inside me. I understood why, once having lived there, nobody wanted to return to their former life. Was Nostalgia, then, a prison for volunteer prisoners? If so, what purpose were these prisoners intended to serve?

Chapter 30

The Trickster House

On returning to Nostalgia, I'd determined to convey my doubts to John. Not easy, working in that hospital room. Whenever I visited, a nurse would be writing up reports at the far end of the room. I couldn't risk the wrong people overhearing but how to know who the wrong people were, if indeed there were any "wrong people".

Musing on this problem, I turned into an unfamiliar street. I knew for certain I had not been down it before because of the unusual front doors, each painted with a distinctive art work. On the first, a brightly coloured abstract; on the second, a view through a classical archway to a romantic vale beyond; on the third, a sailing ship at anchor at sunset; and on the next, freshly painted, an African tribal mask, the sign of the Trickster God. Nothing for it but take a chance and knock.

Sally Macnamara opened the door. She said nothing, ushering me rapidly into a front room. Taking my hands, pushing them down inside her skirt to take hold of her buttocks, she engaged me in a deep kiss.

"Sally! Remember our agreement! This is against the rules."

A man 's voice called out from inside the house, "Who was that?"

"Someone we're expecting," Sally called back.

"Don't worry," she said softly. "My husband has no idea you've been taking liberties with his wife."

She led me to the back room of the house to a family meeting: her husband, Tom, along with her twin sister, Jenny, and Jenny's husband, Patrick.

"It's OK. You're amongst friends," said Sally. "Fellow seekers after the truth."

"We've been expecting you," said Tom, "but we're still waiting for someone to call who knows what the symbol we painted on our door means."

"So *you're* the people the depot manager's been talking to."

"What we can't understand," said Tom, "is why everybody in Nostalgia so accepting of the fencing? The research institute's one thing, but you can't even get to the sea."

"*Couldn't* get to the sea," said his brother.

"Yes, my brother has been to the mouth of the bay."

"Officially?" I asked.

"Strictly unofficial," said Patrick. "I'm an electrician. They contracted me to do maintenance at the power station. They assigned a blue guard as a minder, sticking to me like feckin glue, he was, then he got called away. The equipment room they put me in had a ventilation grille to the far side of the building. I grabbed a screwdriver from my tool bag and had it off the wall in no time. Managed to squeeze through and get down to the water."

"Anything interesting?"

"Not much," he replied. "The rocky stack you see from up on The Knoll is about a quarter of a mile out. It totally blocks the view. There's fierce waves crashing round either side of it."

I asked what the beach was like.

"Large boulders covered with slippy black seaweed," Patrick replied. "Treacherous stuff. You can understand them wanting to keep the townies away."

"Anything along the coast?"

"You can't see. The cliffs curve outwards on both sides."

"What did you do next?"

Jenny said, "There's nothing my husband *could* do next. He was lucky to have been away so long without being missed."

"I was dead lucky," said Patrick. "If I'd delayed any longer on the beach, I'd have been caught. I'd only just got the grille screwed to the wall again when the guard came back."

I confessed to them my doubts about the island and told them of my researches in Dublin, confirming the Trickster symbol to be of African origin. "I have to get to work," I said. "I'm late for my first appointment. We must continue this conversation some other time."

Sally said she'd see me out. As she opened the front door, she said, "Mike. If you're ever in need of help, you will think of me, won't you?"

Her change of mood worried me. "Sally. What's wrong? This isn't like you."

"I never told you," said Sally, "I'm a bit psychic. I've a premonition there's trouble coming."

Chapter 31

A Brick Wall

In the evening, I walked the length of the promenade as far as the Irish cottage and the path leading to where Saoirse had taken me for the abortive first swimming lesson down in the bay. I took the path to the cliff-top fence. The people who'd constructed it clearly had no intention any islander should attain a view of the ocean. Why they wished to do so was a complete mystery. Had Saoirse been right in saying the fence served to prevent any possibility of someone falling off the cliff? Aside from wanting to avoid the human tragedy, having to invite the Irish Garda onto the island to investigate a death would blow the secret the islanders had painstakingly kept for two decades.

Where the fence passed back into the wood, a cleared strip had been created on both sides. It reminded me of a prisoner-of-war film in which an escape tunnel breaks through to open ground and the escapees have to make a dash for cover. Thinking of this caused me to revise my perception of the fences as a dual dividing barrier, firstly between town and research institute, secondly between town and coast. They could be viewed another way — as a complete circle, enclosing the town's inhabitants in a ring of razor wire, the only route out being the railway tunnel. In fact, when the train had departed from Island station, a locked metal barrier closed off the tunnel entrance. So, excluding train arrival and departure, Nostalgia was effectively escape-proof.

I snooped around at random under the cover of the trees, considering whether second childhood was setting in. Not so long ago I had been down in the bay, cavorting naked and erect in the sea with Saoirse. More recently, nearby in the sauna, and up on the ridge, enjoying all the delights Sally had to offer. Now I was reduced to spying in the woods. My life story had become like Enid Blyton — with added genitalia. If I had come across a hidden cave, secret passage, smuggler's hoard or buried treasure, I think I would have booked an appointment with the hospital psychiatrist. My search seemed a ridiculous one.

Regaining the road, I came downhill to the cobbled square by the station. In front of me, the signal box by the level crossing. Eight o'clock. The train ready to leave. I crossed the line and stood at the far side, watching it go past. I saw Tadhg at one of the carriage windows. A pity, as I'd been planning to confide in him the following day.

After the train had disappeared into the tunnel, I wandered down the road, which I assumed must lead back to town, though I didn't recall seeing any such route marked on the map. A hundred yards on, the road came to an end at a brick wall. Why would you want a road crossing the railway to a dead-end? The road apparently served no purpose other than make it necessary to have the level crossing.

Then in a flash, I saw the whole thing. It must have been my musings about second childhood that did it. When I was a small child, my father had converted our spare bedroom to hold a model train set. He'd built staging across the room at a metre height. You'd crawl under the staging and emerge through a rectangular hole cut in the middle. From there, you had control. The trains would run around and around, passing a station, goods yards, a model town, and a road running across a signal box level crossing and terminating in the bedroom wall. No respectable train set can omit the level crossing. There's the excitement of opening the gates and pushing toy cars across before you close them again to let the trains pass. Similarly, Nostalgia's level crossing was a must-have part of a rich man's train set on a life-sized scale. Now other things began to fall into place: the speedboat in the bay — pure James Bond; the guards in their monochrome camp sixties' uniforms — employees of the evil villain; the town wall with its gates and nightly patrols — a castle and toy soldier set. Someone had had enormous fun planning the whole thing, a fantasy town layout. At any moment a giant hand might descend from the clouds to pick up a few trees and bushes and rearrange them for better effect.

Against this theatricality you had to set the genius of what the place had achieved in terms of an economically successful and ethically sound working and living environment, an environment so perfect no inhabitant wanted to live anywhere else. So, why the fences, why the barbed wire, why the patrols, why the searchlight, why the secrecy over the institute? Did the combination of genius and childishness hide a third quality — a madness with a perverted, sinister intent?

Next morning, I got out early. I needed to talk to John. On the way to the hospital, I called in at the office shop to buy more notebooks. While waiting to pay, I saw out of the corner of my eye a green guard. I took a second look, because I had never seen a green guard on the island before. It was Tadhg. The shopkeeper distracted me by asking whether I needed the usual receipt for my expense claims. When I looked back, Tadhg had vanished. I could only think of one explanation for the impossibility he should be back on the island. If he'd gone to the mainland on the train last night, he couldn't return until tomorrow. Therefore, he hadn't left. He'd spotted me at the level crossing, suspected my purpose in being there and had got off the train at the point where the driver stops to put up the shutters for the night's journey. This morning he must have been tailing me, clumsily disguising himself in a green uniform, the very thing that attracted my attention. So, Tadhg could not be trusted; he was a conspirator and had obviously been assigned from day one to watch me. This revelation did nothing for my confidence. As I approached the rickshaw taxi rank, every passing face was the face of my enemy.

A hand touched my shoulder and I turned in alarm.

"Here. You dropped one of your notebooks," said a man.

"Thanks," I said, taking it from him.

Paranoia was beginning to set in.

Chapter 32

The Note

When I arrived at the hospital, I found John working away at his computer. As on all my visits, a nurse sat at a table at the far end of the room, writing medical reports. Now, I suspected spies everywhere.

"You can talk to me," said John. "I'm typing, but I'm also listening." He had the journalist's skill of handling several streams of information simultaneously.

I picked up a document, pretending to be reading it. "I saw a funny thing this morning. A blue guard in green uniform."

I waited for a reaction. John said, "The guards work a rota system. They swap around all the time between green guard, blue guard, night and day shifts."

The nurse chimed in, "The blue guard shifts are a perk — they get the luxury of staying at the hotel — it's an easy number. I wish I had their job."

I tried probing deeper. "The funny thing is I saw the guard on the train going back to the mainland last night. This morning he was already back in Nostalgia, in green uniform."

John replied, "You must have seen wrong. A round trip takes two nights."

Had he not registered my remark or was he covering it?

"Did you cycle here?" he asked.

"No. I've been thinking of getting a push bike."

"You look over-heated. You should take your jacket off. Put it on the chair."

I hung my jacket over the back of the visitor chair at the side of John's bed. Without saying anything, the nurse abruptly left the room, returning a few seconds later with a colleague. "We want to wheel the bed out. We need to clean the floor. Would your friend mind giving us a hand?"

I helped them wheel John's bed to a nearby ward. They left us there while they went back to do their cleaning.

"On no account must they be left alone with your jacket," whispered John.

Prompted by the urgency in his voice I returned to the room just in time to catch a nurse reading a piece of paper. She started when she saw me. "Is this receipt yours? I found it on the floor."

I took it from her. "Thanks. I need it for my expenses claim. I bought some notebooks this morning. It all mounts up, doesn't it?" I put on the jacket, stuffing the receipt back in the pocket, and left them to their floor cleaning. A few minutes later they asked for help returning John's bed. What had just taken place? I had no idea.

At the end of our working session, John said, "I need you to take some photographs. I already took some but the results were disappointing. I'm trusting you can do better. You know the hill with the hill dweller houses? Go up there, past Jim Braben's house, go right up to the top. You get to the fence round the institute land. Now, this is important, because you need to get a good angle on the view. Stand in the centre of the road and walk up to the fence. Don't stray right or left. Get a foothold on the fence and climb up it about three feet. Don't go too high. Three feet will be adequate. Hang on to the fence while you point the camera at the lighthouse. That's the angle I need. Have you got all that? Remember, you need to climb up three feet, no more, and you need to be dead centre on to the road."

"I'll do it now," I said.

"The light's wrong. The best light is evening. Wait for sunset and take the picture just as the sun is disappearing. You'll get a fantastic red tinge. Believe me, it's the best time by far for you to be there."

Armed with these instructions and still baffled by the rigmarole with the jacket, I returned to the hotel for lunch. From reception, I purchased the local almanac, a book full of useful information, including sunrise and sunset times and times of tides. Back in my room, I remembered the shop receipt and put my hand in my jacket pocket to take it out. My fingers felt not one but two pieces of paper. I took out the shop receipt, and a handwritten scrap, which said, "IT WASN'T AN ACCIDENT."

So now I knew John had his own suspicions of the island. Not only that, he believed *they* knew he had suspicions and had attempted to incapacitate him. And he also knew I had formed suspicions, otherwise his terse note would not have made any sense. The nurse at the hospital guessed the business with the jacket. She might even have seen John slip the paper into the pocket. Luckily the receipt prevented her from finding the real object of her search. So, the nurses in the office kept watch on behalf of person or persons unknown. John probably also suspected hidden microphones, which is why he had chosen to communicate through a note.

Something now became chillingly clear. I had not understood why they would invite a friend of John's to the island, going to all the trouble of assigning a guard to keep the friend under observation, when it would be simpler not to invite the friend in the first place. Now I understood all this had nothing to do with me; it had everything to do with John. I still had no idea what was going on behind the facade of the idealised society of Nostalgia. I guessed John knew a lot more than I did. With his journalistic background he'd sensed foul play from the start and had been using the cover of his work to advance an enquiry of his own. They had caught him out and wanted to find out what he knew. Unwilling to stoop to torture, they'd tried to trick him into giving information to a trusted friend, one younger and less worldly-wise than himself, one who might confide in an assumed ally, just as I had been a whisker away from confiding in Tadhg. What concerned me now was the consequence of John or I revealing the information they sought. Would we be deemed disposable? Might Nostalgia Island become our grave?

Chapter 33

The Institute

Taking a rickshaw taxi from the quays, I asked the driver to deposit me at the bottom of hill dweller road. I trudged up the hill, enjoying the late evening sunshine. Many children ran about, playing games in the street. In Nostalgia, the minimal road traffic created permanent safe havens for play, the children here healthier than kids I'd seen stuck in city homes, glued to computer games, traffic rumbling away out front, tiny miserable gardens at the back, with all the aesthetic subtlety of decking and breeze block walls in combination.

Jim Braben sat sunbathing outside his house. "John's asked me to make your neighbourhood famous," I said, showing him the camera.

Jim invited me to take pictures inside his home. I declined, telling him of my instructions not to miss the light at sunset. Jim said it was just as well, as his wife was out, and she'd murder him if she came back and found he'd let a camera into the house without getting it presentable first.

At the top of the hill, the road terminated at a ditch, with the security fence beyond. I knew I'd have only minutes of the right light for my picture and I'd need plenty of preparation to be sure of framing the shot correctly. John had told me to line up with the centre of the road, walk up to the fence, then climb about three feet. More easily said than done, because he'd apparently forgotten the deep downward slope of the ditch. Once down that slope you couldn't judge whether lined up correctly or not. I tried to climb the fence but as soon as I put my weight on the lower wires, it pushed inwards away from me. I tried further along. No problem there, though three foot of height was hardly sufficient to see over the top of the ditch, let alone get a good view of the lighthouse.

John wasn't prone to giving flawed information, and I therefore understood he'd sent me up here for a completely different purpose, a purpose that needed the "right light", i.e. the time between before darkness when there is less light for others to spot you from a distance. He intended me to traverse the fence. Behind it, a network of dry-stone walls led directly to what surely must be the target, the agricultural institute.

I looked more closely where I'd first tried to climb. The wires had been sawn through at the base, which is why they had not supported my weight. A fence of this construction could not be easily compromised. I speculated John had spent many nights under cover of the ditch, patiently working away with tools he must have stolen from one of the town factories. Eventually, the wires succumbed and he got through. Unluckily, he'd been spotted and mown down deliberately by a guard's bike. Whether he'd gleaned valuable information, was something that I, and no doubt they, very much wished to know.

I waited in the ditch until the sun had set and dusk began to draw in, then, squeezing underneath the broken wires, I dived for the cover of the nearest dry-stone wall. I ducked along behind, going uphill till I came to another wall, adjoining at right angles. Vaulting over that obstacle, I continued on in the neighbouring field. After a long upward climb and several vaults, I had come within fifty yards of the institute. The building did not yet have lights on, a pity, as I could not see inside. I had the idea to use the zoom lens on my camera as a telescope. Through the viewfinder the building looked empty but in poor light appearances can be deceptive. I decided to take a photograph, to look at later to try to gauge detail. I clicked the shutter and promptly let off a blinding flash — I had forgotten what the salesman in the camera shop had warned me, to turn off the automatic exposure if I didn't want flash in low light — the camera had unhelpfully decided the light needed a boost. With my heart thumping, I crouched down behind the wall, hoping nobody had been looking out of a window at that moment. I waited five minutes. The building felt unnaturally quiet. A holiday night?

Seeing a side door had been left open, I risked approaching to take a look inside. This part of the building appeared unused. Emboldened, I entered an empty room with a concrete floor and walls of rough block construction, not even plastered. The back wall possessed a single, crude wooden door. With a total lack of caution, I took hold of the handle, intending to open it. Behind me, a light switch clicked and rows of bright fluorescent ceiling lights flickered on. I spun round in terror of discovery. There was nobody, the lights on automatic timer. I found the dial near the window. Why a timer and why light so brightly an empty room?

I reprised my former plan of reconnoitring the building. Turning off the lights, I gently opened the door to give sufficient crack to peer through. I saw not a corridor, office or laboratory, as I had expected, but open countryside. Stepping through, I saw the deep sidewalls enclosed an empty space running the entire length of the building, open to the air at the back, with only the roof to block the rain. No floor, merely rough ground, strewn with builders' rubble grown through with sickly weeds. The wall I had stepped through had crude wooden doors fitted at intervals. Each gave onto an empty shell of a front facing room and each room had a light timer, some rooms with lights on, some not yet. One clicked on as I opened the door, making me jump a mile, even though I knew no person had turned the switch. I was beginning to understand this building. A planned illusion. From a distance, the side walls made it look substantial, even though they enclosed nothing more than space open to the air at the back. The light timers had been set to give the appearance of all-night activity, and therefore, by implication, all-day activity. No doubt a guard came weekly to adjust the times by fifteen minutes or so to keep pace with the changing seasons. I was as sure, as if I had seen it, that the institute building on the mainland was a similarly operated fake. There was no "institute", there was no "research", there never had been any research. Even the "scientists in white coats" weren't genuine, most likely guards dressed up, playing a cliché role to keep up the pretence.

To double-check, I examined the timer settings in each room. As I suspected not identical, but staggered: for realism, you don't want lights in the rooms all coming on together; you want them varied. I tried rotating a dial through twenty-four hours to confirm how it worked. What a fool move! I couldn't have drawn attention better if I had gone up to the roof and let off fireworks. Certain the erratic behaviour of the light would be spotted by the guards, I retreated as quickly as I could, making my way back downhill under cover of the drystone wall, squeezing under the fence, scrambling up the ditch and emerging onto the hill dweller road, hoping and praying not to encounter Jim Braben.

Chapter 34

Conspiracy

I spent a restless night going over and over in my mind the implications of the fake institute. Obviously a blind, to create a buffer zone for something on the other side of the island, something warranting razor wire, watchtowers, searchlights and patrolling guards to protect it from discovery. Less obvious, the need for a similar institute on the Earl's mainland estate. If a cover for criminal enterprise, surely that could be more safely carried out on the island; any parallel activity on the mainland was at greater risk of exposure. Could the mainland institute be genuine, or at least, if a fake, disguising no sinister activity, being merely a way of preparing new island residents for the fences and guards? Having seen the institute on the mainland, I had not questioned the presence of its twin on the island. I imagined how I would have felt, arriving here to find the terrain divided by razor wire, if I hadn't already got used to the idea of fenced-off land. I'm sure it would have given me cause for concern.

This "thing" to which the islanders were being denied access, was it for their own safety or was it some experiment in which they were unwittingly involved as guinea pigs? Or was the island merely an elaborate cover for illegal drug smuggling or some other criminal enterprise? Hard to square the latter with the genuine idealism of Jim Braben and the other key figures but I had to assume all the leading people were in on the plan, whatever it was — given their personal involvement over twenty years, that they'd have no clue as to the goings on was hardly credible.

So, who to refer to for help? Tadhg had been the only person I felt I could trust. I couldn't talk to John, because that would be playing into their hands by risking them listening in and finding out what we knew. Saoirse, I suspected to be an innocent party, an intelligent girl who had sensed something wrong and had broken off a relationship with both John and I out of fear for our safety. At least that's what I *wanted* to believe about Saoirse. Either way, I had no intention of putting her at risk.

Then I thought of Molly.

Molly had been in on the creation of Nostalgia. Harmless Molly, an ex-hippie enjoying her retirement in the town. I could talk to Molly. No need to alarm her by giving away my suspicions. By getting her to reminisce about the old days, she might let slip some clue that would throw light on the mystery. All the initial inhabitants would have been involved in surveying the land. It would be surprising indeed if she didn't know the terrain. For a start, how big was the island? Strangely, a subject I never heard discussed. The words of the old man on the coach came back to me: "There are things you can ask and things you can't ask."

I needed to find out where Molly lived. I'd passed by her in the town many times but we'd talked only briefly. I knew nothing more about her than I had learnt from our conversation on the train.

Next morning, the first grey morning since I'd arrived in Nostalgia, I called in to some shops I thought Molly might patronise. I tried to describe her. "American lady, retired, short and dumpy, a bit hippy."

"Go to the telegraph office on the quays," one shop assistant said. "The woman there knows everybody."

As predicted, the lady identified her straight away. Luckily, Molly was at home and answered the phone when I called from the telegraph. I explained an essential part of my research was to gather historical data from pioneers and I wanted to talk to her about the geography of the island. She asked if I could delay for an hour — she had something to do first.

Leaving the building, I noticed a man on the quays. As I walked towards North Gate, he walked along parallel. To test whether he was following me, I visited a shop. When I came out, I saw the man waiting. Harmless as I hoped my visit to Molly might appear, I preferred he should not observe it. I decided to take the long way round and about-turned towards South Gate. I hoped to shake him off at some point. Further down the quays I met Fierce Hot. While we talked, my tail stood at a respectable distance pretending to be admiring the view. Up on the wall at South Gate, I met one of the blue guards from the hotel. We sat conversing about chess. I noticed the tail walking away across The Commons, no doubt concluding he couldn't continue to follow me — it would have been too obvious.

I carried on round as far as Brew Gate, the nearest to Molly's cottage. Looking through to the other side of the tower, I saw three people deep in conversation — Tadhg, back in his blue guard uniform, Colm and Molly.

At that moment, a fourth person joined them — Saoirse.

There could be no doubt about it: an emergency conference of four. Not expecting me to come by the wall, they had arranged a hasty rendezvous there. So this was Molly's "something I have to do first". I felt stupid for not realising, just as Tadhg was employed to make friends with me early in my stay, so Molly had been employed as my initial minder on the train. Her being behind me in the customs hall queue, then joining me for that first dinner, was no coincidence. And I remembered, when I first pointed out Tadhg to her, how she had denied knowing him. Obviously, a lie. And that business when the customs official took her into his office. Probably briefing her on her task. Worse, I had been duped by Saoirse. She had denied knowing Colm, yet their body language as they talked made it clear that professionally they were well acquainted. Hardly credible the intimate and happy friendship we had enjoyed was just an act on her part but this painful truth was at least an explanation of why she had left me when she sensed the relationship going too far.

What to do next? I had the advantage. I walked out of the tower door as though I had come across them unexpectedly. I wanted to register their reaction. Any awkwardness would give away their guilt. And give away their guilt it did — in spades — they could barely disguise their shock at seeing me. I played the innocent. "Molly, I didn't know Saoirse was back on the island. Could you give us a few minutes? I'll be down to your cottage shortly."

Molly went off, considerably flustered. No doubt she'd arranged the conference for moral support. Now she must be dreading what I would say to her.

"I'd better be going," said Tadhg. "I'm due to take the delivery cart up to the institute." I thought his face registered relief that I hadn't challenged him on his mysterious reappearance in green uniform the previous morning.

"I'll go with you," said Colm.

They walked off in the direction of Centre Gate.

"Did you come back this morning?" I asked Saoirse.

"No. Monday. You were in Dublin, weren't you?"

"Is that why you chose Monday, because you knew I'd be away?"

"I came because I had work to do. I'm returning on tonight's train."

"So, if we hadn't met by chance, you would have succeeded in your plan to avoid me."

The accusation visibly upset her. "That's not fair!" she protested.

Determined to press my case, I said "Is it fair you should play with my affections, build up my hopes, then run away without explanation or apology? Even if, to you, I was no more than a passing acquaintance, is that the way you always say goodbye?"

"It's not like that at all," she replied. She turned and descended the tower steps. "Will you wait for me?"

"Where are you going?" I called after her.

"Only to Molly's cottage. To cancel the interview. The poor old dear's a complete bag of nerves. You can't make her go through with it. I'm going to tell her you no longer need to talk. I'll come straight back."

"Not another disappearing act?"

"I promise."

While I waited on the wall, the sun came out from behind clouds, transforming what had been a dull grey morning into another of Nostalgia's hot summery days.

Saoirse returned. "Let's go to the rose garden," she said.

We walked along in the direction of Rose Gate but in contrast to our walks of old, we kept a distance between us.

"Wait!" said Saoirse. "There's something we have to do. I can't stand the agony any longer. Kiss me. And don't you dare say you don't want to!"

We kissed for a long time.

Saoirse said, "Does that answer your questions?"

I felt elated. I had Saoirse back, as more than friend and colleague; she was *my* Saoirse. At Rose Gate we went down to the rose garden and lay under our favourite tree. I told her how I had lain there in a state of abject misery the day she abandoned me. Saoirse cried so much, I felt guilty for having upset her. But some things could no longer go unspoken.

"Saoirse, that night at Jim Braben's, I saw something worrying. A spy photograph taken of you and I, walking together."

"I know," she replied.

"How do you know?"

"Jim gave it to me. This is the one you mean, isn't it?" She reached into her bag and pulled out the photograph I'd uncovered on Jim Braben's desk. Her total lack of concern astonished me. I asked, "What's going on here? I don't understand. Whose side are you on?"

"I'm on your side," she replied. "Please don't ask me to explain. An explanation is the one thing I'm not allowed to give."

"What do you mean 'not allowed'? Who's not allowing you?"

"If I told you, I'd have to explain, and that's what I'm not allowed to do."

I said, "Everything here is one great riddle. I feel like I've been forced to take part in some fantastic game."

Saoirse looked away from me. I sensed an internal struggle, that she was on the edge of revealing what I needed to know. Eventually, she turned to me and said, "Nostalgia isn't a game; it's real."

"Then please help me grasp the reality."

"I can't," said Saoirse, "You'll have to work it out for yourself. You will find it out. It's what I hope for and dread at the same time."

"Why dread?"

"Because it could mean the end of our relationship."

"Then I'll give up my quest."

"I will lose all respect for you if you do. You must go on."

I said, "I have something to tell you. Something John put me on to. Something I believe you may already know."

Saoirse looked at me with a horrified expression. "Please don't! This is what happened between me and John. I don't want to go through that a second time. Don't you understand it's impossible? It's best you tell me nothing."

With the frustration of losing her so soon after finding her, I asked, "Do you have to go back tonight? Stay with me in my room."

"I have to go," she replied. "Wait for me two weeks. Then I promise we'll make love."

In the late afternoon, we walked back along the wall to Saoirse's lodgings by Canal Gate. I waited while she packed. We took the canal water taxi to the railway station. My last sight of her in Nostalgia was as she waited in the customs hall queue.

Chapter 35

Firework Night

At breakfast next morning, blue guards packed the hotel dining room. It hadn't been this busy since the night of the storm when all the guards, including the off-duty ones, had been called out to assist with the cleanup. The hotel manager entered holding a brass dinner gong, which he proceeded to strike in a slow tolling chime. The room went quiet.

"I have an important announcement to make for yer man in the corner," he said, pointing at me. The guards laughed. "The rest of you know what this is about, because that's why you're working. There will be a late-night firework display in the bay tonight at twenty-three hundred hours." And with a single strike on the gong, he left the room to the applause and mock cheers of us all.

I asked a guard why the short notice. He said the town council never fixed the date in advance, in case the weather turned out unsuitable. Shops would be putting up notices, it would be announced on Island Radio and a town crier would walk the streets. The guards accepted the call to "fireworks duty" as part of their job. They would be out at the seaward end of the bay, setting up the display on anchored rafts. The fireworks would be fired "Nostalgia-style" by a man with a lighter who'd be transported from raft to raft in the guard's speedboat. It sounds clunky but they had developed great skill at coordination.

I'd promised John I would go to the hospital to catch up on a backlog of indexing. "What happened to you yesterday?" he asked, "I expected you to call in."

I quickly diverted the conversation by asking him if he would be attending the evening fireworks. He said, "I have to suffer the indignity of being wheeled about in a chair with this ridiculous plastered foot sticking out in front of me."

I had two reasons not to tell John of my liaison with Saoirse. The first obviously personal — not to hurt him. The second — for Saoirse's safety. Her status with the leading players baffled me. Why had she shown no concern over the spy photo? Was she secretly in league with Jim Braben against the Earl? I wouldn't want information about our relationship overheard and used against her.

"You haven't seen one of our fireworks displays yet, have you?" said John. "It's not the usual, with a ton of rockets. Rockets don't work well here, because of the light in the sky from the lighthouse beam. They use water-level fireworks: Catherine wheels and so forth. It's very good and *very* noisy. The whole town goes out for it. Last time I watched, the guy from the lighthouse stood next to me. I asked him what we would he do if his light bulb went out. He said, 'Then I'll just have to run back up the hill fast, won't I?'"

The lighthouse keeper being willing to desert his post fitted in with his carelessness in leaving both his front and back doors unlocked. I hoped the guy would be on duty tonight, as it would be remiss of me not to make a search inside for anything that might help with my primary aim, to find out what was on the other side of the hills beyond the fake institute.

In the evening I made my way across the harbour wall and along the far promenade. Many islanders had already taken their place on this side of the water so as to get the best vantage point. Leaving them behind, I took the track to the lighthouse. As before, I found the entrance unlocked. One of the ground-floor cupboards had a gap between it and the wall, which offered good concealment and I waited there until I heard the keeper come downstairs and leave the building.

With the knowledge I had possession for an hour at most, I searched each of the three floors by the light of my torch. I found no revealing information of any kind. I had already suspected the lighthouses functioned merely to provide a reliable searchlight.

Disappointing, the view of the firework display from the top floor. I guess fireworks are far more impressive when you are level with them or when they are lighting the sky above you. With the last big bang signalling the end, I happened to look out of the window across to the far hills on the forbidden land at the back of Nostalgia. From behind them a single rocket shot up into the sky and burst into a mass of green stars. I waited as long as I dare, to see if another would follow. It did not. I returned to my hiding place to await the keeper. A quarter of an hour later he entered and I heard the slow tread of his footsteps going upstairs.

Back down on the promenade, I joined the crowds of islanders making their way back home. Their happy mood mirrored my own. That single rocket had given me the proof I had been seeking — there *was* another town on this island.

Chapter 36

Festival at the Darkest Hour

My chance observation from the lighthouse confirmed the existence of a second Nostalgia. The distance I estimated, from the height of the firework above the horizon, to be no more than four or five miles away. This other, was it a place of happiness or of misery? I had no doubt there must be some significant difference between the two towns, otherwise what would be the point of preventing contact between them? My imagination roamed wildly. Perhaps the inhabitants of the second town had been enslaved as forced labour in farms or factories, to augment the apparent economic success of the first. Or perhaps they were Doppelgangers, copies of Nostalgia's inhabitants, perfect but soul-less human beings. Perhaps *my* Nostalgia had the clones. That would explain why the townspeople didn't ask questions about the land beyond the fences — as clones they had been programmed not to ask. Something Fierce Hot said on my first ferry trip came back to me. Referring to the beach sand, he had remarked "Nothing's real here."

Near to my window I heard scuffling. A rat or some other nocturnal animal. Nostalgia had no background noise of traffic, so sounds that in the modern environment would not normally be heard became magnified and clear. I switched on my light to look at the clock. Crazy ideas had been churning around in my head for over an hour. Switching the light off, I lay back, blanking my mind.

Then I heard a sound I had not heard before on the island, a sound that sent through me a shiver of fear. In the distance, a bell tolled, the slow beat of a funeral bell. I knew of no churches in Nostalgia, no place this sound could be coming from, unless from the rocky stack out at sea beyond the cliffs. I pressed the switch of my bedroom lamp but it wouldn't go on. Neither would my room light. In the darkness I dressed hurriedly and left the room. The light switch outside my bedroom failed to work also. I felt my way along the blackness of the corridor. Each bedroom I passed had its door open, was empty and in darkness, no lights working anywhere. I checked all the other floors: not a room occupied, even the hotel managers' quarters abandoned.

Downstairs, I checked the kitchens, which somebody had forgotten to lock up. The back door to the outside banged backwards and forwards in the sea breeze, swung by an invisible hand intent on terror. Suddenly, it clanged shut, confining me in pitch-blackness. I felt something horrifying about to come upon me, an overwhelming urge to escape the building. Throwing open the door, I sprinted along the deserted back streets of Little Island until I came to the sands. The tide was out, the causeway luminous in the light of a full moon, the windows of the town without illumination, the outline of the quayside buildings dark and shadowy against the silvery glow of the wet beach and the moonlit sky. I walked the causeway, not knowing where I should go nor what I should do. From the far end there appeared a man walking towards me. He wore the uniform of a guard but from a distance his face appeared

215

ghostly, spectral, a brilliant white, fixed in an unnatural, devilish grin. As he came close, I saw he'd made up in the mask of a clown. He started to dance. Dancing past me, laughing hysterically, he leaped off the causeway and strode along the beach in the direction of the coloured lights of the funfair. I followed him. As we approached the fair, more guards streamed across the sands to join us, their faces made up with white. Soon, a great crowd of grimacing, clown-faced guards shouted and laughed together.

John, sitting in his wheelchair with his plastered foot stuck out rigidly in front was being pushed along the sands by Saoirse. She looked the epitome of the efficient holiday camp hostess, dressed in a bright red jacket, white pleated mini-skirt and carrying a clipboard. "Saoirse's volunteered to supervise the women tonight," said John. "That way she avoids having to take her clothes off."

While I was trying to take in the meaning of what he had just said, a band struck up on the quays. A great yell of approval went up from the guards as the band, the town musicians dressed in uniform, came marching down to the beach, followed by a long procession of naked young women.

"What the hell's going on?" I asked.

"The Festival At The Darkest Hour," said John. "The guards' favourite night of the year, as they get to see all the young women of the town naked. Attendance is compulsory."

"Look!" cried out Saoirse, "There's always *one*, isn't there?" She shouted at a woman wearing bra and panties.

"Hey! You! That's against the rules! Get them off!" The woman was running away now but Saoirse was the faster. Chucking the clipboard aside, she brought the woman to the ground with an impressive flying rugby tackle. A furious mud-wrestling contest of the two females in a patch of sloppy wet sand ended with Saoirse tugging off the underwear and holding it up in triumph to the cheers and applause of the guards.

The fairground organ started up, the three–four of its waltz time clashing with the four–four marching time of the band in a great cacophony. The women formed into circles, gyrating in a wild pagan dance while the grimacing guards looked on. Had Nostalgia not left the sixties behind after all, everything that happened there just a build up to an hysterical annual sex orgy?

"The bicycle rickshaw will take you as far as the woods," said John. "As a test of your courage, you must cross them alone. If you make it through to the railway station, you will discover the secret of Nostalgia on the train."

I'd lost the will to argue. Nothing made sense any more. The rickshaw took me the mile along the road to the cliffs, the noise of the orgy gradually fading into the distance until you could hear only the rustle of leaves in the breeze. We had reached the woods. I dismounted. The driver said, "Good luck!" turned his vehicle and rode back towards town.

In the open air by the beach, all had been brilliantly illuminated by moonlight. Now, under the cover of the trees, I could barely see the road ahead.

I walked on.

Someone walked behind me. I heard footsteps, faint at first, getting louder.

I stopped to look round. The footsteps stopped. In the pitch black of the wood, I could see nothing. Had they been merely an echo?

I continued along the road.

Footsteps behind me again. I quickened my pace, to no avail, the steps always more rapid than mine.

My pursuer directly behind me now. What had John advised? Courage. I determined to keep walking, that if I once lost heart and looked round, the shock might kill me.

The end of the wood in sight. A fist knocked with three sharp raps upon my shoulder. My heart pounded. The fist rapped three times again. Darting across the cobbled yard, I passed into the safety of the brightly lit waiting room, where a reception committee of smiling, applauding town councillors awaited.

"Well done! Passed with flying colours," said the mayor. "And now, the secret!"

They took me out to the platform, through a guard of honour of clown-faced male citizens each holding a giant chess piece suggestively positioned between his legs at the angle of an erect phallus. I boarded the train. Outside my compartment I found Jim Braben. Too late I saw the gun.

"Finally, we have you where we want you!" he said.

The sight of the gun hypnotised me. It had a long thick barrel marked off with inch and centimetre gradations, the highest gradation marked with the number "8".

"Get your clothes off!" ordered Jim. "You can't be expected to service my wife with your clothes on."

The door of my compartment slid open to reveal Mrs Braben wearing a see-through negligee barely holding in her delicious mounds of flesh. She stared at me as she dragged a brush through her long hair. At each tug her ample bosom wobbled tantalisingly as though at the next her breasts would finally break free and spill over.

"Are you forcing me to do this?" I asked.

"Not at all," said Jim. "You're grand! You're free to do what you want. Everyone is free to do what they want on Nostalgia Island."

He handed me my camera. "Here! Take photographs of my wife while she's removing her underwear. Remember to turn off the flash. You'll get much better pictures and avoid embarrassment."

"Now stand behind her while she bends over," he said, when his wife and I had both undressed. "I am King of the Island and she is my Queen. You see her beautiful body before you in full 3D. You will penetrate her on my orders."

"In!"

I sunk my member into Mrs Braben.

"Out!"

"In!"

As I penetrated her again, one of the train's heating pipes gave out a spurt of steam.

"Out!"

The steam pipe spurted more steam.

"In! Out! In! Out!"

The escape of steam had become alarming.

I said, "The pipe's going to explode. We should stop."

"You can't!" said Jim. "You've got to finish what you came here to do. In! Out! In! Out!"

The vapour from the pipe became one continuous flow, bathing our naked bodies in a hot wet soaking. Then, I felt the satisfaction of losing myself deep inside her.

"I'm going to the bathroom," she said, pulling up her panties.

"Don't be long," said her husband. "You're far too long in the bathroom in the mornings."

"Fuck off!" shouted his wife angrily, slamming the railway compartment door behind her.

The slam of the hotel door next to my bedroom woke me. I went to my bathroom to clean up. That might have been a crazy, mixed-up dream but in twenty-four hours I really would be exiting the hotel in the dead of night. I had my keys, I had my means of transport, I had my security fence crossing point, I had my plan of action. I had a visit to make — to the other Nostalgia Town.

Chapter 37

Escape

Next day, I carried on business as usual since I could do nothing till well after midnight. According to my almanac, the tide would be back in by three. I planned to take advantage of the high-water to travel the greatest distance in the shortest time. My transport would be the rowing boat I'd rescued and hidden in the beach hut after the storm. I needed sufficient darkness to hide my departure but sufficient light to aid my progress once I had crossed under the fence. With the season being high summer and dawn being at its earliest, I judged the timing of the tide perfectly matched my requirements.

My various excursions outside Nostalgia town formed the escape plan in my mind: Row across from Little Island to "swimming-lesson cove"; go up the path and into the wood under cover of darkness; go down towards the railway, cross the line — there would be nobody about at that time with the train not due in till six; take the track past the yards where I'd met Benjamin; from there all the way up to the top of Jim Braben hill; crawl under the fence and get up to the institute under cover of the dry stone walls. Thereon, I would have to rely on my sense of direction. I had no navigational aids; no shop on the island sold them.

At two-thirty in the morning I began my preparations. Into a jute bag I shoved a hunk of cheese, a few biscuits, a wire-corked bottle of island beer, a small torch, notebook, pen and the essential camera. Finally, I squeezed in some

Fifty–Rock bank notes, in case the second Nostalgia worked on identical currency. I tied the bag to my belt. Pulling *Applied Mathematics* from the stack on my bookshelf, I removed from its inside pocket the kitchen door keys. I considered taking with me Sally's golden ankle chain, as a good luck token, but closed the book and left it inside.

I planned to escape via the hotel's back entrance. I guessed they hadn't put it under surveillance, since the only routes off Little Island, by ferry, or by crossing the sands at low tide, could easily be observed from the mainland side. What would be my story on my return? At some point, the people minding me would realise I'd given them the slip. No way would they guess I'd done so by boat. They would assume I'd walked the sands and missed being spotted by a dozy guard. At the hotel in the evening, I'd talk about how I'd spent the day photographing the environment round Nostalgia. I already told John my intention. His quick acquiescence showed me he guessed an ulterior motive.

Opening my bedroom door a crack, I peered through. The corridor was empty. Creeping downstairs as noiselessly as I could, I entered the dining room and from there passed into the kitchen corridor. The kitchen door I unlocked, then locked behind me. Loath to switch on a light, in the darkness I stumbled over something on the floor, instinctively putting out my hand to check my fall and bringing a saucepan crashing down with a noise that would wake a neighbourhood. No time to see if an investigation would follow. I unlocked the back door, cautiously checked for anybody about, passed through and locked it from the outside.

In the cool, still night air, I proceeded swiftly along the back streets to the foreshore hut where I'd placed the boat. All my plans would come to nothing if it had since been discovered and returned to its rightful owner but I could not have checked without risking drawing attention to its hiding place. Luckily, the boat had not been removed. I lugged it down to the water and within a minute felt in my element skimming across the pond-smooth bay.

Had I more diligently studied my almanac I would have been forewarned of the full moon. It shone through a cloudless night sky to illuminate the water a brilliant silver. Emerging from behind Little Island, I felt uncomfortably exposed, as if the whole town must be staring through their upstairs windows at my passage. The lighthouse beam troubled me also. Although aimed at the hills beyond, it scattered its rays over me at each passing sweep. Accordingly, I changed route towards the far promenade, to create a safer distance from the town. Halfway towards my destination, I changed direction again, rowing across more than a mile of open water to the cove. Hauling the boat onto the sands I dragged it above the high tide mark, to be discovered and returned to Fierce Hot as his long-lost rowing boat, presumed swept into the cove on the night of the storm.

Dawn began to break as I left the beach and scrambled up the cliff path. Ahead, the woodland that would keep me hidden as far as the railway. Running under the cover of the trees I felt a sense of exultation with my progress.

I have been told many times by friends and family that my chief fault is carelessness brought about through over-confidence. And so it was on this occasion. As I came in view of the station, I saw with horror the night train had arrived. My escape plan had banked on it not being in till six. I had expected the station to be deserted. The train must have come back early.

Then I realised my stupid, stupid mistake. I had got the number "six" in my head and translated that to "arrives at six in the morning". My own experience confirmed it. Three journeys on the train, I had been woken by the steward at six-thirty with the train arrived at its destination. But the number "six" was the time in hours the train took to travel the tunnel. Leaving at eight, it would be in by two in the morning, which is two thirty-eight in Island time. On my journeys I had been asleep, not waking till after sunrise, oblivious to the train having already arrived several hours before.

From the far end of the station, I heard a throbbing coming closer. The engine car emerged from behind the carriages, travelled towards the tunnel, slowed to a stop, and reverse-shunted to connect to the sleeping cars ready for the evening's return to the mainland. The throbbing of the engine ceased; the night instantly silent. Then, footsteps, as the driver came walking up the hill. He passed within a few yards of where I lay concealed. I waited until the sound of his boots faded into the distance. With the driver gone home to his bed, the passengers asleep, the staff hopefully occupied inside the train, so long as I could get across the railway line unobserved, my plans would be intact.

I strode briskly downhill, but as I crossed the cobbled square a blue guard came out of the station and recognised me. "Hey! Stop!" he shouted. I could have tried to bluff my way through with my cover story of a photographic expedition but the guard's aggressive challenge put me on alert and panic set in. I took flight down the side of the station building, opened the door of the train driver's cab and dived in, locking the door behind me. Crouching down, I heard the guard run onto the platform and call out to another "He's not come your way? He must be on the train. You start that end; we'll meet in the middle." He tried the locked cab door, then moved on to search the passenger carriages.

The cab had an impressive array of control levers. If I could figure out how to start the engine, I might boldly drive the whole caboose out through the tunnel to the mainland. The stupidity of this idea, the many reasons it could end in ignominy, not to mention the cowardice of such a plan, did not take long to occur to me. I had set the task of finding the second Nostalgia and this task I determined to complete, whatever the risk to my safety.

I deemed it advisable to move from the cab to the adjoining windowless engine compartment. I found the compartment empty. What on earth had they done with the engine? Tadhg must have been right, the first time I met him, with his explanation of motors lowered on pods from the base of the engine car to make contact with a magnetic track. The train possessed no conventional

225

engine, as such. Instead, I stood in an empty goods van with the only cargo a 1970's disco sound system and tape deck plus four tall loudspeaker cabinets. I laughed at the idea of somebody planning to play forbidden amplified rock music at full blast with this illegal import in defiance of the island authorities.

I couldn't stay here. The searchers would come back, my only chance to get out now, while their attention was engaged elsewhere. I exited the cab via its trackside door, dashed across the line to the level crossing and made it in safety to the path across the fields. Reaching the summit of hill dweller road, I got down into the ditch and under the fence. Soon the whole place would be on watch. If anything, that was in my favour. They didn't know I could breach the fences and would assume me still within the permitted area. Reinforcements would be called from the restricted area, leaving me a clearer route than if it had been guarded normally.

Running crouched down behind the dry-stone wall, I reached the institute. At the back of it, under the cover of the extended roof, I found the horse-drawn supply cart. It must have been left overnight for someone to pick up and take elsewhere on the island. Could it be there *was* some research activity going on, just not here? The presence of the cart was fortuitous. My failure to escape unobserved meant I would need supplies for a more extensive expedition. I grabbed a loaf of bread and a few apples, as much as I dared without giving anyone cause to suspect theft.

At the top of the hill, I stopped to catch my breath. Dawn had fully broken. On the one side I looked over Nostalgia and the bay, where by now a frantic search must have been launched to find me. On the other side, a scene of peace and tranquillity — a deserted moorland valley with a stream flowing along the bottom. A bright green grassy trench snaked round and round, fording the stream at several points. I had no idea of its purpose, which I could only think must have once been a path for grazing animals. Beyond, another hill, and who knows what beyond that. The view might as well have been the other side of the moon. No chart of Nostalgia featured any more than could be seen from the town walls, which for the forbidden land was limited to the research institute building and the hilltop above it.

I decided to follow the stream. Which way? Uphill to its source in the island's interior or downhill to its inevitable outlet at the sea? Rightly or wrongly, I assumed the other town on this island to be on the coast. And I had an additional motive for going in that direction, my urgent desire to obtain a view of the ocean that I felt certain was being denied to the islanders with a purpose. However, going coastward required me to descend into the valley, where I would be exposed and visible to anyone on the hills above. By going inland, I could keep to the ridge, from where I would be the one with the advantage of observation. In that direction too lay the wooded hill with the mysterious temple I had seen through the fence on the morning of the regatta and had determined a priority to visit. Against it, an unknown risk. The supply cart parked behind the institute had been both welcome and unnerving. If its collector came along the ridge, an encounter would be unavoidable. Would I find friend or foe?

Chapter 38

The Temple of Pan

Dawn had given way to sunrise and another of Nostalgia's cloudless sunny mornings as I put distance from the institute. I saw no pursuing figures in the direction of the town nor in the far valley but I stared more keenly ahead, along the ridge, through my concern of meeting the institute cart collector. I'd decided the moment I saw someone I would descend to the valley and hope to find a patch of gorse or a dip in the ground offering concealment.

My plan wasn't needed. Within half an hour I made it to the cover of woodland. The trees here were taller than any I had encountered in the inhabited part of the island. They might date back hundreds of years. That such a fertile island should have remained uninhabited and unexplored was a mystery to me. Even allowing for access from the sea being denied by the supposedly treacherous coastline, the inland terrain and benign climate would make access by helicopter easy. If the one that crashed near the lighthouse had been sent deliberately, why did no investigation follow when it failed to return home? On the other hand, if no helicopter had ever been sent specifically to the island, why *wasn't* it being explored? I began to suspect collusion at the highest level. Some person or faction in the Irish government conspiring with the Earl to block outside access. A valuable prize must be at risk, something of potentially enormous value. The expertise of the Earl and of his friend, Jim Braben, was first and foremost not agriculture but mining. Suppose they had discovered gold on the island, or uranium, or some other valuable metal, that Nostalgia Town had become an elaborate front for personal profiteering? I shuddered at this prospect. Men might play a desperate game for such high stakes. I could expect no mercy.

The rough track I had been following came to a wide clearing some fifty yards in diameter, in the centre of which stood the white stone temple I had glimpsed between the trees on regatta day. It reminded me of those structures they call a "folly", popular with the owners of eighteenth and nineteenth-century stately homes. A folly serves no purpose other than to exude an air of mystery and stimulate the romantic imagination, a kind of rich man's luxury garden-ornament on a grand scale.

The doorway had been bricked up but when I skirted round cautiously to the other side I saw a second entrance, with a wooden door decayed and crumbling. I tried the handle. It came away in my hand, taking with it a large piece of rotted panelling. However, with my fingers hooked round the door's edge, I managed to prise it open. It yielded more easily than I'd expected, suggesting a recent visitor.

The state of the rotting door in no way prepared me for what I saw inside after my eyes had accustomed to the gloom. From frosted glass windows inset around the circumference of the domed roof, shafts of light shone down, like rays from heaven, onto wall paintings of the god, Pan, and his nymphs, of astonishing beauty and colour. Dead centre in the floor space stood a low, wide stone table. I could imagine hippies, squatting on the ground about, feasting, or participating in a "happening". Extraordinary that the pioneers of the island should have gone to so much trouble to erect and decorate this impressive structure, only to abandon it.

On the verge of concluding the building had no relevance to my wider quest, I saw on the floor something of twentieth-century appearance — a credit card with John's name on it. Now I had definite proof he had come at least this far. Had he dropped the card for some deliberate purpose? I could not imagine what.

Ten minutes after leaving the folly, I reached the edge of the wood. A hundred yards ahead across open land, I saw a security fence, with a gap in it! A whole section had been taken down by two workmen engaged in repair work. I hoped they would leave for lunch, affording me a chance to slip through, or they might go off in their van to get tools or equipment.

The incongruity of seeing a modern van on the island galvanised my thoughts. I am no expert on vans but the small white vehicle looked like a *Ford*. Was the other side of the island motorised? Could the Earl's island fantasy have extended to creating an allegory of heaven and hell: one side light, agrarian, at peace, the inhabitants living in freedom; the other side dark, hellish, the people imprisoned as slaves to work in the Earl's gold or uranium mines?

The workmen didn't drive off for lunch. They sat eating sandwiches in the back of their van. The open back door between us, obscuring their view, tempted me to slip past and steal across the break in the fence but, just as I had summed up the courage for this risky manoeuvre, the men resumed work. I enjoyed no other such opportunity. At dusk, they drove off, the fence fully repaired, topped with vicious new coils of razor wire. I decided to switch to "Plan B": retrace my steps at dawn and go in the direction of the coast.

That night I lay on a bed of dry leaves and foliage on top of the stone table in the folly. Not as uncomfortable as it might sound. On my back, enjoying the vision of two nymphs lit by a shaft of light from the full moon, my imagination substituted them with an image of Sally Macnamara and her twin, both in mini-tunics with bare legs beautifully set off by strappy sandals and ankle jewellery. Then my imagination shifted to their husbands as Druid priests armed with sacrificial knives, and I began to question my vulnerability in this building, sleeping on this stone table, with no means of escape should I be tracked down.

Next morning, my return journey in the direction of the institute was hampered by my concern of meeting the cart collector. Since I had no way of knowing when the cart would be collected, I had no idea whether I might be approached from the front or from behind. I halted frequently, checking the view in either direction. When I reached the institute and looked inside, the cart had been taken away. My caution had not been misplaced.

Chapter 39

The Rebel Inn

Descending into the valley on the far side of the institute hill, I followed the course of the stream, traversing the boggy terrain as quickly as I dare, mindful of the uneven and unpredictable ground. Easy to break an ankle here in a hurry. How ironic to end up prisoner in the same hospital as John and for the same reason. I paused many times in my progress to scan the surrounding hills. I saw no guards. My hunch they would still be searching on the Nostalgia side of the fences was proving correct.

After a frustratingly slow first mile I met my first disappointment. The stream disappeared underground in a noisy gurgling whirlpool. I carried on, hoping to pick it up again, until a further half-mile brought me to rising woods.

The scale of nature can be deceptive. From a distance, what looked like a small patch of gently rising woodland, became, once I had entered it, a steep earth cliff requiring considerable effort of hauling my body from tree trunk to tree trunk to get to the top. I'd hoped the summit would lead to the coast, from where I could look out to sea, but I was to be disappointed a second time. Emerging from the trees onto grassland I came to a great gash, dropping down to rocks pounded by swirling waves. Rising up from the other side, a further cliff blocked the view. The fissure ran a considerable distance in the direction of the far side of the island. I could only follow it in the hope of an eventual view of the ocean.

After some distance the woods on the inland side gave way to a grassy plateau, rampant with wildflowers. Slap bang in the middle of the meadow, with no road leading to it, stood a traditional Irish cottage. I could make a wide detour or risk all and break in. Curiosity got the better of me. I chose the latter option.

The sun had come up, the grassland in this exposed area dry to the touch, alive with the chirping of crickets. Lying on my stomach I edged my way forward under cover of tall grass and wild flower stalks. As I got closer, I saw the vegetation leading away from the back door of the cottage had been flattened by the passage of feet. The question now, whether the cottage was at this moment empty or occupied.

It would have been foolhardy to have just walked in so I attempted a little experiment. Still lying on my stomach, I picked up a small stone and flung it in the direction of the back door. It missed, striking the wall with a clatter. More success with a second, which hit the door with a loud thud. If anyone were in the back room, that would surely bring them out. I lay as flat as I could, my nerves on edge. Nobody came. This didn't satisfy me. I tried a pebble on an upstairs window. Receiving no response, I crawled round to the front of the cottage and repeated the stone-throwing procedure there. Finally, satisfied the place must be empty, I tried the front door and found it to be unlocked. Inside, a typical old-world two-room affair, the door giving directly onto a living room, with an adjoining kitchen at the back. Stairs went from the kitchen to the upper floor. I listened intently for the sound of snoring.

My stone-throwing escapade might not have awoken a deep sleeper. I heard nothing, but I crept up the stairs as lightly as I could, just in case. Despite my care, the wooden risers creaked and snapped with age but I was relieved to find the bedrooms unoccupied. From the contents of their wardrobes, I learned three things: the cottage was inhabited; the inhabitants were male; the inhabitants were guards.

Downstairs I raided the kitchen for food. Opening the larder door, I saw pinned inside a newspaper cutting with my photograph. I relaxed a little when I read the date, the week of my arrival on the island, though the inhabitants of this cottage had obviously been involved in my surveillance.

Keeping a wary eye out of the kitchen window for anyone who might approach, I searched the larder, where I found a large stock of tinned Irish Stew, no doubt smuggled onto the island by a guard with an insatiable craving for meat! My hunger getting the better of my caution I decided one tin would not be missed and within minutes I had the stew bubbling away in saucepan. With my stolen bread and a few swigs of beer, it made a delicious meal.

In the front room I found a pair of powerful binoculars. Purloining them might give away I had penetrated the fences. On the other hand, the inhabitants might simply accuse each other of their presumed carelessness in losing this valuable instrument. The binoculars were too powerful an insurance against recapture to leave behind. I would take them with me.

I left the cottage and progressed along the cliff top. Third time lucky, as they say. I came to a path leading down to a dry rocky area at the bottom of the gash in the land. Scrambling down, I made my way along to where the front cliff terminated. At last, I could look out at the open sea. Literally. That's all I saw. Just sea. No boats, no other islands, no man-made features, no nothing. Just sea and sky.

Estimating the distance I had travelled and comparing it to the size of the land area of Nostalgia town and its surroundings, I calculated I had surely by now come close to the far side of the island. A tall cliff jutted out a mile further on. On the other side, I should find the second Nostalgia.

Once again, I encountered disappointment. A wide sea inlet, two hundred yards across, blocked the way. Cliffs on my side, running out into deep water, made the inlet impassable further inland. To get across, I would have to go all the way back and go overland across the fields to where the inlet came to an end. While pondering this, I saw, on the far side of the water, at the foot of the cliff, an inn.

Positioning myself between a gap in some boulders, I focussed my binoculars. The name on the signboard: "The Rebel Inn", one of Nostalgia Island's historical pastiches, a thoroughly convincing imitation of the genuine article. With the novelty of having the upper hand in the surveillance game, I would stay put, observe this inn, and learn what I may. There would be some hours to wait till opening time but with the warmth of the sun on my back I felt no hurry to leave.

In Nostalgia, pubs stuck to the regular Irish opening time of half past ten but I had to wait until ten minutes past eleven before this publican opened his doors for three old men coming down the cliff path. At quarter to one, a large number of people descended the cliff and went inside the building. The men wore suits, I guessed office or research workers. They came out into the pub garden, carrying drinks. Many had trays of food and sat eating at tables, a typical lunchtime scene such as you might find anywhere. Were these people oblivious to the existence of my Nostalgia or complicit in the conspiracy?

Another large group arrived an hour later, at a quarter to two. The lateness of their lunch puzzled me. I could only assume a special occasion. My musings on this anomaly were interrupted by something confounding all expectations. A man and a woman came down the cliff. I didn't know the man but I knew the woman — Saoirse! I watched, mesmerised, as they entered the pub together. Some minutes later, they came outside with drinks. My intention had been to scan the entire crowd, in case I missed something important, but I returned over and over to watch Saoirse. She had deceived me with her story of going back to the mainland, when all the time she had been here on the far side of the island. Had she been informed of my escape? Nothing in her demeanour indicated concern. She looked happy and carefree. My mind was now more confused than ever about her true intentions.

I continued my vigil until half past two, when the whole party departed up the cliff path, leaving the three old men, now sitting outside, smoking together. Driven by desperation to locate Saoirse and to confront her with her deception, I decided to return along the beach at top speed and find an inland route to the inn and what lay beyond.

I had forgotten the tide. Twelve hours on from my escape by rowing boat, the tide had gone out and come in again. Enormous waves crashed against the cliff face, blocking the way. I had no choice but to wait, a long wait of several hours.

I got back by the cottage at six. A further trek along the high ground in the direction of the inn ended in a mix of triumph and frustration. In the distance I could see a tall security fence, the proof I had been seeking of a second Nostalgia. The fence denied any hope of locating Saoirse. Demoralised, I made my way back to the cottage. I waited till well after nightfall before entering. I figured if no guards had taken up residence by then, the cottage would surely remain empty till tomorrow. Sitting in the dark in the front room, I had never felt lonelier. Here was I, a fugitive, in danger of my life, friendless, betrayed by the woman I loved, trapped on an island a hundred miles out in the open ocean, with no possible means of escape.

Chapter 40

Aftermath

The sudden disappearance of Mike went unnoticed by the majority of Nostalgia Island's inhabitants. The guards had carried out their sweep of the town and surrounding countryside with thoroughness but with the utmost discretion, anxious that nobody should make a connection between the two events, their main problem: coming up with a convincing explanation to give the hotel managers for Mike's middle of the night vanishing act.

A few days later John was taken by ambulance through the fence at Hill Gate, up the rough track and over the hill behind the institute. The local newspapers reported a temporary halt to the Nostalgia history project due to "the coincidence of both staff members having accepted attractive job offers abroad." They quoted the Earl and Jim Braben giving praise to John and Mike for the high quality of their work.

The Tasteless Toys inventor, who had indeed correctly deduced the island's secret, knew different, but the others who had communicated their suspicions to Mike: the canal boat manager, Dave Wilson, the Macnamaras, had no concrete evidence with which to convert their concern into action. Mike's principal mistake, not knowing whom he could trust, was to trust no-one. So the key point of the institute being a fake, which could have brought him powerful allies, was known to himself alone.

Saoirse returned within a fortnight to her lodgings on the island. Her general demeanour, relaxed and pleasant as ever, gave nothing away. A year later, she too disappeared. She returned in a deep depression, her personality change it was rumoured through a nervous breakdown.

Molly read about Mike in the island newspapers. She felt a little hurt he had not called in to say goodbye, though equally relieved — she still held a dread of him asking one particularly awkward question.

Sally Macnamara reacted to the loss of Mike in her own inimitable way. Always resourceful, she teamed up with musician Alice to seduce the two youngest members of the town band in a torrid foursome — at least that's what the lads privately boasted to their friends. How much was an exaggeration, we'll never know.

Tadhg got dismissal from the guards, a consequence of his green uniform security lapse, a warning to the others. He became manager of the barge company stables. Considerably lower pay but a job he loved.

Colm earned promotion to guard sergeant for his part in the organisation of the search for Mike.

Fierce Hot continued to be — "fierce hot".

As for Nostalgia, it carried on for the remainder of the year, and the next and onwards, in blissful isolation, the security and prosperity of its lifestyle as predictable and guaranteed as the twice daily tide cutting off Little Island and the hotel from the town.

It should be mentioned Tadhg married girlfriend Mary. The couple settled into a new house close to Stable Gate. Mary continued in her job as assistant to Doctor Murphy, Nostalgia's environmental manager. Tadhg and Mary's wedding, like all weddings in Nostalgia, was a great occasion, an excuse for the whole town to enjoy themselves.

Chapter 41

The Wedding

Doctor Diarmuid Murphy, the ecologist, was not a happy man. That girl! She'd played him for a fool. And now he'd been asked to give her away at her wedding, "in appreciation of our close working relationship", as she put it. Like most of the specially chosen Nostalgia residents, the bride had no living relatives. The groom, unusually however, did have family off the island. His relatives knew nothing of the Nostalgia ceremony; they'd already attended the official Irish wedding on the mainland.

Tadhg came along at that moment.

"Very smart!" said Diarmuid.

"Aren't I always?" said Tadhg, "I'd better get inside and leave you to wait. Isn't it bad luck to be here when the bride arrives? Except yourself, of course!"

Yes, the doctor was unhappy. The girl's official title was "assistant" but, if the truth were known, *he* was the dutiful assistant, while she, the real boss, had been pulling all the strings. He would just have to put a brave face on it and go through with the ceremony. He'd no right to spoil her special day. In any case, he needed proof, impossible to get until next week. The overnight train. He had to check something on the mainland. Then he would know.

Diarmuid Murphy gave away the bride.

Islanders packed the reception at Nostalgia Hotel, spilling out onto the hotel terrace and garden. Luckily, despite the date being early November, the mild climate prevailed, the day warm, albeit overcast. Murphy had prayed for sun. Not for the wedding, but so he could carry out one more experiment. Next day his prayers were answered. Midday found him high up on the ridge above the reservoir with a homemade contraption having an arrangement of lenses. By one o'clock he'd satisfied his doubts, confirming what he thought he'd seen last month. Not long to go now. One week, then he'd know.

Chapter 42

Deceptions

By the light of my torch, I sketched in my notebook a map of the terrain as I had seen it. Starting from the repaired security fence I drew in first the woodland of the Temple of Pan, then the ridge above the fake institute. On the far side of the ridge, I drew the valley with the stream, continuing towards the coast and terminating in the steep wooded escarpment. The coastal cliffs I traced as far as the open grassland surrounding the cottage of the guards, then onwards to the natural barrier of the river estuary, on the other side of which, tantalisingly close, yet beyond reach, the Rebel Inn. Nothing in these newly discovered areas gave the slightest clue as to those remaining, of a size, shape and composition I could only guess at, helpless as an ancient mapmaker obliged to fall back on "Here Be Monsters."

On top of everything, I had serious concern for my lack of provisions. Yes, I could risk opening another tin of meat stew before leaving the cottage in the morning and I could take with me a small amount from each packet in the larder, a biscuit here, a few dates there, and so on, though I dare not steal too much. My beer bottle I would fill up with tap water. I might also raid the supply cart again. But sooner or later my supplies would run out, with no guarantee of replenishment.

Sally provided my one glimmer of hope. How true her premonition of trouble; how welcome her promise to come to my aid. I decided tomorrow I'd make my way back to the ridge, finding a place of concealment near the institute till evening, slip back through the hole in the fence, find a phone box and call her to arrange a rendezvous. She'd surely find me a hiding place. Knowing Sally, she'd propose a special price for her co-operation, though hardly one I could complain about. I planned to stay hidden while an ally, possibly Dave Wilson, returned to the mainland to get help. How to get back in to a Nostalgia crawling with guards? I remembered the blue uniforms I'd seen in the cupboards upstairs. I fetched one down and packed it for the following day's excursion. Now I could sleep in peace.

The sound of men's voices in the kitchen woke me at dawn.

"There's no trace anywhere."

"Someone must be hiding him."

"The new people — the Macnamaras?"

"We've got them under surveillance in case he makes contact."

"Their phone?"

"We're tapping it."

"And he definitely didn't get away on the train?"

"We swept the goods vans, the compartments, the lot. We even looked inside the baby grand."

"A *child* couldn't fit in that."

"This morning we're getting Tom and Jerry in."

"It's not too late?"

"They'll find him even if they have to search the entire town. Shall I put more toast on?"

"Put the kettle on."

Opening the front door risked alerting the men, so I eased open a side window, slipped through it to the outside and gently closed it behind me. Then I sprinted across the open grassland till I had reached the cover of trees. Too late I remembered I had left behind my notebook.

I put down the lapse to fatigue. The previous evening I should have fully packed my bag, ready to quit the cottage at a moment's notice. Almost certainly, they would find the notebook today and switch their search to this side of the fence. The new circumstance required a rapid revision of my plans. The blue uniform would be my salvation. Wearing it, I could walk down to the fence in broad daylight without attracting suspicion. I would scramble under, find a phone box and ring Sally. They'd tapped her line but they didn't know I knew that. I'd tell her I'd found a way through to other side, was going back there now, that I wanted her to meet me by the egg farm in the salt marsh at eight that evening and, if I didn't turn up, she was to come back at three in the morning. Tonight, I planned to be on the train leaving for the mainland. I anticipated the tapping of the phone would result in most of the guards being dispatched to the other side of the fence, clearing the land for me to enter the train, which I hoped would offer a place of concealment within. At eight, when all the guards in the place should be staking out the fences and the egg farm rendezvous, I would be on my way to safety. When I didn't make the first rendezvous, they'd naturally continue their surveillance till the second, by which time the train would have delivered me to the safety of the mainland. They wouldn't guess they'd been tricked until too late. I need have no concern for the safety of my allies. Once my opponents knew the game was up and the Irish law would soon be due at their doorstep, they wouldn't dare harm them.

Essential I crossed under the fence to Nostalgia before they discovered the notebook, or the whole area would be swarming with guards. I figured the ones who'd woken me at dawn had been on night shift and would be asleep for hours yet but I could take no chances — they might have already made the discovery. I paused only to put on the blue guard uniform.

An hour later found me back at the ridge, scanning the panorama of the institute building with Nostalgia beyond, contemplating the best moment to stride downhill in my new persona of blue guard on duty. Then, my heart fell as I heard, coming from the direction of the railway, a sound that spells doom for any pursued man, a sound I never expected to hear on Nostalgia Island — the sound of barking dogs.

Chapter 43

Dogs

 The sound of dogs overturned my choice of action, my disguise now useless. I turned away from the institute and made a beeline back over the top of the hill to the stream at the bottom of the valley, to wade along it so the dogs would have no scent to follow. Should I go up or down stream? I guessed the guards would think I had gone downstream. So I choose upstream, also because it's easier to run uphill than downhill in water — less risk of stumbling and falling.

Painfully slow progress in the deeper water at the start but as the stream became shallower I found I could splash along at jogging pace. How fortunate, as a stream-wading novice, I had chosen the easier direction. I continued for a mile with only the uneven rocky terrain and low gorse bushes for cover. Several times in my uphill progress a wide grassy trench forded the stream, its purpose no clearer to me down here than when I had first seen it yesterday from the ridge above.

Approaching a copse on the brow of a hill to the right, I craved visual obscurity within, even though I knew it would be no obstacle to a pursuing sniffer dog. I struck off from the stream, scrambled up the slope and entered under the cover of the trees. There, I stopped to listen. In the distance I heard the barking of a single dog. My ruse to deceive them and the sacrifice of laboriously wading water had been a complete waste of energy. They had merely sent one set of guards with a dog downstream and the other guards with a dog upstream.

I raced off again. I had one advantage over the dog. They could not risk letting it off the leash till within sight of me. That meant the dog's sniffing pace would limit their progress. I, on the other hand, could run, and as an ex-college rower I was fit, very fit.

Such is the nature of a wood you could be going round in circles for hours without knowing it. This wood had a path. It might lead me into danger but to trust my sense of direction off the beaten track would inevitably lead to capture. I kept to the path. Half a mile further, to my horror, the way was blocked by a locked gate in a security fence. To one side, a tall tree had fallen and crushed the fence top. The trunk rested diagonally across the wire, forming a bridge to the other side. I agonised over the decision to climb it. Had I come all this way merely to cross the fence back into Nostalgia in the now slim hope I could avoid the guards? Or should I continue my quest, push along into the woods, risking capture in this isolated place where they could do with me as they pleased?

I took a swig from my bottle. The coolness of the liquid cleared my head. At a distance of three miles from Nostalgia, this could not possibly be their fence. It must be the fence enclosing the inhabitants of the second town. I had attained my destination. Negotiating the fallen trunk I nearly slipped sideways onto the vicious coils of razor wire below, before I made it across in safety and continued along the path on the other side.

With the end now in sight, I'd expected a view over a town. Instead, the dirt track crossed, of all things, a railway line. I should have expected it. In my theory of a duplicate Nostalgia, I had not allowed for how such a place might be populated. Suppose the tunnel from the mainland divided into two, one line arriving at the Nostalgia I knew, the other line arriving at the second town. Passengers would innocently disembark, only to find themselves transported to some place of confinement. The Earl himself had admitted they chose people who had no close relatives back home, people *who would not be missed*. To minimise resistance, those passengers must already be drugged and half-conscious before they arrived. I remembered the crowding in the bar before the train set off. Would the drug be administered by spiking the drinks? Not such a fantastic idea.

I heard barking. The guards must be close by. But it was not the sound of the dog bringing me back to reality. I *knew* this place. I had been here before. How and when, I knew not, only this was somewhere I had been at some time in my past.

Across the railway line, the woodland path terminated in a tall, neatly clipped yew hedge with an ornamental gate set in it. Visible over the top of the hedge, the distant roof of a large house. Would the occupants provide sanctuary or betray me? Either way, I had no alternative, anything better than disappearing incognito as prisoner of the guards.

The garden of this mysterious house featured many hedge-lined corridors, which quickly confused my sense of direction. By the time I realised I had entered a maze, I had gone too far. As a schoolboy, I used to boast confidently to my friends of the ease of finding the way out — keep turning right. Now, my childish boast had come back to haunt me. Futile even to try. By the time I had exhausted all the false alleyways, capture was inevitable. They only needed to post a guard at each exit and wait.

Multiple frustrating dead ends brought me not to the edge of the maze but to a twee ornamental bird table at its centre. In my rage at my impotence, I could have kicked and smashed the stupid bird table. Then I noticed the single hedge-lined path leading to a lawn and to the windows of the house beyond. I raced down it, emerging just in time to avoid two guards with their dog coming round the far corner of the maze. Sprinting across the lawn I leaped up a grassy slope to a patio in front of the house and straight in at a door. Inside, the rooms to the left and right were empty but I could hear voices coming from behind a door at the end of the corridor. Flinging open the door and entering an enormous high-ceilinged room, like the great hall of a stately home, I found myself face to face with the Earl.

Chapter 44

Full Circle

My instinct on seeing the Earl was to turn and run but my pursuers blocked the way.

"Are you going to kill me?" I asked.

The Earl laughed. "Sean, show the man your rifle."

One of the guards came towards me, his rifle pointing at my chest. I backed away from him.

"Not like that, you idiot! The poor man's in a state of alarm."

The guard reversed his grip and offered me the rifle. The Earl said, "You'll see the rifle, like all the guard rifles, is unloaded."

"How do I check? I've never handled a rifle before."

"I'll show you," said the Earl, stepping forward. "Don't worry. We'd hardly have given you a loaded rifle, would we?"

He showed me the empty magazine. "Now you know how to do it, check the others for yourself." He nodded to the other guards, who came forward, handing me their rifles one after the other.

"Satisfied?" asked the Earl, "Originally, we had the rifles loaded, even then, only with blanks, to scare off any inquisitive mainlanders who came too near our fences. Once a few fake shots had been fired and the guns had served their purpose of putting fear in the minds of the populace, we judged it better not to have them loaded at all."

"There are other ways of killing people than shooting them"

"True," said the Earl, "but our organisation does not harm people."

"You were willing to do harm to John"

"Not so," said the Earl. "John had an accident, which we took advantage of."

"John doesn't see it that way"

"How do you know?"

"He passed me a note in the hospital saying it wasn't an accident"

"Ah, yes. My security staff slipped up there. They *thought* an attempt had been made to communicate. You realise the nurses in the dispensary office aren't actually nurses?"

"I thought they were the real deal but they'd been told to keep an eye on John in addition to their nursing duties."

"Well, it's a credit to their acting abilities, I suppose," said the Earl. "Pity their detection skills aren't up to equivalent standard. However, back to the subject of John and his accident. We got him to the hospital; they took an X-ray and found no broken bones. He was lucky. Then, we saw an opportunity. We'd already figured out John had entered the secured zone deliberately. You can't wander onto it unintentionally — it's impossible. When he clumsily pretended the collision had caused him temporary amnesia and he couldn't remember how he'd got onto the land, we knew for certain he was lying and was going to keep to himself how much he knew. That's when we devised a plan to make up a story about hairline bone fractures, immobilise him by encasing his leg in plaster, and suggest we employ a former colleague to assist in his work. We hoped John would confide in that person and thereby be tricked into giving away what he knew and, more importantly, giving away what he intended to do with his knowledge."

"So, John is not in any danger?"

"No."

"And I am free to go?"

"Yes."

"To go back to Nostalgia."

"You will never be allowed back to Nostalgia. You know too much."

"What about the second Nostalgia?"

"I'm not following you. The *second* Nostalgia?"

"There are two Nostalgias, right?"

"Oh, I see! You still don't know where you are. I meant you are free to go home — Dublin, or England, or wherever you call home now."

"I had begun to think of Nostalgia as my home."

"That happens to everyone who goes to live there. They quickly grow accustomed to the place. They cannot imagine wanting to live anywhere else. You can appreciate why we are so protective of it."

"So, I am not in any danger?"

"Absolutely not!"

"I could leave this minute if I wanted?"

"As I said, you are free to go home. You were an excellent employee. I'm sorry we have to lose you. We will of course give you a month's pay in lieu of notice."

"I passed my interview with the bank in Singapore. They have made me an offer."

"I advise you to accept it. Get right away from here. It will be the best medicine."

"I can't abandon John. I need your promise he's not under threat."

"You have my word."

"I've been in mental and emotional turmoil. I need answers."

"The mental turmoil we can relieve," said the Earl. "The emotional turmoil we're not qualified to deal with. There's somebody here who can help. You can go to her later."

"Saoirse's here? Is she safe?"

"She is safe. She was never in any danger. *You* were never in any danger. *John* was never in any danger. It is *we* who are the ones in danger."

"I don't understand."

"That's because you have been successfully brainwashed. Don't be alarmed. It's nothing that can't easily be cured by what I am about to tell you. It is clear your grasp of reality has been usurped. Even now, with the truth staring you in the face, you haven't seen it. Let me first of all protest our innocence. You were not brainwashed by anyone in this room. That was carried out by our agent."

"Who is your agent? Is he someone I have met?"

"It's nobody you know. No further questions please. Let me explain."

With that, the Earl began the following narrative:

"Every two days, in the early evening, the night train is made ready for its long journey through the salt tunnel connecting the mainland to the island. On the mainland side, goods are loaded, being those items that cannot be farmed or manufactured on the island. On the island side, the goods we send back are the organic vegetable produce — the mainstay of the island economy. It's simple import and export, with the balance of trade in favour of export, keeping the community happy and prosperous, as you have seen for yourself. What you have also seen is the island has a thriving *internal* economy with its own currency, with many people running small businesses that trade with each other. Full employment, lucrative employment, *meaningful* employment, are the necessary pre-conditions for a harmonious and safe society, free of the social dysfunction characterising the modern world. Of course, the need for local enterprise was born of necessity, born of the island's *isolation.* Notice I emphasise the word *isolation*. You may not remember your remark but the thing that most impressed me at your job interview was your astute observation, despite your youth, that the insidious influence of the modern world will always work against the creation of a better society. That was precisely our thinking when we came up with the concept of an isolated community on an island.

Now we have to come back to the subject of the train. In fact, everything that happens on the island, everything that *has* happened on the island, comes back to the train. Without the train, the concept of Nostalgia Island would not have been possible.

You've never been to San Francisco? No doubt you've heard of the famous cable car. Many people think the word 'cable' means electric cable, like an overhead electricity wire. It does not. The San Francisco system is mechanical, not electrical. An endless loop of thick steel cable runs in an open channel under the street. The cable is kept moving by an engine house. When the cable car wants to move, it lowers a pod into the channel and grabs the moving cable, which pulls it along the road. When it wants to stop, the pod lets go of the moving cable and the driver applies the brakes. If you go to San Francisco, I recommend you walk the cable car route. Cross the road and walk over the channels. You'll hear the noise of the cable running underneath the street."

"What's the relevance of the San Francisco cable car?"

"Our train uses the same propulsion system. It's the original salt-mine railway system. We adapted it."

"I was told your train was driven by electric motors. I stood by the engine the night of my first trip. I heard the noise the motors were making."

"You heard what we wanted you to hear. You in fact heard electronically synthesised engine noise played through a quadraphonic sound system in the compartment behind the driver's cab."

"I saw those loudspeakers when I hid in the train."

"My guards told me they searched the entire length of the train, excepting the driver's cab, which had been locked up."

"I locked the door from the inside after I hid in the cab."

"Of course you did. You showed great presence of mind."

"Not that great. I forgot to lock the door the other side. I don't understand. Why disguise the way the train is propelled?"

"It's a matter of simple arithmetic, one of a number of small impressions that add up to create one big impression. We wanted the sound of the engine to suggest to your subconscious the sound of a train about to confidently embark on a ninety-mile, all-night journey."

"But the train *was* moving? You can't tell me I imagined seeing it leave the station"

"No, you didn't imagine it. At eight o'clock precisely, the train grabs onto the moving wire under the track and is pulled one mile into the tunnel, at which point it releases its hold of the wire and comes to rest. The driver gets out of his cab and works his way down the outside of the train, closing all the window shutters. This is our next small impression, part of our big equation. We tell the passengers the purpose of the shutters is to shield them from the regular flashing caused by the movement of the train past the tunnel lights. Implication: they have a long journey ahead and we don't want the flashing to disturb their sleep. That's not the reason. The purpose of the shutters is to hide what the train is *really* doing."

"What is the train is doing that you don't want the passengers to see?"

"It's doing precisely nothing. That's the point. The train is at rest, with each carriage parked on top of a motion-simulation rig. Moving rollers engage the underside of the train to simulate the vibration of wheels, and each simulation rig independently rocks its carriage to create that instability you experience when you try to walk down the corridor of a moving train, particularly when you try to cross from one carriage to the next. On each side of the train, with its light only just visible through gaps in the shutters, is a single lamp moving round on a looped belt, to complete the trick of movement being played on the mind, which assumes the train is passing from one tunnel light to the next."

I said, "How do I know what you are telling me now is true and not a clumsy attempt to hide from me the real truth? I have been three journeys on the train. Many times I felt it accelerating in the tunnel. Twice in the dining car it braked and the waiter came flying down the aisle with his tray of drinks. You can't simulate that on a stationary rig."

The Earl smiled. "But you can! Each rig is fitted with a hydraulic ram to occasionally tip its carriage slightly up or down at one end, so it's not level. The pull of gravity on your body as you walk along the sloping carriage makes you think the train is accelerating or braking, depending on whether you are being made to walk slightly uphill or slightly downhill. If you could see out of the window, you'd know the carriage wasn't level but you can't see out of the window, can you? Your brain has told you that you are on a moving train, so it interprets the force on your body as the train changing speed. The simulator even changes the speed of its rollers in sync with the hydraulic jack, so your ear gets additional wheel noise feedback persuading you a real acceleration or deceleration is happening."

"Assuming for the moment you're not telling me another elaborate story, what then?"

"The simulator continues to run for the duration of the six-hour journey. Then it is switched off, the under-track wire is re-engaged and the train is drawn from the tunnel and into Island Station. You arrive on what you think is an isolated island where you have already, without knowing it, been psychologically prepared to accept the challenge of its isolation from modern civilisation.

You see, there is no island; there never was an island. And there is no ninety-mile tunnel, only an old salt mine tunnel, two miles in length. The tunnel leads under the hills to an isolated corner of our family estate, with no roads leading in or out, cut off by high hills and with the handy feature of a narrow sea inlet that makes it easy for us to deny access to the coast. All other escape routes are blocked with our research institute fences. I assume your capable researches took you to the institute buildings, so you will know they are fakes?"

"I sussed out the one on the island — I mean, the one closest to Nostalgia Town."

"You see how difficult it is not to think of it as an island? And all because of a train."

"So, this building I am in is your house?"

"Of course. You came in by the back entrance. Had you come round the front you would have recognised it and the game would be up."

"But I *didn't* come in the front entrance. You didn't need to tell me the truth. You could have bundled me back over the hills and I'd have been none the wiser."

"Too risky. You've seen too much. We need absolute control of what the islanders know. A person who knows even a little is a threat to us. As with John, they'll get inquisitive and they won't rest till they've found out the whole truth. And they might tell others what they know. We can't take the risk."

I asked, "The sculptress who moved to Dublin — I think her name was Mary somebody — did she guess the deception?"

"Amazing you managed to find out about her!" said the Earl, "She came to me and challenged me. She hadn't got everything right but her suspicions were uncomfortably near the truth. We terminated her residency immediately and gave her a generous compensation in exchange for her silence. There *are* a few people on the island who know everything: Jim, Molly and the other founding members, a few railway staff, the guards of course — and Saoirse."

At the mention of Saoirse's involvement, I felt a rising anger, "And how have you persuaded her to keep quiet? Because she's your mistress?"

The Earl laughed. "Who told you that one? Saoirse is the daughter of a best friend. He died many years ago. Saoirse is the oldest of the children brought up on the island. She has lived there most of her life. Her mother died when she was a toddler. That girl has learnt to cope with a lot of tragedy. I suppose that's what makes her so exceptional, plus her upbringing on the island until she went away to university."

Simultaneously, questions and realisations crowded in on my mind. "The railway tracks I crossed in the woodland before I entered your garden; they are the tracks between the tunnel and the mainland station?"

"Yes"

"Why is Island time thirty-eight minutes ahead of mainland time?"

"You like our little riddle? We did it to add to the disorientation, to help people feel far from the mainland"

"And the telegraph continues the charade of being cut off?"

"Yes. Plus, the lack of external phone lines avoids the problem of weather coincidences. Imagine somebody on the island regularly telephoning a friend on the mainland and each finding out the other enjoying identical weather. Somebody would put two and two together, sooner or later."

"Do telegrams have their contents edited?"

"Sometimes."

"What about letters?"

"Our postal department have got skilled at opening and resealing letters. Though, so far, there has only been one we needed to conveniently 'lose in the post'."

"And the confiscation of cameras at customs with people only permitted to use film processed in Nostalgia, is a further means of controlling information?"

"Yes"

"One thing I don't understand. The fake institute. What happens to all the supplies delivered by horse and cart?"

"Transferred to a Land Rover at night and driven back to our warehouses on the estate. Non-perishables are recycled as wholesale stock, to be sold back to the island. We repack them in cardboard boxes stamped with new serial numbers. My accountant does the necessary disguising in the books. Some perishables have to be composted. We don't like wasting anything, but it's a necessary evil."

I said, "That explains the mystery of the recycled centrifuge. Myself and someone else — I won't say who — couldn't understand why the same centrifuge was repeatedly delivered to the institute or how it managed to get off the island."

"Our security staff appear to have slipped up yet again," said the Earl. "All recycled goods are supposed to be fully repackaged to disguise the fact they are the same goods previously delivered."

"The packaging didn't give it away. Someone had scratched a doodle on the centrifuge base. It was spotted repeatedly coming into the goods yard. I thought it was the symbol of a secret society. I even managed to find it in a reference book in Dublin, the symbol of the African Trickster God."

"Well, in a sense, we were all tricked by it, weren't we?" said the Earl.

I asked, "I understand the purpose of the institute fences. I assume the fences on the cliffs and around the lighthouse were to deny a view of the sea."

"Not the sea, but the Irish coastline, which stretches for miles into the distance northwards, the sight of which would immediately tell anyone they weren't on the small island they were supposed to be on."

"And the lighthouse beam assisted the guards in preventing any night time breach of the fences?"

"Correct."

"I got inside the lighthouse on firework night. I saw a rocket in the sky. About four miles away."

"The town here announced a special firework celebration. We had to hurriedly arrange our Nostalgia display to coincide, to mask the distant sound of flaring rockets. You know, the threat of discovery from the air is the threat that worries us most."

"Is that why you cancelled the hot air ballooning festival and took legal action to prevent over-flying of your estate?"

"Yes. Though we couldn't prevent any government high altitude aerial surveys. That's a reason for the roof gardens and their greenery that we don't tell the townies. Camouflage. To make it look like an agricultural complex from above, rather than a town."

"And the cancelled motocross?"

"Too noisy. You could hear it for miles. Also, we needed the valley between here and Nostalgia to be deserted and unused, to act as a buffer zone. That's where we used to hold the motocross. The stream made a great race obstacle. You can still see the course, although what used to be dirt track is all grown over with grass now."

"He's seen it," said one of my pursuer guards.

264

"Oh. I see," said the Earl. "You came here up that valley."

I asked, "Is noise the reason you abandoned the clock tower project?"

"You were told about that, were you?" said the Earl, "I flew to Italy with my architect to look at an historic tower built halfway up a hill, just like we had proposed. I was horrified to find out how far the sound of the chimes travelled with the wind in the right direction."

"People in the town here might get curious as to the source?"

"Worse!" said the Earl, "Imagine an islander arriving at mainland station and hearing the familiar chimes of their island clock tower."

I thought for a few seconds. "The helicopter crashes. Were they genuine?"

"Helicopter *crash*, you mean. The year before the foundation of Nostalgia. Two people killed. On the hill where the lighthouse now stands"

"I discovered the wreckage, uncovered by the storm. I covered it over again"

"Did you, indeed? Most resourceful of you."

"Why didn't you get the wreckage removed?"

"A crazy legal quirk of the crash investigation. We had to leave it just as it fell. So we covered it over and left nature to do the rest."

"What happens if they re-open the investigation?"

"We'll meet that when it comes. However, I think it's unlikely to happen twenty years after the event."

"I investigated newspaper archives in Dublin. A second helicopter crashed at sea, never found."

"I don't know anything about that one. You thought the second crash must be the helicopter on the island, because you naturally assumed you were not at the site of the mainland crash?"

"Yes. Can I ask — the story you told me at my interview — ?"

"The tunnel digging story was all lies, of course. We didn't need to excavate, because the old salt mine tunnel already ran the two miles from end to end and the old nineteenth century mechanism for driving the wagons was, incredibly, still functioning. You may or may not have noticed the tall sheds at each end of the line. They hold the original winding gear, which we still use to drive the under-track cable. They are the oldest buildings on the estate."

I couldn't help exclaiming, "So that explains the noise!"

The Earl gave me a puzzled look. "Explains the noise?"

"Nothing. It's not important," I said. "Please go on."

I was thinking of Ben's report of the night time noise. What he'd heard in the middle of the night was the winding gear pulling the train off the simulator and into the station. But he wouldn't hear a noise when the train was going out, because it must be a two-engine system, the winding gear at the *mainland* end of the line needing to do the pulling in the other direction. Similarly, the fifteen minutes of noise he'd heard on the evenings the train was not on the island was the sound of the island winding gear

266

pulling the return train out of mainland station until it came to rest on the simulator.

The Earl continued, "We'd had an idea for the tunnel before: to create the world's biggest ghost train experience, a ghost train for adults. At the end of the line, you'd get to stay in the 'Amazing Floating Hippy Hotel', psychedelically floodlit at night, the latest thing in 'far-out' tourism. The floating hotel idea came about when we had the idea of making use of the harbour wall and port scheme from my father's time by channelling the sea to flood the land, creating an enormous artificial bay. And it might interest you to know that Nostalgia's town walls pre-date the town. Volunteers from a commune living on the land in the mid-sixties built them. They had a plan to create a fantasy medieval community, their one and only achievement, building the walls. They fell out with each other and the commune disbanded. A case of too many lords and ladies and not enough serfs. All these elements came together with a purpose when we planned our secret town."

"And the tidal sluice gates of the power station served the additional purpose of preventing people from getting through to the seashore? More convincing than running a barbed wire fence across the water?"

"You have everything well worked out," said the Earl.

"I do now. Before this morning, I'd have drawn a whole different set of conclusions. I feel like an idiot"

"No more than five thousand others, all of them intelligent and capable people. It just shows the power of suggestion."

"What I don't understand is why the need for secrecy? You admitted yourself nobody who goes to live in Nostalgia ever wants to leave."

"All this talking is making me thirsty," said the Earl, "and these lads need to get back to their duties. Come through to the library. I'll explain over tea."

The guards collected their rifles and left by the corridor to the garden. The sniffer dog, which previously I had been in such terror of confronting, a dirty and muddy, brown and white cocker spaniel, lay flat-out asleep on the mat behind the door. It made a sad whining noise when I bent down to stroke it, looking at me with pathetic eyes. It revived instantly, sitting to attention when I produced a lump of cheese from my bag. Meanwhile, its owner carried on walking into the garden, leaving the door open behind him. Inevitably the strain of disappearing owner got the better of the desire for more cheese and with a yelp the dog charged down the corridor, skidding on the floor matting, leaping from the doorway, racing, barking, across the lawn.

The Earl opened a door for me to pass through to the library, the scene of my job interview, all those weeks ago. Outside the window, the Type 39 Bugatti.

"So, you see, no more tricks," said the Earl. "You have no more doubts as to where you are, do you? Excuse me, while I go and report to the young lady as to how we are progressing."

"I'd like to speak with Saoirse," I said.

"Of course. She insists I tell you everything first, so you can understand why she had to act as she did, then she will meet with you in private."

I was left alone with my thoughts, my principal emotion being a dread of the impending showdown with Saoirse. I desperately wanted to see her again, to hold her, to hug her, to kiss her. At the same time, I felt intense bitterness over the great lie of Nostalgia, in which she had been actively and coldly complicit. A door opened and I stood to greet her but it was only the housekeeper bringing in the tea tray. After my long ordeal in the open, hot tea never tasted better. As I munched my way through a plate of biscuits, I felt physically and emotionally drained.

The Earl returned to the library.

Pouring some tea, he said, "There are two reasons for the secrecy, one external, one internal. Which do you want first?"

"The external"

"The easy one. Imagine the suited assholes in the corporates getting wind of Nostalgia. What an opportunity! A town of five thousand with money to spend? The supermarkets and DIY stores would have set up shop nearby in no time, decimating the economy, decimating our full employment statistics. How would that have played out with our youth? Forget the skills you have learned, forget the dignity of satisfying work; we'll give you a dumb-ass job stacking shelves. Either that or move to the big city, or emigrate like everyone else, and be grateful for any work you can get."

The Earl spoke with both passion and contempt. For him this was no capitalism versus socialism issue. The Earl was a confirmed capitalist, no doubt about that, an enormously rich and successful capitalist also. What infuriated him was not capitalism but the blind, thoughtless application of capitalism — the career ladder where every employee is protecting their own backside, all decisions must be in the interests of "the company", responsibility to the wider world doesn't come in to it, except as a cynical, insincere marketing ploy. I thought of Ma Thatcher and her cronies in my own country and their decimation of the social fabric of whole communities in the north of England, all in the name of economic reality. There had to be a more responsible, less one-sided way of practising successful economics than that.

"And the internal?"

"More difficult to justify. We were certain our experiment would stand no chance if people could simply drive down the road or up to the cities for what they needed. We had to enforce a collective reliance for the community to have any chance of establishing itself. So the founder members agreed a pact. Each new person invited to the island would be told the story about the tunnel railway. The simulator we installed at the outset. Old technology now; cutting-edge twenty years ago. Hugely expensive, as you can imagine, but I'm a multi-millionaire, I don't sail yachts, I don't go to casinos, I have to have something to spend my money on."

"You spared no expense on the inside of the train either."

"Also part of our big equation of impressions. Make it a special occasion for people, emphasising the special nature of the journey they think they are undertaking. Furthermore, we had to justify setting an expensive ticket price. With cheap tickets, people would be asking for more trains to be laid on, so they could travel more frequently. We couldn't risk people becoming fond of the mainland, taking the island for granted. So we used price to effectively restrict their travel to once a year."

"When did the fences go up?"

"We had the fences, the lighthouse and the fake institute buildings all in place before our invited inhabitants took up residence."

"Did any of the new residents guess the secret?"

"None. Many of the island's founders were sceptical the deception would work. We were all amazed, I think, that we got away with it so easily."

"Jim Braben showed me his photograph albums with the pictures of Nostalgia gradually being built."

"It took ten years for the building work to be completed. We brought in building materials by dirt road, stacking them near the train station to give the impression they'd been delivered by railway. Secret lorry loads arrived nightly, supposedly by goods train. Of course, our guards had to be in on the deception, the train drivers too, all paid generously to keep their mouths shut. They knew they'd never get such an easy, well-paid number anywhere else."

"How did you hide all those people on the payroll and all the town's commercial profit from the tax man?"

"We didn't. We accounted for everything. We'd not risk drawing attention to ourselves by cheating on our public obligations. From the taxman's point of view, the declared activity represented one subsection of the total commercial activity on my estate land. Which of course, it was! Only the residents of Nostalgia thought they were working elsewhere."

"Don't you feel guilty about deceiving all those people?"

"Yes. Of course. On the other hand, look what a wonderful life they have been given by the deception. The founders originally agreed to reveal the secret after five years, but the longer we went on, the more the town grew, the more success it demonstrated, the more precious it became for us, the more difficult to risk everything by telling all. After so long deceiving people, we were stuck with maintaining our deception. Then we made our first mistake."

"Which was?"

"Employing an outsider. Employing John. If I can explain it to you, it's similar to when people join a religious cult. Because they personally get benefit from the cult, they become immunised against seeing the faults of the cult so transparently obvious to outsiders who have no vested interest. As I told you at your interview, people become islanders by invitation; they are already highly motivated to make a success when they join the community. Effectively they become self-censoring and won't ask awkward questions. With John, we hadn't understood that as a former journalist the island was no more than another investigative assignment for him."

"Couldn't you have got somebody from your own community to do the work?"

"We tried and failed. What's unique about John is his command of the English language mixed with his high level of technical understanding, plus his skill at organising information, professionally just what we needed. Then we compounded the first mistake with a second: employing *you*. Although we had no direct evidence you knew anything, it became clear you weren't going to be as easily fooled into giving away information as we had hoped. We had no idea you'd advanced your suspicions so far, nor that you could evade our surveillance so brilliantly. We had you followed in town, and the ferry and causeway watched when you were back on Little Island. We still don't know how or when you managed your vanishing act."

"At three o'clock in the morning. I guessed the front of Little Island was being watched, so I left from the back, by rowing boat, across the bay to the cliffs."

"That's a substantial distance to row."

"I rowed for my university."

"Saoirse never told me."

"She doesn't know."

"Isn't it the sort of achievement a young man can use to impress an attractive girl?"

"I have my reasons. They're personal."

"We didn't know whether you had detected our surveillance. Even after Tadhg put a spanner in the works by letting him see you when he was supposed to be on the mainland, my spies tell me you acted like you weren't concerned about it."

"Why was he following me?"

"He wasn't. He left on the overnight train for the start of his mainland shift. Next morning he'd put on his green guard uniform, when he realised he'd mislaid his surveillance book. He'd taken it to the hotel the previous day to report to the guard sergeant. He panicked, thinking the hotel cleaner would find it and give it to you, as it was full of photographs of yourself. He broke the number one rule for guards. He crossed the buffer zone between the two fences. Guards are only permitted to travel to and fro by train, for precisely the reason they might slip up and show their face in the town when they are supposed to be ninety miles and a six-hour journey away on the mainland. We wouldn't have found out the incident if one of our spy nurses hadn't overheard you talking about it to John. Tadhg was lucky. The only reason he avoided instant dismissal was because we needed to keep him available to test your reaction to meeting him again. Next time you did see him, with Colm, Saoirse and Molly as witnesses, they said you kept your cool admirably. You gave nothing away."

"That's because I had been observing them from inside the gate tower. I had plenty of time to compose myself. *They* were the ones who were flustered. I was the last person they were expecting to see at that moment, I imagine."

"I think we're done," said the Earl. "Thank you for being so cooperative with this little inquest on our security procedures. I'll go and ask Saoirse to come to you now. If you have any further questions, she will answer them."

He shook my hand warmly. "As a Nostalgia resident, you were exemplary. A real asset to the community. Believe me when I say I am personally devastated we cannot allow you to stay, but it's a risk we can't allow ourselves to take, even for someone of your ability and resourcefulness."

The Earl left the room and once again I gathered my emotions in anticipation of meeting Saoirse.

Chapter 45

The End of the Road

I'd decided to play it cool with Saoirse, I suppose because of my bitterness over her knowing the truth from the outset and allowing me to go on being deceived. However, at the sight of her, all resistance melted. We held each other tightly, crying with relief we could finally put the deception behind us.

I asked, "Why didn't you tell me the truth?"

Saoirse replied, "It's my job to protect the secret of the island. It's not mine to give away. I didn't know I was going to fall in love with you."

"And when you felt yourself getting in too deep, you went back to the mainland?"

"I didn't know what to do. I'm so sorry for all the hurt I caused you."

"It reached a real low point yesterday. I watched you at the Rebel Inn. I guess it's somewhere down the coast from here."

"Yes. I took one of our suppliers to lunch. How on earth!"

"I was determined to verify what I thought was on the other side of the island. I stole some binoculars from a guards' cottage and got down to the beach. I'd been scanning the inn from across the water for hours, when you and the guy came down."

Saoirse hugged me close. "My poor darling. What you must have thought of me. That I'd lied to you yet again."

"I didn't know what to think. Seeing you confused me completely. If it hadn't been for that, I might have picked up on three vital clues. The pub opening, the first lunch party and the second lunch party all happened around forty minutes later than normal. Why? Because of the Rebel Inn being a *mainland* pub. My watch was set to island time, thirty-eight minutes ahead. It should have told me I was looking at the mainland, not the island."

"What would you have felt there?" asked Saoirse.

"Extra determined to get to the other side of the water. I might even have risked swimming across. Saoirse, a few days ago you said you dreaded my finding out the truth. Now I've found out the truth, you know the Earl's told me I can never return to Nostalgia?"

"*That's* what I was dreading."

"Will you come away with me? To Singapore? I've been offered a job there."

"I can't. My whole life is Nostalgia. I can't possibly go anywhere else."

"Then I won't go to Singapore. I'll live in the town here, and when you have to be in Nostalgia for work it'll be like you've gone up to Dublin for the fortnight."

Saoirse shook her head. "That wouldn't do at all. You'd hate it. And where would you get suitable employment in this area, with *your* skills? You'd end up resentful. Nostalgia would come between us. I don't want a repeat of that pain."

"But there's going to be pain if we have to separate, yet again."

Saoirse sat for a few seconds, deep in thought. She said, "Go to Singapore. Take the new job. I'll keep pleading with them here till I can find a way to get you back."

"Is that what you want? What's the likelihood I'll be allowed back?"

"Zero. But I'll not give up without a fight. Here! I've got some photographs to show you."

Saoirse handed me a set of photographs of the two of us walking round Nostalgia, laughing and joking together. "Jim gave them to me. His wife said we make a lovely couple and it's wrong for the estate to keep them as surveillance photographs, because they're personal."

 "Who took them?"

"Tadhg. I spotted him taking one from inside a gate tower. I was terrified you might have seen him."

A plaintive meow interrupted us. Saoirse picked up a grey bundle from behind the sofa. "Remember this? The Earl's adopted her."

The animal began to purr as I stroked its head. "That was all a story about it hiding on the train? More likely it strayed across the fields and scaled the security fence."

"The other strays also. Though we'll never know for sure, as we can't ask them."

With the arrival of the cat, our conversation made the transition from controversy to reminiscence of all the times we had enjoyed together in Nostalgia, a place that, now I could no longer go there, had already become a memory from a past life. Midday, the housekeeper brought Saoirse and I lunch in the Earl's dining room, after which Saoirse said she had "things to organise" and would be leaving me for two hours. She suggested I get some sleep, to recover from my early morning ordeal. I slept on one of the couches in the library and dreamt of a Trickster God party. One by one, each trickster removed his mask, revealing the benign visage of the Earl, laughing uproariously at his success in fooling everyone with his elaborately devised schemes of misdirection.

I would have gone on sleeping the rest of the day and the night, had I not been awakened by my farewell committee. I wasn't ready for the calculated thoroughness with which they packed me off. Tadhg and Colm arrived with my suitcase, hastily filled with the things from my hotel room, minus my Nostalgia research notes and photographs, which they kept out. The estate manager had been busy booking me in for an overnight stay at a Dublin airport hotel, prior to a flight taking me back to England the following morning. From the local bank he had obtained several hundred pounds in sterling to cover any hotel or travel expenses I might incur on arrival.

I asked what would happen to John. Tadhg told me the hospital had removed the plaster cast from his leg and tonight under cover of darkness he would be taken through the fences to the fake institute. From there they would drive him by Land Rover to the estate, where, tomorrow morning, the Earl and Saoirse would tell him the truth about Nostalgia. I wrote a note for John, reassuring him of what he would be shown, that I had successfully crossed the land from Nostalgia to the Earl's home. In the hope of easing any doubts John might have,

I attached his lost credit card, telling him precisely where I had found it.

We went out to the front of the house, where they'd parked the car to take me to Dublin. Tadhg apologised for having been my principal minder. I said I understood he was only doing his job. We shook hands. Saoirse and I got in the car and we sped off up the driveway.

On the old road network, you journeyed to Dublin slowly and laboriously. We stopped twice, first at a quaint country café, later at a pub, painfully reminding me of the many times Saoirse and I had met for a meal in Nostalgia, occasions that would be no more.

We arrived at the airport hotel in the evening. Before we got out of the car, I asked, "Saoirse, does it have to be this way?"

"The more we prolong it, the more impossible it will get," she replied. "It's almost impossible already. Don't think of this as the end of the road. There's still hope for us."

I said, "Stay the night with me."

"I can't," she replied. "I'm meeting with the Earl and John first thing in the morning. I'm driving back tonight, getting a few hours' rest at a friend's house on the way."

She came in to reception to put the booking on the Earl's account. The hotel clerk gave me the usual form to fill in: signature, phone number and so on. I turned to say something to Saoirse but she was no longer standing beside me. "Excuse me," I said to the clerk, "I'm going to say goodbye to my friend." A party of tourists, laden with bags, were pushing their way into the hotel entrance. Only a few seconds wait but an agony of a delay. When I got outside, Saoirse had gone out of my life.

Chapter 46

Return to Europe

 "I know you're going back there," said my wife, Fionnuala.

The week I commenced work at the bank in Singapore, I met Fionnuala. She worked on the floor below mine, floor 58 to be precise. We met in the express lift one morning. Next morning, we met again and I asked her out. A whirlwind romance. A year later, we married.

Three years older than me, Australian, of Irish ancestry, and beautiful, I told Fionnuala of Nostalgia the night we got engaged. Although I had made a promise not to reveal the secret to anyone, it hardly seemed fair to my future wife not to share it with her. The story fascinated her, as she had never been to Ireland. However, I took care to play down my relationship with Saoirse, describing her merely as a colleague, my supervisor on the island. Neither did I tell Fionnuala of the letter I sent from Singapore informing Saoirse of my marriage, a letter in which I cruelly omitted to include my new address.

Four years on, still working for the bank, rapid promotion had brought me a high salary and a pension plan. We had two young children, a boy and a girl. I was content. At least that's what I liked to pretend at the time.

My parents emigrated to Melbourne after travelling over for our wedding in Australia and falling in love with the climate. My grandparents also emigrated to join them. My grandfather said he had no regrets leaving a home town no longer the thriving seaside resort he had known in his youth. With none of my family remaining in England, I'd no reason to return to Europe, until my company asked me to represent them at an international bank security conference in Dublin.

"It's no use pretending. You want to find out what happened to *her*," my wife persisted. "Ever since you received the invitation to the conference in Dublin, you've been distracted."

"That was all four years ago."

"Four years is not that long a time," said Fionnuala, leaving the bedroom. From down the corridor she called out, "Just remember when you are over there, you have a wife and two children waiting for you back in Singapore."

I called back, "I don't understand what you're saying."

Fionnuala returned, carrying a suitcase. "I'm being hard on you, I know. Why *shouldn't* you be curious to know how their experiment is progressing?"

"I'll be in Dublin. I don't know that I'll have time to get down to West Cork."

Drawers were being opened and assorted items of clothing rapidly and efficiently filling the suitcase. "How can you not go a few hundred miles more after travelling all that way?" said Fionnuala, "I don't believe you!"

"There's no guarantee they'll let me in to Nostalgia again. You know what I told you. They're paranoid about outsiders revealing the secret to the inhabitants."

Fionnuala looked at me with a searching expression. "But you could still get to meet with *her* though, couldn't you — at the Earl's mansion?"

283

I decided to use humour, as a decoy from questions getting uncomfortably close. "I don't know she'll still be there. She may have met somebody from outside Nostalgia, got married and moved away. She could be living anywhere. She could be here in Singapore. I might know her husband. I know who it is! It's your old boyfriend, Philip."

Fionnuala look at me wide-eyed. "Philip!"

"Yes. Didn't you say you'd heard he'd got married? We'll meet him in the street and he'll say we must come to dinner, and when we get there it will be Saoirse, and you'll ask how married life's treating him, and he'll say he's disappointed and he'd like you back and would your husband like to swap wives, and I'll say yes please!"

Fionnuala laughed at my joke at her doleful old boyfriend's expense but I knew she had formed doubts over the veracity of my version of my Irish past. As appeasement, I offered to take her and the children with me but she thought it too long a journey to inflict on the little ones.

I arrived in Dublin in the middle of May. The Irish weather felt decidedly chilly after the heat and humidity of Singapore. It's funny; until that moment I had not considered the extent to which a freak spell of exceptional weather back in 1990 may have coloured my impression of Nostalgia. I'd believed I had arrived on an island ninety miles from the mainland, an island that had its own microclimate, not subject to Irish weather rules, with cloudless blue skies and uninterrupted summer sunshine the norm for the place. Fancifully I imagined now if ever the weather angels smiled on a developing relationship, it was back then.

The conference in Dublin initially engaged me but, as the week dragged on, I found my thoughts increasingly distracted. The hurt and pain of the enforced separation from Saoirse began to intrude once more. How ridiculous to be reliving an old passion when I had such a beautiful family and secure, happy life in Singapore. Foolish to entertain hopes that might be dashed by finding out she no longer lived in the area. I imagined tea in the library with the Earl, my looking at the door, thinking Saoirse might enter at any moment, then being told she had married and emigrated, and nobody knew where she lived or what she was doing.

On the penultimate day of the conference, the suspense overcame me. At lunchtime, while one of the attendees regaled me with a tedious monologue on the subject of computer viruses, I decided to check out from my hotel and forgo the final day. I took a late train down to Cork, where I stayed overnight. On a grey, wet and blustery early morning, I collected a car from a rental depot and drove the three-hour journey to the coast.

My destination town looked exactly as I remembered it when I'd stood on the pavement waiting for my luggage, with Saoirse speeding past in the Bugatti. Driving out towards the Earl's estate and entering the driveway through the gates, immediately the state of the security fences indicated something seriously wrong. At several points, great gaps had been made and dirt tracks bulldozed through. Sheep and cattle grazed in the fields, ironically a sight never seen when those fields supposedly belonged to an agricultural institute.

My heart sank when I came to the house, the windows pasted over with "For Sale" signs, giving the phone number of an auctioneer in Cork city. On the hill opposite, the institute building was no more. I drove on in the direction of the railway station. Neither security fence nor guard post blocked my way. I found the station empty, the side gate to the platform unlocked, the railway-track overgrown with weeds. I walked the line, crossing the point where the woodland path goes on down to the maze. Last time here, I ran in terror of pursuit. Half a mile further, I came to the entrance to the tunnel, blocked by a sturdy metal grill.

A manic desire gripped me to get through to the other side. I could have tried to navigate the hills but, wary of the distance and the stormy weather, I knew what I desired to be only a two-mile walk through that tunnel. I might find a place like this, derelict, abandoned, grey and windswept, a mirror held up to my heart. Whatever I should find, I had to know what had become of her. I drove back to the town at top speed. In a hardware shop I purchased two powerful torches, the strongest pair of bolt cutters they had in stock, a woolly hat to protect against the cold and damp, and a small carpentry tool bag, into which I threw a selection of tools in case I should need them: pliers, jemmy, claw hammer, screwdrivers and so on. A real house burglar's kit. The shop man looked at me dubiously. As I returned to the estate, I could hear the voice of my wife saying to me over and over "Just remember you have a wife and two children waiting for you back in Singapore." Was the tunnel safe? Would I be overcome by fumes half way through and be brought out as an unfortunate corpse, like a nineteenth century salt miner starved of oxygen? I took no notice of the warnings of my mind. Desire drove me on.

As it happened, I had no need of wire cutters, nor torches, nor jemmy. Arriving back at the estate gates, I spotted what I had not seen before, a signpost labelled "Nostalgia". That surely meant the community had gone public. I followed a smooth and recently tarmac'd road. Two miles along, I passed a large supermarket. The Earl won't like that, I thought! Then, just as the road came over the brow of a hill, the clouds parted and the sun came out. I stopped the car and got out to survey the scene before me: Nostalgia Town, Little Island, the wide bay, the golden sands and the calm blue water. The weather angels were back on side.

I had never seen the town from this angle before. Where I stood had been one of the far hills beyond the security fences when I lived in Nostalgia. In the past I had looked this way many times, wondering what lay beyond. The new road swept down through what had previously been heath land, crossing the canal on a bridge and entering through a cut in the walls near South Gate. It took me a moment to figure out why the town looked so different. The surrounding fences had gone. My eye followed the cliffs down from the lighthouse to the power station and up to the cliffs on the other side. No evidence of a fence anywhere.

I got back in the car and drove down, eager to discover what had happened, for better or for worse. Passing though the new gap in the wall, I drove onto a paved area having the signage "Commons Car Park". Although I knew the street plan of Nostalgia intimately, this development confused my sense of direction. Taking my bearings from South Gate I could see a large area of the former allotments had been taken over in the service of the motorcar, which, in this part of town at least, had been given precedence over self-sufficiency. Going up onto the wall and walking round, I noted that, outside of the spoiled land at The Commons, little had changed, the same familiar buildings, water flowing in the rooftop solar panels, the roof gardens still cared for. My spirits rose. The state of the railway and the addition of a car park had prepared me for catastrophe.

I stopped first at Canal Gate cottage where Saoirse had been a lodger. I rang the doorbell several times. No answer. I thought of leaving a note with my mobile phone number. Was their clunky old telephone system even connected to the outside world yet?

Back up on the wall I continued round to Centre Gate, then descended to the main shopping street, as busy as ever, but with people conventionally dressed, the distinctive fashions of Nostalgia having been replaced by conformity to the outside world. Though many of the shops were as I remembered, several were empty, with "To Let" signs stuck on their windows. On the other hand, a conspicuous new arrival, a butchers, was doing a flourishing trade, with a queue of people waiting to be served, the butcher moving animatedly behind his counter, picking up and holding out for inspection large slabs of blood red meat. Outside the door of the shop, an aged spaniel looked mournfully in: my sniffer-dog pursuer. I patted it, fussed over it, hugged it, a tear in my eye.

On the quays I enquired of a fisherman whether Fierce Hot still worked the ferry.

"He passed away last year," said the man. "The ferry stopped running when the hotel closed. No trade. Little Island is cut off at high tide now to anyone who doesn't have their own rowing boat. Funny how people got used to it. They adapted their lives to fit."

I climbed down the old ferry steps and walked across the dry sands of low tide to the hotel. I fully expected to find it boarded up, the garden overgrown with weeds, a sorry sight. Not so. The garden had tables and chairs out; people sat outside in the sunshine with drinks. Chalked up on a notice board by the door: "Under New Management. Grand Opening Dance Party Tonight. Vacancies."

The manageress greeted me at the front desk. I had the honour of being their first guest of the re-opening, so no problem obtaining my old room. Strange to be back in the room I had last seen at three in the morning on the night of my escape. The decor had changed but otherwise everything was as I remembered. Opening the wardrobe to hang up my clothes, I found inside the pile of books that had once adorned my bedroom shelf, including *Applied Mathematics*. I fully expected Sally Macnamara's gold ankle chain to have been removed from its cut-away hiding place, but it had not. I considered taking it home as a souvenir but hesitated, because of the difficulty of explaining the object to my wife, so I returned it to its secret hollow, to be discovered and puzzled over by posterity.

From the hotel I walked the length of the sands towards the coast. The families on the beach and the children playing in the water reminded me of happier times past. Would it have been better, knowing what I knew now, not to have undertaken my expedition that night? I'd expected to be safely back by evening and out and about on my work assignment for the next two weeks, awaiting my reunion with Saoirse and the lovemaking we had pledged.

The fairground displayed a notice saying it would be closed at the end of the school holidays. The ghost train had gone, replaced by a modern ride. As I passed by the hospital, someone called out my name. I kept walking. I had no desire to talk. I wanted to delay the inevitability of the unwelcome news to the last moment. This was not Saoirse's Nostalgia, the town she had loved and for which she had sacrificed our relationship. I could not imagine for one moment she had wanted to stay.

Reaching the end of the beach, I took the road past the Irish cottage. Somebody had parked an expensive Mercedes outside the garden gate. How times had changed! I decided to make a sentimental journey through the woods. Last time here, I ran with the exultation of my quest. No way did I think the next time I would tread this path would be as a bank security consultant, married with two kids and a pension plan.

Halfway through the woods, I lost heart. I couldn't face the depressing sight of a yet another derelict railway station. I would go down to the cove. It might be as in a romantic novel. I'd find *her* there, waiting for me.

A man came from the Irish cottage with a suitcase and put it in the Mercedes. "Great weather, isn't it," he said, as I passed. "In fact, just like four years ago. You've brought the sun with you again."

It was John, now severely balding, which made him look a lot older, so I hadn't recognised him. We shook hands.

"What an amazing coincidence finding you here," I said. "I'm only here a short while."

"And I'm just off for the weekend," said John. "We almost missed each other."

"You live here?"

"Our second year in the cottage. My wife and I have a kid now. And you?"

"Married with two children. Living in Singapore"

"You had an interview, didn't you? I remember. So when they wouldn't let you back in Nostalgia, that's where you went?"

"Yes."

"Come inside and meet the family." He ushered me inside into their kitchen. "Here we are. You two know each other, of course."

Saoirse was sitting on an chair, facing away from me, feeding a small child from a bottle. She turned to look and her face broadened into a smile of welcome. "Hello! How lovely to see you again! Wait till I've finished giving little Timmy his bottle, then I'll come over and give you a big kiss."

Hiding a disappointment more bitter than if I had found out Saoirse no longer lived in Nostalgia, I remarked, "The baby looks just like you, John."

"There you are, John! See! He *does* look like you!" said Saoirse, "John thinks little Timmy's more like me than him."

"I'd say both," I said tactfully.

"John's going with Timmy to his parents for the weekend."

"Aren't you going?"

"His mother and I had a falling out. It's awkward. I expect we'll patch things up but I'm happy to get a break."

Saoirse handed Little Timmy to John. We embraced and kissed each other on the cheek.

I said, "Something went seriously wrong here."

"You can say that again!" said Saoirse.

"We were found out," said John. "The second year after you left us."

"By an outsider?"

"An insider."

"Someone who'd formed suspicions?"

"A complete innocent," replied Saoirse. "Pure chance he found us out."

"All those miles of fencing," said John, "all those guards, all that security, and in the end given away by something the size of a One Pebble coin. Anyway, that's a long story. We'll tell it to you some time. As you have seen, Nostalgia has succumbed to the automobile."

"What *have* you seen?" asked Saoirse.

"I drove to the estate first. I found the house and railway station boarded up and derelict. What happened to the Earl?"

"He died last July, leaving nobody to inherit," said Saoirse. "The legal tussle over the fortune might go on for years."

"He wasn't that old."

"He had a heart condition. That and the strain of the collapse of his dream killed him."

John said, "As soon as the secret of Nostalgia was revealed, it went from the sublime to the ridiculous, one day living peacefully on a remote island, the next back to 'civilisation' with hordes of mainlanders driving across the hills in their cars. The sports fields on The Commons became one giant car park. TV crews here, the lot. Good for business though."

"Initially *very* good for business," added Saoirse. "The bank made a pile from the currency exchange, because of course people were fascinated by everything unusual, wanting to buy it all up: the electrical goods, the cameras, the beers, the confectionery, anything that made a souvenir. And, of course, the designer handbags. And the clothes, *especially* the clothes."

"The economy collapsed?" I asked.

"The problems started with the simultaneous shutdown of several of the staple incomes of the island," replied John. "The town no longer needed guards, only a few retained as traffic wardens. So all their spending money went away. And without the guaranteed income from accommodating guards the hotel only limped along, eventually closing. The railway suffered the most. The train stopped its fake overnight runs. Who'd pay a fortune for the train when they could walk or drive across the estate land? No longer any need to employ all those stewards, chefs, waiters and railway workers."

Saoirse added, "The shops suffered next, not just because of the unemployment but because the inhabitants of Nostalgia were now purchasing cars and using them to drive to neighbouring towns and beyond for their shopping."

"I suppose they lost all those orders for the fake institute?"

John laughed. "They were furious when they found out they'd been duped into supplying the same goods over and over, and outraged at all the quality food ending up in compost bins. Even though they'd profited handsomely, the wastage offended their conservationist sensibilities."

"I see there's a big supermarket the other side of the hill now."

"That came as soon as we got a tarmac'd road," said John.

"But it's not doing well," said Saoirse. "Serves them right. There's starting to be a backlash. I've been running a sustained campaign for people to buy local. Nostalgia's beginning to revive."

"You've got the local papers on your side, I expect?"

John and Saoirse both laughed.

I asked, "Did I say something funny?"

Saoirse said, "There's only one local paper now and it's not difficult to get it on side when your husband is editor-in-chief."

"We won a national journalism award," said John.

I said, "With you in charge, that doesn't surprise me at all! I see somebody's taken over the hotel."

Saoirse said, looking at John, "We don't have a lot of faith in the woman, do we? She's very nice; I'm sure it will be clean and well run but she's clueless about marketing. The sluice gate mechanism is still operational, so the hotel still looks like it's floating at high tide. If I owned the hotel, I'd be marketing it as the 'Incredible Floating Hotel'. It doesn't matter how good you are at running a place, it's nothing without customers. Tonight's the opening night. They're having a celebration dance. I don't know if she has any room bookings yet."

I said nothing.

"Are you here long?" asked John.

"My flight for Singapore leaves tomorrow." I lied. The flight left the day after that.

"So you're driving back today?"

I thought of John going away for the weekend. "Yes."

"That's a pity. You could have stayed at the hotel. You and Saoirse managed it once, didn't you? Why don't you persuade your wife to move over here and come and manage the hotel with you?"

We all laughed at this suggestion.

"Would you like a coffee?" asked Saoirse, "I'll put the kettle on. I'm sorry, we're going to be very rude and abandon you while we finish packing. I have to make sure John's got the baby's feeding gear."

"*I* know what he can do!" said John, "He can read Diarmuid's letter."

"Who's that?" I asked.

"Diarmuid Murphy," said John, "is the guy who blew Nostalgia's cover. The first person after yourself to discover the secret."

"The week after we got married," added Saoirse. "We came back from our honeymoon to find everything totally changed. Ironic really. Diarmuid was one of the people who I'd worked most closely with, so I asked if he'd give me away at my wedding. We didn't know at the time but apparently he and his wife had already figured out Nostalgia wasn't on an island. They were only waiting for the opportunity to confirm their suspicions."

John said, "The Nostalgia archives you and I worked on you'll be pleased to hear have become part of an officially curated archive in the town museum. One thing missing, though. We didn't have the story of how the experiment came to an end. I wrote to Diarmuid and he sent me a detailed letter explaining how he uncovered the secret by the merest chance. The original of the letter is in the archives. I have a copy here."

So saying, John opened a drawer and took out some photocopied sheets, which had been stapled together.

Chapter 47

Diarmuid's Story

Dear John,

I am writing this letter to you under protest, as you tell me you and your former colleague knew the secret of Nostalgia Island long before anyone else but did nothing about your discovery. Excuse me if I accuse you of cowardice and duplicity, washing your hands of the affair, leaving the rest of us to go on being deceived. We made great sacrifices for that place, cutting ourselves off from friends, denying ourselves travel opportunities we might otherwise have had, forgoing the pleasure and freedom of owning and driving a car, all because we were tricked into believing we had no access to the outside world beyond an expensive ninety-mile undersea train trip once a year. It's amazing we were taken in by the deception but the fact we *were* taken in does not excuse those who conspired to deceive us.

However, that said, I will accede to your request, only because I understand you are writing a detailed history of Nostalgia Island from its beginnings up to the present. Such a history cannot be called complete without telling how the whole caboodle unravelled, and, since I was the chief agent of the unravelling, you need to hear my story.

Firstly, to clarify some relevant details that people need to know. I trained as a biologist, my doctorate obtained through a study of the ecology of salt marshes. I wrote the occasional article for the journals, not only about salt marshes but also on general topics of interest to ecologists.

After I had published an article about managing the interaction between towns and the local natural environment, for the benefit of both, the Earl contacted me. He made a generous offer of sponsorship for research on salt marsh ecology, with only two conditions attached: the work must be done in Ireland and I should visit him in person to report on progress. However, whenever I met the Earl, he asked only token questions about my research. Instead, he showed more interest in discussing with me the relationship of towns to their environment. Later on, his questions became more personal, probing my life story, asking about my closest friends, how many of my relatives were still alive, and so on.

I challenged him on what I considered to be entirely inappropriate questioning and that's when he told me the story of Nostalgia, the ninety-mile tunnel, the isolated island, the idealistic community. He offered me a job as their environmental manager. So I went to live on the fascinating island, got bitten by the "Nostalgia bug", got married there, had a child there and lost contact with my former "mainland" friends, replacing them with friends from my new life on the island.

My work frequently took me in close proximity to the security fences. I was not at all happy about these military installations but, as for everyone else, life was good, so it was convenient to explain them away as a necessary evil. The fact they did no actual farming on the land near the institute did not worry me. I assumed it functioned as a neutral buffer zone between island agriculture and institute research projects on the other side of the hills.

In October of the particular year relevant to the downfall of Nostalgia, I received an invitation to give a paper at a scientific conference in Dublin. I contracted food poisoning when away and was not at all recovered when I got back on the Nostalgia train, extremely annoying, as the chief pleasure of travelling on the train, as you know, was the excellent cuisine, which I had to decline. I had to be content with a brandy, which I took back to my compartment.

Missing dinner wasn't the only annoying thing. My rucksack had been stolen in Dublin and I had been obliged to buy a replacement in a camping shop. This I now took off the luggage rack, placed on the bedside table and took out a paperback novel to read. As the train left the station, a movement distracted my attention. Attached to one of the shoulder straps, I saw something I hadn't noticed when I bought the rucksack: a miniature compass. As the train curved round on the track, the needle moved so as to continue to point to magnetic north. It implied the train was pointing north-east, which would have taken us inland.

The train stopped where they fix the shutters for the night journey. When it started off again, I expected the direction of the train indicated by my compass to change. The needle stubbornly refused to move. I concluded the compass must be faulty, the usual cheap rubbish you might expect to buy in a cut price store, and thought no more of it.

Awake the whole night due to my upset stomach, anytime I happened to look at the compass it still indicated travelling north-east. Six hours later, we arrived at the point where the train stops prior to exiting the tunnel. My compass still pointed in the wrong direction. Then a curious thing happened. As soon as the train began moving, the compass needle moved round as the train followed the curve of the tunnel and came out to Island station. Too much of a coincidence my compass was working only up to the shutters going up and then only starting working again at the end of the journey. The inescapable conclusion was for six hours the train had been travelling the wrong way!

When I got home, I plotted on a map where the train would have arrived, assuming a minimum speed of one mile an hour and a maximum speed of fifteen miles an hour. No way could a train in this speed range be anywhere off Ireland's coast; it would have to be inland. It was possible the train travelled faster than we had been told and had come out beyond the east coast of Ireland. This would imply a tunnel of improbable length for the technology of the time — even a ninety-mile tunnel was already a fantastic achievement.

I told my wife the puzzle. She suggested the compass needle might be slightly bent, so it had got stuck on north east. She asked, "How did the old sailing ships navigate?"

I explained they could determine their north–south location by measuring the angle between certain stars and the horizon.

"Could you pick out those stars?" she asked.

I said that I could, as astronomy had been a teenage hobby of mine.

"Why don't you try it?" she asked.

Such an obvious suggestion, amazing that nobody on the island had thought to do it out of curiosity. We had to wait several nights for a clear sky. When one came, I calculated us to be at the exact same latitude as the Earl's estate.

"That's settled!" I said. "The compass is faulty. The train travelled neither north nor south but directly out to sea. The compass indicated the train moving north-east when it should have been indicating west."

My wife asked again, "How did the old sailing ships know their east–west position?"

"That was a big problem which, until solved, caused a vast number of shipwrecks. They could only calculate longitude by comparing the time of their midday sun to the time of the midday sun at the port where they began their journey"

"Surely that was easy," said my wife. "They had clocks, didn't they? Couldn't they just set their clock to the time at the port of embarkation? As long as they remembered to keep the clock wound up, they'd be OK."

"An ordinary clock's no good at sea," I replied. "The damp salty air, the extremes of temperature, the rocking of the old sailing ships, made them unreliable. Only when they invented the chronometer did they have a reliable instrument for measuring time."

"You haven't been at sea," said my wife. "You've only been in a tunnel, and your watch is digital, not mechanical. You could find out the time of the midday sun tomorrow."

Next day, we measured it using my watch. "About forty minutes later than the mainland," I said.

With her penchant for spotting the obvious, my wife corrected me, "The *same* as the mainland. Island time has the clocks put forward by thirty-eight minutes, so the astronomical midday point would seem to be lagging the mainland by thirty-eight minutes. You set your watch forward last time you arrived back from the mainland, didn't you?"

I confirmed that I did.

"But, if according to the stars we are no further south or north than the estate, and, if according to the sun we are no further east or west of the estate, there's only one place we *can* be," said my wife. "Still on the estate!"

This was too outlandish an idea to accept, particularly when set against the experience of all-night travel on the train. I devised some experimental apparatus to make an accurate measurement of the sun's angle above the horizon but we had to wait an infuriating number of weeks of typical overcast Irish weather before being able to test it out. Eventually I set up my equipment on a sufficiently sunny day, on the ridge above the reservoir. The measurements confirmed our worse suspicions.

I suggested to my wife we could be on an island a short distance off the coast bordering the estate land.

She replied, "More difficult to understand is where the train goes all night?"

I said, "My theory is the train moves slowly east for six hours. At the end, it starts to travel west again, but faster, to get back to the estate and then travel the extra mile or so off the coast. The idea is to trick us into thinking the island is a long way off and isolated."

My wife said, "If only we could get over the fences we could confirm where we are."

Then, the penny dropped. The fences had been constructed precisely to stop anyone making that discovery. We agreed a way had to be found through them. The other idea we came up with was to hire a boat when back on the mainland and go up the coast fronting the Earl's land. We'd either find an island, or if Nostalgia were indeed on the mainland, at least the lighthouse on the cliff would be visible from the sea. Hiring a boat was an easier option than breaching the fences, so we agreed I'd give it a try when I had to travel to a management meeting held at the Earl's home.

In fact, it was the week following your wedding to Saoirse when I boarded the train back to the mainland. On arrival, I collected my Polaroid camera, which the railway customs men had kept locked up in their safe, and took a taxi to a village on the coast south of the Earl's land. After enquiring at a nearby pub called "The Rebel Inn", I found a local boatman willing to take me northwards along the coast. With no islands at that point, I scrutinised the mainland cliffs. At the place where I judged would be the opening to Nostalgia bay a stack of rocks jutted out to sea, blocking any view. I did observe up on the cliff the glassed top of a building of similar size and shape to the Nostalgia lighthouse. I'd hoped we could get a closer look but this part of the coast is fringed with vicious jagged underwater rock formations. The boatman told me it had the distinction of being the most inaccessible stretch of coastline in the whole of Ireland. No boat could safely approach. I asked him whether the building on the cliff was a lighthouse. He told me it had never shone a light out to sea in all the time it had been there. I took photographs, but on the whole a disappointing trip, thoroughly inconclusive.

On the taxi ride back to the estate, two fire engines raced past with sirens blaring. As we entered the gates a cloud of smoke was visible. A major electrical fire had broken out in the vegetable packing sheds. At a security fence gate, I noticed no guards on duty. I assumed they had been called away by the emergency of the fire. I called for the taxi to stop, paid off the driver and, entering the unattended gate, stood for the first time on prohibited land.

It was now or never. I set off, walking up into the hills, taking a connected series of Polaroids, the purpose being to prove the route from the Earl's estate to what I hoped would be the outskirts of Nostalgia. As navigational aid I had the tiny compass, which I had cut from my rucksack and hidden in my shoe to evade customs.

The view from the top of the first hill disappointed: open countryside with more hills in the distance. I decided I should carry on until I'd proved our theory one way or the other. Attaining the top of the next hill I saw below a broad valley with a stream running down the middle and some grassy ditches snaking up and down and across the terrain. After crossing this valley and climbing up the far side, I finally stood triumphant: the institute building, Nostalgia and the bay spread out below.

Until that moment I had not considered how to escape from this no-man's land. If I retraced my steps, the chances were the missing guards would be back at their post but, if I went on, how to explain to the Nostalgia guards my presence on the wrong side of the fence? Then, I had an idea. First, I scrambled downhill, cross-country, out of sight of the guard post. Next, I sidled along tight up against the fence, hoping not to be spotted. As I came into view of the security gate, I strode up to the guards, who were much astonished by my sudden appearance.

I said, "Did you know there's a feckin great hole in your fence? A hundred yards down. Go and see for yourselves." I pointed, and as they walked down to investigate, I ran like crazy to gain the cover of Nostalgia's streets and alleyways. Luckily, I reached my house in safety.

My wife asked. "How did you get back so soon?"

I laid out my Polaroids in sequence on our kitchen table. "The camera doesn't lie!" I said.

We invited some neighbours of ours to look at the pictures. To reassure them it wasn't a hoax, we had to tell them about my experience with the compass on the train and of our subsequent measurements proving Nostalgia could not be ninety miles from the mainland. Our neighbours telephoned their friends, who telephoned other friends. A queue of people gathered outside our house to hear our story and see the evidence. Somebody said, "I want to see this for myself and I want to see it now!" Fifty of us converged as a mob on the security post. The guards locked the gate on seeing our approach. They must have guessed the game was up. When they refused to unlock it, we threatened to bring round the town fire engine and use it as a motorised battering ram till we had brought down the fencing. The crowd steadily grew as other townspeople joined us. They'd been watching from the wall, astonished at the scene unfolding before them. Eventually, the guards had no choice but to unlock the gate. Like the Pied Piper of Hamelin, I led this great procession of people over the hills and valleys to the fence on the Earl's estate. Here, by force of numbers, we pushed aside the guards and let ourselves through.

What to do next? We agreed the priority should be to create a track across the land, so anyone could easily drive in and out of Nostalgia. While some of us organised with a local builder to cut a gap in the fences and bulldoze a dirt road, others went to the town, to expose the fraud to the local newspaper and make calls to national TV and radio.

It's difficult to say who was the more amazed; the islanders for having thought for twenty years they were living on an isolated island; or the townies, for not knowing there'd been for two decades a flourishing community of five thousand only four miles distant. Whichever way the balance went, Nostalgia was much more a novelty for the townies than the mainland was for the islanders. Next day, a solid line of cars crossed our newly commissioned dirt track. People wanted to see for themselves what had been on their doorstep for twenty years.

A fortnight later the islanders organised a meeting in Nostalgia's theatre, to call Jim Braben and other Nostalgia notables to account. The mood was mixed, with some supportive of the Earl's vision, despite the deception, and others furious with the Earl for having toyed with their lives. I am sure you must have been at that meeting so there is no need to go into further detail nor to describe any of the subsequent happenings, about which you will also be well informed.

I give my permission for you to include this letter in your historical archive of Nostalgia. If you have any questions about my story or about any other aspect of my experience of Nostalgia, I will be happy to answer them,

Yours sincerely, Dr Diarmuid Murphy.

Chapter 48

Unfinished Business

John came into the kitchen, his hands grubby with oil. "Trouble with the car. I'm driving down to the mechanic. I'll be about half an hour or so. You don't have to leave just yet, do you?"

I said that I didn't.

"Stay and keep Saoirse entertained. You must have a ton of stuff to talk about. She can fill me in on the news after my weekend trip. Where's your car?"

"Parked down at The Commons"

"So, how did you get up here? Taxi?"

"I walked. It's great to be out in the sunshine and sea air after being cooped up in a technical conference."

"I'll give you a lift back to your car when I've got my own sorted out."

I thanked him but said I'd walk back to Nostalgia along the beach. "This letter tells an incredible story," I said.

John nodded his head in agreement. "The conclusion to the archives you and I worked on. We can be proud of the work we did. It's all on display now, in the museum building, which the town eventually got up and running. After the Earl died, it became imperative to preserve his legacy for posterity. Saoirse's the museum director, in fact."

Saoirse came into the kitchen carrying little Timmy, not too happy about having been stuffed into his outdoor coat. "I'm only there part time," she said. "I don't want to miss out on my child's formative years. I have a first-class personal assistant. Sally Macnamara. You remember her?"

I asked, "Is she still with her husband?"

Saoirse looked at me quizzically. "Of course. Why would you think not?"

I said nothing, pondering the irony of the one woman in Nostalgia I had enjoyed having sex with now working as personal assistant to the one woman I'd wanted to have sex with. How would Sally react to my being back in town?

John gathered up his car keys. "Sorry I have to leave you. See you shortly."

I heard him at the front door, talking to Saoirse, then the sound of the car driving off. Presently she came back and sat down with her child on her knee. We smiled at each other. Who was going to say first what needed to be said?

Saoirse said, "It's fantastic to see you again."

"And you," I replied. "When I saw the Earl's house, I was sure you'd moved away and we wouldn't get to meet."

"Well, we *did* get to meet. Fate has thrown us together once more."

"Are you happy here, despite it no longer being the Nostalgia we both once knew?"

"Very happy. I never want to have to move from this place." She spoke without conviction. She asked, "Are *you* happy, so far away in Singapore?"

I evaded the question. "Singapore is home now."

We were both silent for a moment.

Saoirse said, "I pleaded with them to let you back in. Finally, I persuaded them to put aside their misgivings and offer you a permanent role on the island."

"Then you found out I'd got married."

"I cried for weeks after I got your letter."

"Then you met up with John again?"

"When you couldn't come back to Nostalgia, I asked them if I could contact John."

"Were you planning to revive your former relationship?"

"Not at first. The work he'd done had been left unfinished and we couldn't find anyone as good as you or him to finish it. By the time we invited him back he'd overcome his anger against us for faking his injury and confining him to a plaster cast. The Earl compensated him with a big payout. How else do you think we can afford to buy a top of the range Mercedes? Twelve months after we started working together, we married."

Something bothered me, the contrast between my treatment and that enjoyed by John. I asked, "How did he get round the stipulation a person can't be a Nostalgia resident unless their near relations are dead?"

Saoirse said, "Look after Timmy for a few seconds while I go and get something." I heard her in another room opening and closing cupboard doors. She came back holding an estate agent's leaflet advertising a flat to rent. "You and I, that is, I mean, John and I, were to live in this flat in the Earl's home. We'd have another flat in Nostalgia. Whenever his parents visited, we would be at this mainland flat. If one of us were away, working in

Nostalgia, the other would say we'd gone 'abroad'. Once Nostalgia went public, we moved here permanently and bought the cottage."

I looked with regret at the pictures of the cosy little flat that could have been the beginning of our life together: the sitting room, the kitchen, the bathroom, the balcony with its potted plants — and the bedroom, with its king-size double bed. All the bitterness of four years ago welled up inside me. I said, "You'd had sex with John before you met me, hadn't you?

"Yes."

"But you wouldn't make love to me?"

"I didn't want to cause you the hurt I caused John. His growing suspicion of the place made a close relationship impossible. He obviously thought me innocent of any participation in the deception. Of course, I couldn't tell him the reason for breaking off the affair. I did it clumsily, which made it worse. Then I made the mistake all over again with you. You know how sorry I am about that."

"You didn't act sorry at the time."

"I just had to harden my heart and get on with it."

Saoirse stood, gazing out of the kitchen window, with her back to me. I took her hand in mine. "Saoirse, I'm sorry. Let's not argue. You're the last person in the world I want to argue with."

She turned and smiled. "What's your wife's name?"

"Fionnuala."

"That doesn't sound Asian."

"She's not Asian. She's Australian, of Irish descent."

"Do you have any photographs of her and your children?"

I took out my wallet. "I have a fancy studio portrait of them all together, done in black and white, and I have a colour picture of Fionnuala on her own."

"Let me see," said Saoirse.

I handed her the black and white photograph.

"What a lovely picture," she said. "When you said it wasn't colour, I thought what a funny idea, but it's beautifully lit. We'll have to get one done. And what sweet children. Your wife looks like me."

"She does a bit."

"And the colour picture?"

"It's not as good as the other. Fionnuala would be cross if she knew I'd shown it to you."

"Why should she be cross? Don't be silly. Let me see it."

I hesitated.

Saoirse looked at me intently. "I understand. You said your wife has Irish ancestry?"

"Yes."

"She has the same hair colour as me, doesn't she?"

"Yes."

"How alike is it?"

"Almost identical."

I showed her the photograph. Saoirse gasped at the resemblance between them.

We were silent for a while, neither sure what to say next.

Saoirse asked, "If I said that I wasn't happy, would you leave your wife and children to be with me?"

I replied, "I love my wife, Saoirse, but she's not you."

Saoirse said nothing.

I asked, "Would you leave your husband and child to be with me?"

"I'd leave my *husband*. "

"So, it's not over?"

"No."

We were silent again. The desire for her I felt at that moment was overwhelming.

Saoirse said, "Promise me you won't be sad. When you think of me, promise me you'll think of all the times we had together. If you're sad, it will spoil the memory of it."

I said, "We should have made love, then we wouldn't be feeling so strongly the loss of what we might have had."

Saoirse took my hand. "If we had been intimate, our parting would have been much, much worse."

The sound of the Mercedes announced John's return from the mechanics.

"False alarm," said John. "Did you have an interesting talk?"

"Saoirse tells me she never wants to leave this place and have to live anywhere else."

"This cottage, or Nostalgia?" asked John.

"Nostalgia, of course," said Saoirse, "but I'll be sorry if we have to leave the cottage. The next place we live will have to be extra special to compensate."

"She's mad on swimming," said John. "There's a path opposite here, going down to a cove. She swims down there in the nude. Crazy! I know this is southwest Ireland and we have the Gulf Stream and it's exceptionally mild, but it's not the Mediterranean. I don't understand her obsession with the place. The water feels bloody freezing most of the time."

"Because you're not fit," said Saoirse.

"I have to go," I said. "I'll be in the way of your departure."

"Here's our card with our address and phone number," said John. "Send us a postcard from Singapore with your contact details. We must keep in touch."

We shook hands. I left him in the kitchen, packing the baby clothes and feeding gear for his trip.

At the cottage gate Saoirse asked, "You're looking round the town before you go?"

"It's my last chance to see close up what's changed and what hasn't." I asked, "How much does John know? He seems remarkably nonchalant about my being here?"

"I decided not to tell him," said Saoirse. "Telling him would spoil the special friendship you and I had. It's my memory, it's precious to me and I want to keep it that way. Does your wife know about us?"

I laughed. "I thought I'd done a brilliant job of keeping it quiet but you can't hide from a woman's intuition."

Saoirse said, "You don't know how much it means to me, to know you still feel the same way."

I said, "I do know, because it means as much to me that you still want me."

I kissed her tenderly on her lips. Saoirse turned and ran into the cottage. She didn't look back.

I could have told Saoirse of my hotel booking. Instead, I planned to make use later of the phone number John had given me. I'd ring and say I'd changed my mind and decided to stay for the hotel celebration. Would she guess the deception and be furious? One thing certain — John should not know I was still in town.

A few yards down the road, I came to the path to the cove. I couldn't leave without going there, but first I followed the path to the top of the sea cliff. A low wire fence stood where the security fence had once been. I climbed over, stepping as close as I dare to the cliff edge. To the north, the Irish coastline stretched for miles into the distance. No wonder they had been so anxious to block this view from the gaze of the islanders.

Down on the sandy beach, the intense sunshine reminded me of the time Saoirse had brought me to the cove for that memorable first swimming lesson. I lay on the warm sand, looking up at a cloudless blue sky, closing my eyes, imagining being back ther.

I heard someone coming down the cliff path — Saoirse, wearing the flimsy cotton dress she had worn the first day we worked together. "John and Timmy have left," she said.

"How far are they going?"

"John's parents live thirty miles away."

"How did you know I'd be here?"

Saoirse smiled. "What were you saying about hiding from female intuition?"

I asked, already knowing the answer, "Why have you come?"

"Unfinished business," she replied, removing her dress.

I asked, "Saoirse, what about ...?"

"I'm two months pregnant. John doesn't know yet. I'm going to tell him when he returns from his parents."

After we had made love, I confessed I had already booked a room at the hotel and didn't intend to leave till the Sunday. Saoirse cried tears of relief we didn't have to immediately say goodbye.

Back at the cottage, she changed into a dancing dress. We walked together, hand in hand, along the beach to the hotel, just as we had done four years previously after that first swimming lesson. At the opening night celebration, we met many of the people I had interviewed for my work on the island. Of course, they knew Saoirse and I as a pair, having seen us together many times in the past but we took care how we behaved. We didn't want any rumours getting back to John.

Around ten o'clock, Saoirse said, "Let's go to your room."

An hour later, when we came downstairs, we met Molly. "Hello, Molly," I said. "Saoirse and I have been for a walk on the sands."

"That must have been difficult," said Molly. "At high tide."

A good friend, Molly. We knew she would be discreet.

I told Saoirse of my concern for John's reaction if he found out we had attended the hotel opening night together. She said she would play down the revelation; she'd pretend it was nothing special.

Saturday, we walked the town, taking in our old haunts, the harbour wall, the canal stables (the barge horses semi-retired and a tourist attraction), the roof gardens, the fairground, the rose garden, as if none of the intervening events had happened: we'd been living in a dream and now we were back together again. But this was the dream — tomorrow we would both have to face reality. Saoirse announced she'd be going up to Dublin with me. "To erase the memory of the dreadful time I abandoned you at the airport hotel. The biggest mistake of my life. I'm going to say goodbye properly this time."

That night, we made love at the Irish cottage, and again in the morning. Saoirse asked, as I had gone still, "What's the matter? Are you spent?"

I said, "This is the last time ever I can feel what it's like to be inside you. I want to prolong the moment."

After breakfast, Saoirse telephoned John while I returned to the hotel to pack my luggage. I found Sally Macnamara sitting on my bed. "Such a nuisance Tom and I were away. Lucky I met Molly. She told me you were here. I couldn't let you go without seeing you. The hotel said you were out. I guessed where. I waited downstairs, then I saw you coming back alone, so I came up."

There are some older women whom age increasingly favours. In her long white dress and high heels, she looked even more desirable now than that first time I'd passed by her on the beach. We reminisced about the past and caught up on what we had been doing since. I told her I knew she had become Saoirse's assistant.

317

"She's a lovely person," said Sally. "Mike, she really misses you. She may have hidden it from that husband of hers but she can't hide it from me."

I said, "I miss her too but I have a beautiful wife and two beautiful children waiting for me in Singapore. What can I do?"

I opened the wardrobe and took out my clothes to pack my suitcase. "Sally, I have something here that's yours." I threw over to her *Applied Mathematics*.

"This isn't mine!"

"Open it."

Sally laughed when she saw inside. "I never did find out whether it should be right or left ankle," she said, "but *you* don't need to be told what sort of married woman I am, do you?"

She walked towards me, fixing me with that sexy stare, swinging the chain rhythmically round her finger, like a prelude to a striptease act. "Mike, there's something we have to do. For old times' sake." She sat at the window seat and pulled up her dress, exposing a great deal more bare flesh than necessary. I fastened the chain, took her ankle in my hands and kissed it tenderly. She leaned down and kissed me on the mouth. A long sensual kiss. "Always remember me."

Through the window we saw Saoirse coming across to the hotel. "Go down to her," said Sally. "I'll stay up here till you've both left."

I picked up my case and opened the door to the corridor.

318

Sally was crying. "Mike, she might never see you again."

Chapter 49

Postcard from Ireland

Ten months after I had arrived back home, I received a postcard. Saoirse was delighted to tell me her second pregnancy had gone without problems. She was writing the postcard three days after the birth and hoped the post wouldn't take weeks to convey the news from Ireland to Singapore. Little Timmy now had a baby sister. John was apparently already complaining of another child looking more like the mother than himself. "But," said Saoirse, "I can see the father each time I look at her."

I called out to my wife. "It's a postcard to say Saoirse and John have had their baby. It's a girl."

Fionnuala came into the room. "That's nice for them. Now they have an older boy, and a younger girl, just like we have."

The front of the postcard featured a photograph of Nostalgia Hotel, lit by moonlight, magically floating on the water. What better picture for Saoirse to send as a symbol of the precious times we spent together.

Fionnuala said, "The post from Europe is very slow. You told me she was already two months pregnant. She must have had the baby about three months ago."

I looked at the Irish postmark on the back. The date, nine months from my rendezvous with Saoirse in Nostalgia.

Chapter 50

Revival

The following years were not happy. Outwardly, Mike Denning, married man, successful at his job, with a good home, who loved his wife and children, who took family holidays in Australia; inwardly, a man for whom Saoirse had become an obsession. I would think about her while travelling to work, during solitary lunchtime walks in the park, at night when going to sleep, sometimes when making love to my wife. The worst thing, having no photograph. I'd shot dozens with my Nostalgia camera but these had not been returned to me after the escape, because they showed details of the secret town. My only memento, the postcard. I kept it at the bottom of a drawer, taking the precaution of tearing off the corner with the postmark's incriminating date. Should my wife find it, I'd say I gave the postage stamp to a collector colleague.

Just as I had patiently laid plans for escape from Nostalgia, I devised plans for Saoirse and I to rendezvous. My best hope would be another technical conference in Ireland. When it became obvious that wasn't happening any time soon, I contemplated taking the family on holiday to Europe. I didn't dare suggest Ireland directly, instead sounding out Fionnuala on the possibility of visiting England, from where I hoped to make the quick hop over to Cork.

Even should a trip be possible, I had to consider the added complication of the child. Did she resemble me? If John hadn't already guessed the real father, his seeing us in close proximity might trigger realisation. And many in Nostalgia might put two and two together. Molly, for one, knew we'd been having sex that night at the hotel.

As the Internet came to prominence, I used search engines to try to locate Saoirse. I found nothing, until one day at work there it was: her beautiful face smiling out at me from my screen; Nostalgia's museum now had a web site. Many times I composed an email, only to delete it, fearing John might intercept the message. I had no wish to upset Saoirse's marriage, nor create a situation further decreasing the chance of our meeting.

They'd done the web site brilliantly, covering the origins of Nostalgia, the philosophy behind the experiment, transcripts of the interviews we had carried out, descriptions of the business enterprises, the cultural life, the restaurants, pubs, and so on. An article about John and I told of our respective escapes and capture and how it had taken the third attempt, by Diarmuid Murphy, to fully expose Nostalgia's secret. The article revealed information I had not known before: that John had actually made two forays onto the forbidden land. The first, he'd avoided getting too close to the institute for fear of being seen. He did not of course know the building was unoccupied. The second, in the middle of the night, he'd planned to look in the windows but had collided with a guard on a bike before he could attain his goal.

In a section dedicated to biographies of the museum staff I read Saoirse's life story, from her birth in a hippy commune, through her moving to the island as the only child of a pioneer couple, to her going away to college and her eventual return as a dedicated worker for the Nostalgia project. I'd hoped also to find a bio of Sally. What it would say (and not say) could make fascinating reading but another lady had since taken the role of Saoirse's assistant.

It occurred to me Saoirse also might be searching the Internet. I tried my name to see what she could find and instantly pulled up my photograph on the bank's public web site. Would she email or call me? Surely, she would have done so by now. To protect our child would she never make contact? As the years went by, I came to accept this as the compelling reason I too should never attempt to contact her, that altruism had fully conquered desire. How quickly did my faux nobility evaporate on receiving the letter from Sally Macnamara.

March 2004. Almost ten years on from my return to Nostalgia. I had reached thirty-six years of age. Saoirse would be almost forty by now. Would she still be beautiful? I resisted all temptation to search for a picture or news. That activity had been abandoned long ago as causing too much pain, too much dissatisfaction. Sally's letter arrived at my office, marked "Confidential". The envelope contained a postcard view of Nostalgia, with the cryptic note: *See you soon. Sally. xxx.* Was she coming here to Singapore? For her own purpose? To deliver a message from Saoirse? Or was she merely on a holiday trip with her husband? A further message would surely follow.

The following month, my manager called me to his office. "The I.T. department is being sold off, Mike. Don't worry. It's a good deal. Nobody's getting fired. We'll carry on as before, in new offices down the road, nearer the park. We'll still provide software to the bank and we'll have other clients — international clients — we'll be expanding to meet their needs. Our first client will be the bank that has purchased our operation. I have their brochure in this envelope. Take it back to your desk and read it."

I expected to have to wade through a lot of dull takeover propaganda but the contents of the envelope galvanised my attention. Our I.T. department had been purchased by the Bank Of Nostalgia. I could hardly believe it. Had Nostalgia's tiny bank with its theatrically inclined manager really grown to such a size and power that it could afford to purchase our Singapore operation? According to the brochure, the Earl's estate had been settled on a distant relative, an economics graduate. An idealist like the Earl, he reconstituted the Bank Of Nostalgia as a new kind of bank, a humanitarian bank. It would invest in big business in the normal way but profits would be ploughed back into low interest loans for third world projects, to raise up the world's disadvantaged, who would benefit from the bank's success. The new owner's shrewd investment policies, aided by vast wealth inherited from the Earl, had rapidly expanded their operations, such that in anticipation of future growth they needed access to superior technology, hence their purchase of our entire I.T. operation.

Left unexplained, why they had chosen us over the many other businesses they might have purchased closer to home. Surely, no fortuitous coincidence. Someone,

324

somewhere, somehow, had planned this with me in mind. I scoured the brochure for a telling detail I might have missed. I found it in the small print listing the bank's directors, "Managing Director: Sally Macnamara". So, clever scheming Sally, who had once contrived to trap me in a sauna for an afternoon of steamy sex, had since worked her way up the bank hierarchy to the ultimate position of influence and had taken hold of it to get me back to Ireland.

In less than five weeks, I boarded a plane at Singapore airport, for a month of work in Nostalgia, and hoping, I knew not how, to detach Saoirse from her family and spend time with her alone. My flight took me to Dublin, from where I hired a car. Seven in the evening, I passed the Earl's estate gates and turned onto the new Nostalgia road, though curiously the signpost had been taken down. Two miles along I noted the supermarket business had gone, the building and its litter-strewn car park deserted, a decaying commercial wasteland. The road became a dual carriageway, with my lane looping to the left, passing through an underpass and coming out on the opposite side, returning in the direction I had just come. Stopping the car, I clambered up the grassy bank above the underpass. To my astonishment the view at the top revealed not only the distant town of Nostalgia but, close by, an obstacle I had never thought to see again. The fences were back. A large notice said "Private Estate. No access by road. Parking available at railway station, through estate gates." The fence could imply only one thing: Nostalgia had isolated itself anew from the world.

I found the station reopened, with the addition across the road of a multi-storey car park. The ticket office man told me the last shuttle service had departed but I could, if I wished, book a sleeper on tonight's "Express", which in true Irish fashion took six hours to traverse the tunnel, as against the twelve-minute shuttle. The revived luxury train now ran as a novelty for tourists attracted by the romanticism of the past and the experience of a simulated train journey indistinguishable from the real thing. Arriving at Island station next morning, we even got heavy sea fog, the genuine article, not stage mist. On the barge to town, the tourist passengers marvelled at the same phenomenon of the mysterious illuminated eyes of the hill-dweller windows as I had done all those years ago.

We crossed the water to the hotel in a substantial motorised ferry with a glassed-over top for shelter in bad weather. Evidently, an old guy in an open rowing boat no longer sufficed for Nostalgia's new busy industry of tourism. After checking in and unpacking my stuff, I headed back across the water to Nostalgia town. Sally greeted me in her office, her manner informal but brisk, the old flirtatious Sally turned off, at least during business hours. Trapped in meetings, I had no opportunity to thank her for manipulating the takeover situation in my favour nor to quiz her about Saoirse. And I had to contain my impatience several hours more when she and Tom and Jenny and Patrick took me to dinner at *The Refectory* restaurant.

"We have the fifth earl to thank for the town's revival," said Tom. "His idealism has restored Nostalgia to its former glory. He wanted to ban all cars but that caused an outcry, so they compromised. Residents keep their cars in an indoor car park at mainland station. A ten-minute shuttle train runs back and forth. So the residents get freedom of travel and Nostalgia once again gets freedom from traffic."

"The other major change," added Sally, "is the return of the fences and the guards. We're living in a hundred percent secure environment. And there are customs men at the railway, to protect our restored economy."

I described how I had encountered the new fence blocking the road.

"The fences aren't like before," explained Patrick. "Instead of two spans with a no-man's land in between, there's only one fence, which runs along the edge of the estate, far from Nostalgia town. That's freed up land for agricultural development, and the valley with the old motocross course is being developed as a second urban area."

"They wanted the bank to finance the development," said Sally. "Unacceptably high risk in my opinion. I had a better idea. Each new building showcases a green technology company. They have to finance their own project. In return they get the international prestige and exposure Nostalgia offers as a successful experimental ideal town, and we get, bit by bit, a second town to be proud of, at no cost to ourselves."

I asked what was driving the new urban development; was it the Irish tourist industry?

"No feckin way!" replied Patrick. "If you want to live in Nostalgia, you have to *work* in Nostalgia. We won't allow ourselves to be turned into a soul-less theme park, like Venice for example, with genuine locals priced out of town by greedy holiday-let vampires."

We ate and drank and talked and laughed for three hours. Jenny invited us back to her house but Sally said she and I needed to go to the hotel to discuss our schedule.

"That job of yours is making you boring," complained her sister.

Sally and I walked arm in arm along the wall to South Gate and across the causeway in the moonlight to Little Island. We made small talk or discussed business. Saoirse wasn't mentioned. Something wasn't right.

"Mike, it's all gone wrong," said Sally, as we sat together in the hotel bar. "I don't understand it. Saoirse's disappeared. I thought she'd be delighted to hear of your return but, when I told her, I sensed distress. And now she's left town."

"Does anyone know where she's gone? Have you spoken to John?"

"That's the thing," replied Sally. "They've all gone — John and the children went with her."

I confessed to being the father of the daughter. I suggested Saoirse feared my visit would reveal the truth.

"It can't be," said Sally. "When I rang John's newspaper, the deputy editor said his boss wouldn't be back for at least three months, possibly as long as six months. He didn't know where they'd gone either. I feel it's all my fault. I should have kept my mouth shut."

I told Sally not to worry, because my next trip over should coincide with Saoirse's return.

Saoirse's absence clearly bothered Sally. By contrast, I felt content. I finally possessed what I had sought: a legitimate excuse to visit. But, as my four weeks there drew to a close, I couldn't avoid a growing suspicion that Saoirse wanted to terminate our association once and for all. For that she was willing to make the ultimate sacrifice — moving away from Nostalgia altogether. They could even now be in some other part of the world, far from Ireland, John working on a temporary contract, Saoirse putting down roots, establishing a new home for her family.

Chapter 51

Saoirse's Story

Back in Singapore, Fionnuala asked about my trip. "How was Saoirse?"

"Fine. I had dinner at their cottage one evening. A great couple of children they have." I couldn't bring myself to admit to the disappearance.

"Mike, I had a scary experience while you were away. I saw my ghost. Our neighbour asked me to baby-sit Peter, you know, their seven-year-old. I took him shopping in the city. He wasn't on his best behaviour, moaning about the heat, so we went to a cafe to get an iced drink. He suddenly said, 'That woman's staring at you.' I looked over to where he was pointing and got the shock of my life. It was like seeing myself in the mirror. A woman a few tables away, my age, my hair, everything, except, Mike, her skin — deathly pale, and such an expression of grief. I cried out in shock. People were looking at me. So embarrassing! I got cross with Peter. I told him it was rude to point at people. When I looked again, the apparition had vanished."

I suggested Fionnuala had seen a mirror image, probably a distorted reflection of herself in a glass door that had been momentarily opened. However, she insisted she'd seen a ghost.

Next morning at the office, I checked in at reception to collect the post arrived in my absence. "Just these," said the secretary, handing over a bundle of commercial circulars. "Oh! And this letter. Someone said your wife brought it in."

"My wife? Are you sure?"

I took the letter from her and my pulse raced. Written on the envelope, my name in Saoirse's handwriting. I slung the circulars back on the desk of the astonished secretary and rushed down the street to the park. There, I opened the letter:

My darling Mike,

The most terrible set of circumstances has occurred. Fate is conspiring against us. I've been diagnosed with a rare illness. The doctors tell me there's only a ten percent chance of survival and even that depends on getting the right treatment. In desperation I asked the new earl for a loan to cover the medical expenses. He refused, saying he would pay all costs, on one condition: that I seek out the best obtainable medical care. The only hospital in the world with a specialist centre for the disease is in Sydney, Australia. That's what has brought us to Singapore, on a flight stopover. Last month, when I heard about the purchase of your bank's software business, I asked Sally for your home and office addresses. I hoped somehow to get in contact and meet you, though without our respective families present, for obvious reasons. Imagine my disappointment when she told me you would be visiting Nostalgia during the same time, unbeknown to her, I would be in your part of the world.

John left the hotel early this morning to take the children to your famous Singapore zoo. I said I would stay in bed. As soon as they had gone, I took a taxi to your home address. If I couldn't see you, I at least wanted to meet your family. Your wife came out with a little boy, jumped into her car and sped off before I had a chance to intercept. I ordered my taxi driver to give chase and we ended up in the car park of a shopping centre. I followed them into a cafe. She got a drink for the boy and they sat down. I sat a few tables away, wondering how to speak to her. Watching her, I felt overwhelmed with regret. That could have been me sitting there, in her place, as your wife. Then, she suddenly looked straight at me, and Mike, I think my appearance startled her. She cried out. Her reaction upset me so much I got out of there immediately.

I have been walking in the park down the street from your office. Do you go there? I am sure you do. Do you ever think of me when you are there? Different trees and flowers but it reminds me of our garden at Rose Gate. My darling, I may not survive the next six months. I'm so sorry Nostalgia came between us and the perfect life we could have had.

Yours forever, Saoirse.

Epilogue

Entering the second-class cabin of the jumbo jet, knowing he had a window seat, one of a pair, Steve Davis speculated whether the airline's computer system had chosen to shape his destiny with an interesting travelling companion, preferably of the young, female and available variety, or had evaded its sacred duty and saddled him with yet another oversized traveller too voluminous to fit neatly and politely in the allocated space. To his surprise, the adjacent seat was occupied by a slim young lady, aged about twenty, with a cute face, flaming red hair and a pleasant, natural smile. Thanking the patron saint of I.T. for heeding his prayers, Steve silently promised to baptise his computer mouse with holy water, then, taking up his seat, he tried to act as cool, nonchalant (and available) as possible.

"Going far?" he asked.

"The same distance as you are," answered the girl, "unless you've brought a parachute."

"I'm Steve."

"Catriona."

They shook hands.

Picking up on Steve's American accent, Catriona asked, "Have you been to Ireland before?"

"I'm a post-grad at Dublin UCD. I'm from Portland, Oregon."

Catriona said, "I know Portland. I'm an exchange student at Oregon State."

"Going back home on vacation?"

"My father's taken over the management of a hotel. He's meeting me at Dublin airport. We're driving down to County Cork for the opening party."

Not wanting to seem a jerk, more interested in tapping away at a phone than talking with a pretty girl, Steve put away his smartphone. "Course work?" he asked, pointing to a folder on her lap.

"It's the manuscript of a novel," replied Catriona.

"Yours?"

"It was written as a therapy by a man suffering intense psychological trauma. He wrote it as a work of fiction. In fact it tells the story of a real place he once knew."

"What's it called?"

"The title hasn't been decided yet. He says he might just call the book 'Nostalgia', because that's the name the inhabitants gave the place where it all happened."

"Have you read the manuscript?"

"Yes."

"So, what do you think?"

"There are personal things in the narrative to do with me and my family. The author says if I'm uncomfortable with what's written he'll respect my wishes and won't publish. I'm ambivalent. I wonder what somebody who had no connection with the people and with the events would make of it all."

Steve said, "If you're needing a volunteer, I'll read it. How long will it take?"

"I should think the whole flight," replied Catriona. "Only promise me you'll read it thoroughly, and not skim it." Sizing him up, she added, "Do you have the stamina?"

"I can't sleep on flights," replied Steve, "and I've gotten bored with in-flight movies. And I'm a student of English literature, so I'm motivated."

Catriona handed Steve the manuscript. "Wake me up when we're ready to land." She busied herself arranging the airline blankets and pillows. "These seats are never comfortable for sleeping. Would you mind me borrowing your shoulder?"

"Help yourself!"

She rested her head against him as naturally as a long-term girlfriend. Steve's ego significantly boosted, he set about returning the favour by dutifully reading the manuscript he had been given.

#

"Finished!" said Steve, closing up the manuscript.

"Perfect timing," said Catriona. "There's only ten minutes to landing. Do you time everything so well?" She laughed. "That question isn't a prelude to taking you to bed. Come on! What's the verdict'?"

"I'd say publish! Yeah. People need to know the story of that place."

"You've realised I'm the baby girl born at the end?"

"I guessed so."

They shared a luggage trolley and went through to Arrivals together. Steve weighed up whether to drop a clumsy hint like "I've always wanted to see County Cork," in the hope of getting an invite to Catriona's party.

They stood in the middle of the Arrivals hall, waiting for Catriona's father. "Where is he?" she said, scouring the sea of waiting faces, "There he is!" She waved to a man standing at a sandwich counter in a shop. They went over to him.

"Mike, this is Steve. He's from Oregon. We sat next to each other on the plane."

"Hi Steve," said Mike, embracing Catriona. "My lovely daughter. Every bit as beautiful as her mother in her twenties."

"I made Steve read your book. You don't mind, do you? He thinks it's brilliant. Mike, would you mind if Steve joined us for the weekend?"

Mike hesitated briefly. "Er... Yes, there's room for one more in the car. Steve, you're welcome, if you want to travel down with us."

Steve opened his mouth to answer but Catriona said, "Of course he'll come. Now he's read all about Nostalgia Hotel, he has to see it for real."

They waited outside the shop while Mike joined a long queue at the till.

Steve said, "When you said you were meeting your father, I thought you meant the other one, not the man who wrote the book."

Catriona sighed. "That's a story! I've had a difficult time coping with all the upset in our family."

"Yes, I'm sorry about your mother," said Steve. "I can understand how Mike too would have been devastated by her death."

"What!" exclaimed Catriona, "That's not what I meant. My mother recovered from her illness. Mike came over twice a year, then it went up to three times a year. Although genuine work trips, his wife was deeply unhappy about the situation. She started an affair and she and Mike split up. Then it came out John wasn't my father and my parents divorced. Though the real reason for the divorce is what my mother once admitted to me: she was never happy in the marriage."

Mike emerged from the shop and waved to someone across the other side of the Arrivals hall. Catriona called out "Mum!"

"Mike. You pig!" she said, laughing, "You didn't tell me Mum would be here."

"Surprise!" said Mike.

A woman of striking appearance, aged about fifty with voluminous natural red hair, even more richly coloured than her daughter, came walking towards them. Catriona gave her a big hug.

"Mum. This is Steve. We met on the plane. I've invited him down for the celebration."

Saoirse said, "Pleased to meet you, Steve. I'm Saoirse. I see you've already met my husband."

#

Afterword

I finished the final version of this book in County Cork, Ireland, at the end of a long hot dry summer, which like the Nostalgia summer of 1990 did not seem to want to end. Some of the story is based on events in my life. Yes, I was brought up in a small English seaside town on the south east coast, yes I was a student at the University of Birmingham, yes I did fly to Ireland for the first time in the summer of 1989, yes I did work in an office in Dublin with several I.T. men called John, and yes, there was a "Publishing John", a former journalist, who mentored my early technical writing efforts. At that point, his story and mine depart, as does the book's, because of course it is a work of pure fiction. There is no Nostalgia (unfortunately). In the future there may be a Nostalgia but only after sufficient people have woken up to the disadvantages of the living and working environments we currently find acceptable, and show the will to change to something better, for their sake, and for the sake of future generations.

Acknowledgements

Firstly, to my wife, Hossanah, for listening to the outline plot on a romantic weekend and encouraging me to temporarily switch from writing plays to writing novels. Secondly, to our daughter, Melina, for reading draft chapters and making several useful plot suggestions. Thirdly, to my friend, John Daly, for working through my first drafts and giving useful feedback. Fourthly, my friend, Michael Irwin, of Western Canada, who diligently critiqued my early attempts at writing. Finally, my other Canadian friend, Rosalind Priestley, sadly now deceased, whose expertise in the use of the English language helped me appreciate the importance of getting it right.

Also, my thanks to the following professionals, who, amongst others, helped critique this novel. Any faults remaining are mine, not theirs:
Doug Watts (Jacqui Bennett Writers Bureau), Janet Laurence (Writers Workshop), Dea Parkin (Fiction Feedback), Stephanie Hale (The Oxford Literary Consultancy), C.S.Lakin (livewritethrive.com).

Thanks also to my friend and business colleague, Marcus Bolt, professional graphic designer and fine artist, for the front and back cover design, Trickster God sandcastle and the excellent map of Nostalgia.

For The Love of Alison

(Finalist 2020 "Indies Today" awards)

Journalist, David Buckley, walks into a murder scene. Only one problem — the murderer doesn't exist, so now Buckley's the chief suspect, and he's on the run. Can he prove his innocence – and his sanity?

"A wonderful read! You know you are onto something fantastic when you feel sad upon reaching the last page!" Alexandra Williams at LoveReading.co.uk

Sixty Positions with Pleasure

Twenty-something IT worker, Charlie Gibbs, has a problem – several problems, in fact. His boss has just been killed in mysterious circumstances. Replacement boss, fifty-year-old Dutch cougar, Ilse Teuling, is writing a sex manual and wants Charlie to help with "the practical work". Populists have declared a coup; people are seeing visions; the clock is counting down to environmental disaster, and a murderer is on the loose, providing Charlie with the biggest problem of the lot – he's the intended next victim and he doesn't know why.

"… a fun read … with an enormous cast of characters, most of whom are not what we think they are … Very enjoyable." Lucinda E Clarke for Readers' Favorite

https://www.businessassistant.biz/novelsandplays.htm

341